Lethal Risk

Jane Blythe

Bear Spots Publications
Melbourne Australia

Paperback
ISBN-13: 978-0-6456432-1-3

Cover designed by RBA Designs

SOME QUESTIONS HAVE NO ANSWERS
SOME TRUTH CAN BE DISTORTED
SOME TRUST CAN BE REBUILT
SOME MISTAKES ARE UNFORGIVABLE

I'd like to thank everyone who played a part in bringing this story to life. Particularly my mom who is always there to share her thoughts and opinions with me. My awesome cover designer, Amy, who whips up covers for me so quickly and who patiently makes every change I ask for, and there are usually lots of them! And my lovely editor Lisa Edwards, for all their encouragement and for all the hard work they put into polishing my work.

CHAPTER ONE

February 14th
4:28 P.M.

Every parent's worst nightmare.

His daughter had disappeared.

Asher "Mouse" Whitman spun in a slow circle, sure that if he kept looking, his seven-year-old would suddenly reappear.

Where was she?

She'd been right there, playing on the swings with a few of her friends. The Valentine's Day party picnic in the park meant there were families and kids everywhere. It was winter and cold in Manhattan, but that didn't seem to have put a dampener on the fun. All the kids from his daughter's class were there along with their parents and siblings, but he couldn't see Lolly anywhere.

Lauren had been nicknamed Lolly when she was about eighteen months old and trying to learn to say her own name. It had stuck. Mouse believed sooner or later she'd drop the childish nickname, but for now, she was his sweet little Lolly.

They'd been at this very same spot just ten days ago celebrating her seventh birthday.

Away more often than he was home, Mouse had been thrilled to be able to celebrate his daughter's birthday with her. He'd missed two in her short little life, and while Lolly never complained about the fact she spent more time at her grandparents' Long Island home than at their Manhattan apartment, he hated missing out on any of her special days.

The life of a single parent was full of guilt over the things you had to miss because you were the sole provider. Added to that, his job with Prey Security was dangerous and required extensive travel, and he missed much more than he should.

Definitely much more than he wanted.

"What's wrong?" Luca "Bear" Jackson asked, appearing beside him. The two of them had been friends since childhood, served together in Delta Force, and now worked side by side on Prey's Alpha team.

"Where's Lolly? I can't find Lolly," he said, barely sparing his friend a glance as he continued to spin in circles searching for his daughter.

"She's gone?" Bear asked, his voice immediately snapping into his work tone. No one else on his team had kids—although Bear and his fiancée Mackenzie were expecting their first child in five months—but they were all close with Lolly. They were her uncles in every way but blood and had decided to come and join the party.

At first, Mouse had intended to take his daughter out for a special daddy-daughter day to celebrate Valentine's Day. Shopping and lunch at a fancy restaurant had been his plan. Lolly was starting to become much more independent and had been asking for a while now to be able to choose all her own clothes. So, he'd thought he'd take her out, let her pick out a few new things for her wardrobe, but then he'd gotten the note from her school about the party.

Lolly loved parties. His little girl was sweet, friendly, and outgoing, and she'd been so excited about the picnic that he'd scrapped his plans to join the rest of her class in Central Park.

Now he wished they were out, just the two of them, enjoying lunch and shopping.

"When was the last time you saw her?" Caleb "Brick" Quinn asked. Apparently Bear had summoned the rest of the guys over.

Even though the question was a legitimate one, and one that anyone investigating a missing child would ask, Mouse felt a zing of guilt hit him straight in the chest. He should have been watching his daughter more closely. It was his job to protect her, keep her safe, and he knew better than most how much evil lived in this world.

Keeping his eyes on his daughter should be a given, but he'd caught sight of a pretty blonde out running. Other than a couple of nondescript encounters there had been no one in his life since his wife died giving birth to Lolly. While he wasn't on the lookout for a new partner, he was still a man, and when a beautiful woman caught his attention, he couldn't help but take a look.

Stupid.

Because of that split-second mistake, his daughter could be gone forever.

No.

He'd find her.

He had to.

There was no other choice.

Shaking himself, Mouse forced his brain to leave panicked father mode and slip into trained operator mode. Lolly's life might depend on him holding it together. He'd already lost his wife, there was no way he was going to lose the only piece of her he still had.

"She was playing by the swings with three of her friends," he replied.

"What's she wearing today?" Antonio "Arrow" Eden asked. Although all the guys had greeted Lolly with hugs and Valentine's Day gifts when they'd arrived at the park, he wasn't surprised they hadn't paid attention to her outfit. He knew exactly what she had on today because Lolly loved the new dress he'd given her as a Valentine's Day gift. Loved it even more because he'd given her a pair of new boots in the same color. Apparently, matching your outfit was important once you hit seven.

"She's wearing a black long-sleeved dress that hits just above her knees with red hearts all over it. She has on black leggings and red boots, a red knitted beanie with a pompom on top, and she's wearing a red jacket. Or at least she was, but she was begging to be allowed to take it off so everyone could see her new dress, but I told her it was too cold." Lolly had pouted and sulked as they'd walked from their apartment to the park but once she got here and saw her friends her bad mood evaporated. It was one of the things he loved the most about his daughter, she was almost always happy.

"I'm going to call in a description of her to the cops," Arrow said.

"You're going to report her missing already?" Mouse asked. It was the smart thing to do, he knew that. If they found her playing with her friends, they could always let the cops know it had been a false alarm. Better safe than sorry. But reporting her as missing made the fact that he still couldn't see her anywhere a reality.

It meant she was really gone.

"We don't want to waste any time," Arrow said, his expression full of sympathy.

Dominick "Domino" Tanner jogged over from the direction of the swings. Mouse hadn't even noticed that the man had left their small group and gone over to the last place he'd seen Lolly. "I found this," he said, holding up a red jacket. "Is it hers?"

Holding out his hand, Mouse took the jacket and checked to see if Lolly's name was on the tag. He already knew the jacket was hers, recognized it, and could smell the scent of her strawberry shampoo lingering on it, but he needed one last moment of denial.

The moment ended when he saw Lolly's name written in his mom's cursive script on the tag.

His daughter's jacket.

But no Lolly.

"We'll find her, man," Christian "Surf" Bailey said.

The empty words offered little comfort.

There was no way to know if they would find Lolly because they had no idea where she was. If she'd been lured away from the group of children playing, if she'd wandered off on her own, if she'd been taken, and if she had by who and for what purpose.

His ex-in-laws had been making plays to get custody of Lolly ever since their daughter died, their last attempt just a couple of months ago. Could they be behind this?

No.

They'd never hurt their own granddaughter like that, would they?

There was something off about the family law firm they'd hired in that last petition for custody. Something he hadn't been able to figure out other than to know that the money running in and out of the company was a whole lot more than it should be.

Were they behind Lolly's disappearance?

"I'll wait here for the cops to show up," Arrow offered. "I have photos of her on my phone from her birthday party, I'll give them to the cops. I'll also call Eagle and let him know what's going on." Eagle Oswald was their boss and founder of Prey Security, the company he now ran with his five younger siblings.

"I'll ask Mackenzie to start asking her friends if they know where she went," Bear said. Being a woman, Mackenzie would be less intimidating to a bunch of seven-year-olds than a team of huge, muscled special forces operatives. "I'll talk to the parents."

"The rest of us will start searching the park," Surf said with an encouraging nod.

"She can't have been gone long," Domino added. Only they all knew that it only took seconds to complete an abduction if done right.

Unable to stand around doing nothing productive to find his missing daughter, Mouse merely nodded at his teammates, then took off running. He was glad he wasn't here alone today because despite his training, he was pretty sure he would have fallen apart and that could have meant the difference between life and death for his little girl.

"Lolly! Where are you?" he screamed as he ran, praying for an answer he knew might never come. His daughter had been the only reason he'd survived losing his wife. How would he survive losing his sweet little girl?

* * * * *

February 14th
5:00 P.M.

Phoebe Lynch ran like the devil was chasing her.

Maybe because that was how she felt.

It had been two months since she'd moved from California to New York City, and so far, everything had been quiet.

Well, not completely quiet. She'd had the feeling of being watched for a few weeks now and had it just a minute ago as she ran past the playground. And someone was sending her creepy letters. The letters were addressed to her place of work not her home, and while they weren't threatening in any way, actually they were nothing more than a blank sheet of paper, they had definitely creeped her out.

Her cousin had helped her get the new job when she moved here and had even set her up in an apartment owned by her husband's family. Since she wasn't renting in the traditional sense, it made sense that her ex didn't know where she was living but did know where she was working. There was no way to completely hide her identity, not unless she told her cousin everything and allowed her contacts to help.

That wasn't something she was ready to do yet.

Part of her was hoping it would all just blow over and her life could go back to the way it had been before.

Before she met the man of her dreams.

A man who had slowly morphed into the demon of her nightmares.

Phoebe hadn't thought she was the kind of woman who would

find herself trapped in an abusive relationship. She was strong, smart, and had a good sense of self-worth. She'd worked hard through law school and gotten a family law job at one of California's most prestigious firms. She had lots of friends, enjoyed a healthy sex life, and had strong bonds with her family. The idea of letting a man hit and control her seemed so absolutely foreign that she could hardly believe the last eighteen months hadn't all been some horrible bad dream.

The lingering pain in her shoulder told her it was no dream.

The opposite in fact. It was horrifyingly real.

But you're free now, she reminded herself. *Hopefully.*

Even as she had the thought, she knew it wasn't true. He'd told her she would never really be free of him. That he wouldn't let her go. That she was his and the only way out was death.

Fleeing to the other side of the country should have reassured her that she's escaped from his clutches. It might have if it wasn't for the letters and the feeling that someone was watching her, following her.

Maybe he was right.

Maybe she would never truly be free.

It was stupid not to have told her cousin everything, but she was embarrassed. Her cousin was so strong and had survived something so horrific it was the stuff of horror movies. Only it was no movie, and she'd almost lost her very best friend in the entire world. They were more like sisters than cousins, had grown up together, and she knew that her cousin had the resources to help free her from her ex.

But to get access to those resources, she'd have to admit how stupid she'd been not to see him for who he really was.

How weak she'd been not to leave the first time he put his hands on her.

Phoebe wasn't ready to do that yet. Wasn't ready for anyone to know her deepest, darkest shame. She'd turned into a person she barely recognized, one who was just a shell of the woman she used to be.

It was becoming harder to pretend that nothing had changed, that she was still the old Phoebe, the one her cousin knew and loved. Sooner or later, everything was going to come spilling out, she knew it and accepted it, but wanted to delay the inevitable for as long as possible.

There was no way her cousin would understand how Phoebe had gotten to a point where she had allowed a man to control and abuse her. She'd let down the one person she loved the most in the world, and that was motivation enough to keep her mouth shut.

If she was lucky, her ex would get bored and move on eventually.

With a sigh, she shoved away the voice in her head that told her that would never happen. That men like him didn't let go of what they believed to be their possessions.

She'd never be free.

Ready to head back to her apartment, Phoebe pushed her body harder. Running had been her thing for as long as she could remember, it settled her, centered her, and catered to her need to always be active and busy. It had also been her life saver during the last eighteen months.

Her ex hated running, but he wanted her to look her best, so he indulged her desire to go for a nightly run after work. Those couple of hours away from him might only delay the inevitable of what happened when she got home, but they also gave her the strength to endure it.

As she approached the road, her attention was snagged by a little girl in a red beanie flanked by two large men gripping her arms and marching her along between them.

Something wasn't right.

Phoebe didn't know how she knew that, but her gut told her the child was in trouble.

Increasing her speed, she ran past the trio then stopped up

ahead and pretended to stretch. They were on one of the roads that cut through the park and maybe a dozen or so yards from the road.

As surreptitiously as she could, Phoebe glanced around. Her gaze fell on a white van pulled up at the side of the road right where this street ended. The destination of the two men all but dragging the child between them?

Was this an abduction she was witnessing?

The little girl's gray-blue eyes met hers for a second and she saw the terror in them. Recognized it because she knew for a fact it was the same look she'd had in her own eyes when she looked at her tormentor. There were tear tracks on the child's face, and the two long blonde braids that peeked out from under her red beanie were messy. There was also a tear in the black dress with the hearts on it.

The child had fought.

More than Phoebe could say for herself.

Anger flared to life inside her. Her ex had started off slowly, at first, she hadn't even noticed the signs. When she had she'd tried to leave, but when he found her, dragged her back, and punished her, she'd let her fear take over. It had become about staying alive, nothing more.

But she'd fought through her fear, run after that last time, determined that she wasn't going to be anyone's punching bag any longer.

That same determination filled her now.

No one was taking this little girl on her watch.

"Excuse me," she said, taking a step closer as the trio prepared to pass her.

As his gaze swung toward her, she noticed the man closest reach for the inside of his jacket almost on instinct.

She caught sight of the weapon there, and if she'd had any doubts that these men intended to abduct the little girl they vanished.

Phoebe had no idea what came over her. All she knew was that she wasn't a victim anymore and she wasn't going to allow this innocent little girl to become one.

After what happened to her cousin, they'd both taken self-defense classes. While what she'd learned had done little to help her with her ex, she hoped it was enough to save this child.

Slamming her foot into the closest man's groin, she was pleased when he groaned and released his hold on the child, dropping to his knees. He had been unprepared for her attack, and she'd caught him unawares, but now the other guy knew to expect trouble.

Still, she wasn't giving up.

Dodging sideways as the man pulled out a weapon, she kicked him in the side and when he stumbled, she followed it up with a one-two punch to his head.

The little girl opened her mouth and let out an ear-piercing scream, and as though afraid the sound would bring more witnesses than they could safely take out and make it away without getting caught, the two men ran to the van, jumped in the back, and it took off into the traffic.

It had worked.

She'd done it.

Phoebe almost couldn't believe it, but she felt a piece of herself that her ex had stolen return.

"Are you okay?" she asked the little girl.

In answer, the child flung herself into Phoebe's arms and began to sob.

"Lolly!" a male voice screamed.

In a blur, a large body came flying toward her, knocking her down. Her head slammed painfully onto the concrete, hard enough that she saw stars, and the next thing she knew she was being flipped onto her stomach, her arms wrenched behind her back, and secured with handcuffs as her body was pressed ruthlessly into the ground.

CHAPTER TWO

February 14th
5:11 P.M.

After forty-three agonizingly long minutes, Mouse heard the most beautiful sound.

Lolly screamed.

While the terror in her voice about destroyed him, Mouse would know his daughter's voice anywhere, and she was close by.

As he rounded a corner and saw a woman touching his child, he didn't think, just reacted.

He and Brick moved at the same time. While Brick snatched Lolly away from her would-be abductor, Mouse slammed the woman onto the ground. Her cry of pain as her head likely hit the concrete barely registered, an anger like no other he'd ever experienced clouded everything.

This woman had tried to take his child from him.

The most precious thing he had, and she'd tried to steal it.

Yanking her arms behind her back, he secured them with handcuffs, then shoved her into the ground to hold her in place even though she wasn't fighting him.

"Here, I got her, go to your daughter," Domino said.

Not needing to be told twice, Mouse handed the woman off to Domino—he'd deal with her later—and reached for his daughter. Lolly's thin arms wrapped around his neck, holding on with a grip that belied her small size, and sobbed into his chest.

His own eyes misted. He hadn't cried since the day his wife died and he realized that not only had he lost the love of his life, but he was also solely responsible for a tiny human being who relied on him for everything.

Today he had failed that tiny human being.

It was only because his daughter was a fighter that he was still able to hold her in his arms.

When she tried to move, he tightened his hold on her, not ready to let her go yet. There were things he needed to do, question Lolly, interrogate the woman before she was handed off to the cops, but right now he just needed to hold his baby girl for one more minute.

"I'm okay, Daddy," Lolly said. Although her voice was a little hoarse from sobbing, she sounded stronger and more in control than he felt.

"Are you hurt, baby girl?" he asked, pulling back but keeping his hands on her shoulders.

"No. And I'm not a baby." The disgruntled face she shot him was one he'd seen dozens of times before. While he still saw her as the little baby she'd been the day she'd been born, she saw herself as a big girl now, and she got annoyed with him when he didn't agree.

"I know you're not, bumblebee," he said, tweaking her nose. Bumblebee was his very own nickname for his daughter. As an infant, she'd made a buzzing sort of snoring sound that reminded him of bees. "I need you to go with Brick for just a little while. He'll take you back to the picnic. I just need to talk to the lady first before I come find you, okay?" Mouse did his best not to let his fury show. Once his daughter was safe, he was going to find out exactly what the lady's plans had been, no matter what he had to do to get her to talk.

Nobody messed with his child.

Lolly looked around him, presumably to her abductor, and her little brow creased into a frown. "Why is the lady wearing handcuffs? Only bad guys wear handcuffs."

His own brow furrowed. "What do you mean, bumblebee?"

"She saved me," Lolly said, her voice calm and confident. "She kicked the bad men and they let go of me, then I screamed, and the bad men ran away."

"She saved you?" he echoed.

Lolly shot the woman a warm smile. "She saved me, Daddy. She's not a bad guy." The reprimand in his daughter's tone was clear, and Mouse felt a stab of guilt. He hadn't even attempted to be gentle when he'd taken the woman down, he'd thought she'd tried to kidnap his little girl.

"Okay, bumblebee, go with Uncle Brick now." It was hard but he lifted his daughter and handed her off to Brick. He was sure Lolly would complain about being carried, but he needed to know his child was completely safe.

Once Brick and Surf had disappeared with Lolly, he turned to look at the woman who was standing beside Domino. She was dressed in black leggings that hugged long, slim legs that seemed to go for miles, a bright pink hoodie, and matching hot pink sneakers, with her blonde hair pulled back into a ponytail.

She had large blue eyes that were currently wide with fear as she stared at him, and he could already see a large lump forming on her temple from where her head had hit the ground when he'd knocked her down. From the way she hunched her shoulders, it was like she was trying to fold in on herself and disappear, and Mouse got the distinct feeling that she'd been hurt before.

Nodding to Domino, his friend produced the handcuff key and unlocked the cuffs from around the woman's wrists. Very carefully she brought them around in front of her, wincing and then rubbing at her wrists.

"You saved my daughter?" he asked, stepping closer. The woman took a step back and he stopped, hating that she was afraid of him but completely understanding why. She'd risked her life to help a child in trouble and had been assaulted and cuffed for her trouble. "How did you know she needed help?"

Terrified eyes darted from him to Domino and back again. It was obvious she was still afraid of them and didn't trust either one of them. "I … the way they held her … then … I saw her eyes. She was scared."

"So, you risked your life for her?"

The woman straightened her spine, and he got the feeling he'd offended her somehow. It wasn't his intention, if anything he was in awe of her bravery, and eternally grateful. Because of this woman, he still had his sweet little girl.

"My cousin and I took self-defense classes, I guess all I was thinking was that she was just a little girl, and those men were dragging her toward a van," she said, her voice a little stronger now.

"You and your cousin obviously learned from the best," he said, hoping to put her at ease with a genuine smile.

She nodded once. "My cousin Hope is married to Falcon Oswald. I don't know if you've heard of them, but Falcon and his siblings run Prey Security."

Mouse's mouth dropped open. Of all the things he'd expected her to say it wasn't that. Sometimes it really was a small world. "I'm Mouse—Asher—me and my friends are part of Prey's Alpha Team. You must be Phoebe, right?" He'd heard about the woman, who had given Falcon the shove he needed to go after Hope when the two had first met but had never met her. Although she had attended a few Prey get-togethers with her cousin, they were ones he'd been unable to attend.

Phoebe looked as shocked by the connection as he was, but she nodded again. If he'd still had any doubts about whether or not she was somehow involved in his daughter's near abduction they were gone now. Falcon had nothing but good things to say about his wife's cousin, and he trusted the Oswalds completely.

Noting the thread of pain in her blue eyes he winced. "I'm sorry about hurting you. I just saw you with my daughter and lost control."

For the first time, Phoebe's expression softened. "It's okay," she said softly. "I understand. You were just thinking about your daughter. I hope she's okay."

"She is. Thanks to you."

A slight blush added a little color to Phoebe's cheeks, and he took a moment to really look at her. A delicate nose, plump pink lips, smooth creamy skin, she was beautiful, and the first woman that had stirred something inside him since his wife's death. Too bad she was afraid of him because …

Was he really considering asking her out?

That seemed ridiculous given he'd knocked her down, made her hit her head, and possibly inflicted other injuries. Although she seemed to understand that he'd been out of his mind with fear for his daughter, it didn't mean she was willing to forgive him and go on a date.

"Are you okay?" he asked, nodding at her head.

She seemed surprised by the question, her gaze skittering away. "Fine."

The murmured word did little to reassure him, but before he could press further a couple of cops appeared. Now that he knew the woman wasn't the kidnapper he didn't really need to hang around and question her, he had to get back to Lolly, be there with her when she gave her statement.

"Again, I'm sorry, and thank you so much for what you did. If you hadn't intervened, I could have lost her." Impulsively he closed the distance between them, touched a kiss to her cheek then turned and walked away. For some reason there was an odd kind of ache in his chest as he left Phoebe behind.

* * * * *

February 14th
9:34 P.M.

Finally.

Phoebe let out a sigh of relief as she stepped back inside her apartment, closed and locked the front door behind her, and sagged against it, completely and utterly drained.

Home at last.

This place might not really feel like home, not because she hadn't been here long, but because it was furnished with nothing that belonged to her. It felt more like a hotel to her than a home, but she was glad to be here, alone, away from prying eyes.

After the little girl—whose name she had learned was Lolly—had told her father and his friends that she'd saved her and not tried to abduct her, nobody had looked at her with suspicion. The medics who had checked her out had been kind, the cops who had interviewed her had been gentle and made sure she was treated like a witness and not a suspect, but it hadn't eased the knot of fear in her stomach.

Maybe it was because she'd recently been abused by a man bigger and stronger than she was, that she was having trouble separating her ex from the men who had tackled her today, hurt her, and restrained her. Knowing they were actually good men and had—in their minds—a good reason for being rough with her wasn't helping.

She'd been terrified.

Battled not to fall apart.

Memories of her ex hitting her and tying her up, making her do things she didn't want to do had assaulted her mind, and if they hadn't uncuffed her when they did she might have embarrassed herself.

"It's over now." Shoving off the door, Phoebe winced at the ache in her shoulder. Her ex had dislocated it in early December. The assault had been awful, one of the worst he'd inflicted on her, then after leaving the joint out of place for hours he forced it back in. Afraid to go to the doctor to have it looked at because she knew she'd have to give an explanation, she had left it to heal on its own.

That event was the catalyst for her leaving.

Today the men had apologized—something her ex had never done—when they realized she was innocent, and they had a good reason for what they'd done.

Although her ex always thought he had a good reason for abusing her too.

"No, it's not the same and you know it," she rebuked herself as she wandered through to the kitchen and grabbed a bottle of water from the fridge. She knew the men from Prey were good men. They'd served their country and now continued to risk their lives to make the world a safer place, they wouldn't hurt her just for fun.

Still, they were big, strong men, fierce and capable of inflicting pain. Definitely not the kind of men she was interested in. The last thing she needed in her life was another man who could crush her if he wanted to.

Phoebe truly believed that but still she couldn't forget the feel of Asher's lips on her cheek as he'd thanked her with a kiss.

Stupid really.

It was unlikely she'd ever see him again. Hope had invited her to a few Prey functions, so she had met some of the men and women who worked there, a lot of them at Hope and Falcon's wedding, but Alpha team had been called away just before the wedding so she hadn't met them.

Today's meeting should be more than enough to turn her off them. To turn her off men in general actually.

Bath.

She needed to soak in a long, hot bubble bath. The heat should ease the ache in her shoulder, and maybe it would help her relax enough that she could get some sleep.

Wasn't likely she would sleep much, there were too many bad memories churning inside her. It would be a long day at work tomorrow but since it was a new job, she didn't want to call in sick. As much as she was grateful to Hope and Falcon for letting her stay in this apartment that was usually used as a Prey safehouse, she wanted to find her own place. The apartment was too ostentatious for her tastes, and she could never hope to afford something in this building on her own, but she wanted to get control of her life back.

Phoebe wandered listlessly through to her bathroom and added a generous amount of her favorite bubble bath. She added lavender-scented salts as well, and then turned on the water, getting it nice and hot.

Just as she'd slipped out of her clothes her phone rang.

As much as she wanted to ignore it, her cousin's name was on the screen and since Hope had done so much for her these last couple of months, finding her a place to stay and getting her a job, she didn't want to not answer.

"Hey," she said, attempting to inject some energy into her voice.

"Were you going to call and tell me?" Hope demanded, sounding angry.

"Call and tell you what?"

"About what happened today."

Honestly, the thought hadn't occurred to her. Maybe it would have eventually, but right now her nerves were stretched tight, she was exhausted, and her focus had just been getting back home so she could let go. "How did you find out?"

"Mouse called to apologize and ask us to pass on how sorry he was again for knocking you down."

"He told me he was sorry already."

"He feels so bad."

"I believe that." She did. She had accepted his apology and meant it. It was understandable that he'd been out of his mind with fear for his child, and then he'd seen her with his daughter. Of course he thought she was involved. As far as she was concerned it was over and done with, and she just wanted to forget it and move on.

"He said he hurt you, that you had a lump on your head and

seemed like your shoulder was sore. He wants to make sure you're okay."

"If he wants to know he should call and ask himself instead of going through you," she snapped. It wasn't until the words were out of her mouth that she realized what she'd said. Asher having her number and calling her were the last things she wanted. No more big, strong men in her life. None. If she ever got up the nerve to date again, she was going with a sweet, kind of geeky guy, who couldn't hurt her if he tried. Before, she'd always gone for hot guys with great bodies, it was the first thing that had caught her attention with her ex. Now all she wanted was a man who made her feel safe.

"Ah," Hope said, and Phoebe immediately knew her cousin had gotten the wrong idea.

Rubbing wearily at her temples, wincing when she brushed against the bruises, she reached over, turned off the faucet, and sat on the edge of the bath. "I didn't mean that. Don't go giving him my number. I just meant there was no need for him to go to you just because we're cousins. I get that he didn't mean to hurt me, that he was just worried about his daughter, honestly, I just want to forget about today and move on."

"I know you're not over your ex yet," Hope said slowly. All Phoebe had told her cousin when she'd arrived in Manhattan was that things hadn't worked out with her ex and she wanted a fresh start. She knew Hope believed that her ex had cheated on her and that was the reason for the move, and Phoebe hadn't bothered to correct her. "But Mouse is a great guy. He's a devoted father, a great friend, he's smart and funny, and a really nice guy."

"No matchmaking. Please, Hope." There was no way she was ready for any sort of relationship. Not when she was still terrified of her ex and unsure if he would follow through on his threats to kill her if she tried to leave him. Just because she'd been gone for two months didn't mean he'd forgotten about her. When she was ready to move on there was no way it was going to be with another super-hot, chiseled muscled, panty-melting man.

No way.

Definitely not.

Hope sighed. "Okay. No matchmaking. But he really does feel bad."

"I know he does. The important thing is that his little girl is all right, that she wasn't taken."

"Thanks to you. You're a hero." There was pride in her cousin's voice, but Phoebe didn't want praise, she didn't want anyone to make a big deal out of it. She'd done what she could to save Lolly because she didn't want the child to be hurt and because she needed to prove to herself that she wasn't the weak woman her ex made her believe she was.

"It was nothing."

"It wasn't nothing. It was amazing. You're amazing, and I love you so much. Are you okay? Do you want me to come over?"

Phoebe smiled despite everything, she was lucky to have her cousin. Hope loved her unconditionally, and she appreciated that so much. "I'm okay. I'm just going to take a bubble bath and go right to bed, I'm exhausted."

"All right, but you'll call if you need me?"

"Of course."

"I love you."

"Love you back."

"Night."

"Goodnight, Hope."

Once she ended the call, Phoebe climbed into the bath and sank down, submerging most of her body under the bubbles.

This was usually her happy place, but today she didn't get any enjoyment from the hot bath. How could she when she was running from a man she thought she'd been in love with, a man who had abused not just her body but her mind as well. Phoebe didn't know if she could ever learn to trust anyone, including herself, ever again.

CHAPTER THREE

February 14th
10:01 P.M.

"Can I have hot chocolate?"

Mouse couldn't help but smile. His daughter was remarkably resilient. Despite everything that had happened today, Lolly was still her usual happy, bubbly self. She certainly hadn't hesitated to try to take advantage of the situation. Unable to say no to her, they'd had ice cream for dinner, he'd bought her some video game she'd been asking for for weeks and let her stay up way past her bedtime.

As much as he'd love to say yes to hot chocolate, maybe whip up a batch of cookies and eat them fresh from the oven, one of Lolly's favorite things to do on a cold winter evening, it was ten and she needed her sleep.

"Tomorrow night, bumblebee," he assured her as he pulled back the covers so she could climb into bed.

"What if you have to leave?" Lolly looked up at him with serious blue eyes. Her mother's eyes. His daughter never complained about his job, that she spent more time with her grandparents than with him, that sometimes he missed important events in her life, her mother hadn't either. With his black hair, dark eyes, and tanned skin he didn't look like his daughter, Lolly was absolutely her mother's child. She had Emily's dark blonde locks, gray-blue eyes, and pale skin, she even had her mother's dimple in her left cheek. Mouse knew he was lucky to have had Emily and lucky that he hadn't lost Lolly along with her mom.

"I won't have to leave tomorrow," he assured her. Eagle had

grounded Alpha team for at least the next week so he could be there for Lolly.

"Do you promise?" Lolly asked as she climbed onto her bed. For the first time since he'd first found her, he saw a vulnerability in his daughter that said she wasn't quite as okay as she was pretending to be. She was a tough little thing, and he knew that with time and some therapy she would be okay. He had already booked an appointment for her with a therapist for tomorrow afternoon. He was taking no chances when it came to his daughter's mental health, so he'd rather deal with it now than allow potential issues to fester.

Sitting down beside her, he looped an arm around her shoulders. "I pinkie swear."

That drew a smile out of his suddenly too-serious little girl. To seven-year-old Lolly, a pinkie swear was the ultimate proof that you were telling the truth. "Can we make cookies to have with the hot chocolate?"

"We sure can."

"Yay," she cheered as they locked pinkies and shook on it.

"All right, it's time now for you to get some sleep."

"Can you read me a story first?"

It was on the tip of his tongue to tell her not tonight. It was late and she had school tomorrow, she needed her sleep, but there was no way he could turn down an opportunity to spend a few more minutes with his little girl. Mouse had asked Lolly if she wanted to sleep in his bed tonight, but his daughter had told him she'd be okay in her own room.

"I can read you one chapter," he offered.

"Deal, Daddy," Lolly quickly agreed.

They were currently reading The Babysitters Club, his sister's favorite as a child. When Lolly had found them in a box in his parents' attic she'd become obsessed. They were onto the tenth book, and even though Lolly was a great reader for her age, she still loved to have him sit beside her on her bed and read to her

JANE BLYTHE

each night when he was there to tuck her in.

Far too soon they reached the end of the chapter, and it was time to kiss her goodnight and leave. Normally he looked forward to a little downtime after he tucked his daughter in for the night. Between his job and being a single dad, his life rarely allowed time for him to just chill out, not that he was complaining. Mouse loved his life, but he wasn't getting any younger, and he was starting to wonder if perhaps he wanted more.

Tonight though he didn't want time on his own, he wanted to hold his daughter and never let her go. While she might have bounced back quickly after her forty-three-minute ordeal he hadn't. The fear of not knowing where his daughter was or what was happening to her would forever be imprinted on his mind.

But his daughter needed him to be strong. If she knew how afraid he had been—still was—then it would set off her own anxiety. She might be growing far too quickly, but she was still only barely seven years old, and she still took a lot of her cues from him.

"All right, sweetie, that's it, time to go to sleep," he said, trying to sound upbeat when all he wanted to do was gather up his daughter and keep her glued to his side for the rest of her life.

"Night, Daddy," Lolly said on a yawn as she snuggled down under the covers.

"You sure you're going to be okay in here tonight?" he asked as he set the book on the nightstand and stood.

"Yes."

"Want me to put the nightlight on?" Around Christmas, Lolly had started to insist that she was too old for the Minnie Mouse nightlight. Unable to go cold turkey, some nights she still asked for it to go on and he thought tonight might definitely be one of those nights she needed it.

"No, I'm fine, Daddy. Can you get Mr. Whiskers and Mrs. Fuzzy?" she asked, gesturing to the toybox that was filled to overflowing with dozens of stuffed animals. Lolly usually slept

25

with her favorite teddy bear and a ragdoll that Emily had made while she was pregnant, but sometimes she liked to pile her bed high with pretty much every one of her stuffed animals.

"Here we go, bumblebee." Mouse retrieved the two cats and set them beside Lolly, who immediately took Mrs. Fuzzy and pulled it under the blankets with her, holding it close.

"Mrs. Fuzzy makes me think of Phoebe. They're both pretty," Lolly said.

With the cat's golden fur and blue eyes, he could see how Lolly saw Phoebe Lynch in the toy. It was clear his daughter had been thinking of the woman who had without a doubt saved her life. He had been too. Hadn't been able to forget how she'd selflessly put herself in danger to save his daughter. How he'd hurt her when he'd knocked her down and how there had been genuine fear in her eyes.

The woman was strong and beautiful, yet there was a vulnerability in her that called out to the protector in him.

Of all the women he'd met since Emily's death, Phoebe was the only one to spark any interest inside him. Had he finally reached a point where he was ready to start dating again? How would Lolly feel about him bringing another woman into their little family? Would Phoebe even be interested in him given the fact he'd tackled her and slammed her into the ground then had her handcuffed the first time they'd met?

"Daddy?"

"Yeah, sweetie, Mrs. Fuzzy is pretty just like Phoebe," he agreed.

"I like Phoebe," Lolly said on a yawn. His daughter had been full of questions about the woman who saved her, and when she'd learned Phoebe was Hope's cousin, she'd been extra excited. To Lolly, everyone at Prey was an uncle or an aunt, they were her family, and between them, his parents, his sister and her husband and kids, she had lots of people who loved her.

Didn't stop him from wishing she had a mother.

Emily would always be Lolly's mom, the woman who gave her life, who loved her from the second they knew about the pregnancy. But Emily would also be the first one to tell him to move on, give Lolly a mom who could be there for her, who would love her like her own.

Could that woman be Phoebe?

"I like her too," he admitted. "Sweet dreams, sweetie. If you need me you just call out, okay?"

"'Kay, Daddy." Lolly's eyes closed, and her breathing evened out as she drifted off.

Mouse stooped to kiss the top of his daughter's head, then crept out of the room, leaving the door cracked and the hallway light on. Lolly liked Phoebe, he liked Phoebe, when he'd called Hope earlier to let her know what happened and that Phoebe might need a shoulder to cry on, he'd also asked for her number, her home address, and her work address.

If he called, she might not even answer since his number would show up as an unknown caller. Maybe after he took Lolly to school in the morning he'd go and see Phoebe. He did want to check on her and make sure she was okay. She'd had a traumatic experience today as well, but it was so much more than that.

Something deep in his gut told him that Phoebe was special and he shouldn't let her go.

* * * * *

February 15th
8:48 A.M.

Someone was watching her.

Phoebe had that feeling again.

Why wouldn't it go away?

No matter how many times she looked she could never see anyone who appeared to be paying any sort of attention to her, yet the feeling persisted. She was starting to think that she was losing her mind.

Her ex was managing to torture her even though they were on opposite sides of the country. Just because he'd threatened that he would never let her go didn't mean he intended to follow through. Maybe he'd already moved on.

One could only hope.

Sipping her coffee, she stood outside the cute little bakery across the street from the building where she worked and did her best to scan the street without looking like she was doing so. Everyone appeared to be going about their business, no one was looking at her, no one seemed to care about her at all.

Was she really losing her mind?

Phoebe felt exhausted, completely wiped out. Eighteen months of dating a man who took pleasure in her pain, everything that happened yesterday, and no sleep last night. It felt like the life she'd built was quickly slipping through her fingers. She didn't even know who she was anymore, but she knew the woman she'd been for her whole life had disappeared and she didn't know if she could ever find her again.

With a long sigh, she headed for her building. The quicker she got to work the quicker she would get through the day and go home. Maybe by the time she climbed into bed tonight, she would be tired enough to actually sleep.

Someone came up behind her. Phoebe went to move out of the way, but instead of going around her they loomed over her.

Panicked, she spun around so quickly she lost her footing and stumbled.

Phoebe would have landed flat on her backside in the middle of the dirty sidewalk, where she likely would have been trampled, but a pair of hands darted out and caught her.

"Sorry I startled you," Asher said.

What was he doing here?

Was he the one who had been watching her?

Why would he do that?

A terrible thought occurred to her. Had he been following her because he thought she really did have something to do with his daughter's abduction? Maybe he thought if he followed her, she would lead him to the men in the white van.

"I wasn't involved," she blurted out. Pushed to her limits it wasn't going to take much to shatter her completely.

"In what?" he asked, looking genuinely confused.

"With your daughter. I wasn't working with those men."

His face softened, and she wished he didn't look quite so deliciously handsome. Her life was a mess, and even if it wasn't, the relationship she'd run to Manhattan to escape had turned her off men completely. Especially a man like Asher who was all hard muscle and strength.

"I know you weren't, Phoebe," he said. "And I hope you know how sorry I am that I hurt you." He reached out and brushed his knuckle under the lump on her temple.

Why did her pulse have to triple its pace at his touch? Her skin went tingly, and she got that swirly feeling in her stomach.

Okay, don't panic. You're just attracted to him, it's no big deal. Just because you find him attractive doesn't mean you have to do anything about it, she coached herself.

"Phoebe, you okay?"

Asher's voice drew her out of her thoughts, and she quickly took a step back. He couldn't touch her like that, all sweet and gentle, if he did, she'd give in to the urge to throw herself into his arms. He was big and strong, he'd be able to hold her up, just for a little while, until she got her feet beneath her again.

The temptation was almost more than she could bear even with the distance between them. Why did Asher have to be everything she'd always thought she wanted in a man? The package had always been important to her, but she wasn't so shallow that she thought it was all about a cute face and a six-pack. Intelligence, a sense of humor, a good heart, she thought all those things were just as important, and unfortunately Asher Whitman had them all.

"I'm not really hurt," she said, mostly to reassure him. Her head did still hurt, and the hot bubble bath hadn't helped her shoulder at all, but she didn't want Asher feeling bad about it. What else could he do given the circumstances as he saw them but restrain the person he thought was trying to steal his child? "How's your little girl?"

At the mention of his daughter, it was like Asher's entire being softened further. It was clear that his daughter was the center of his world. "Lolly seems to be doing fine. I was worried she might have had nightmares last night, but she slept through. This morning she was excited to go to school, she loves learning, and she always looks forward to school, but I was worried she might have reservations since we'd been on a school picnic yesterday. But nope, not my little Lolly, she was her usual self, excited, chattering away ... like I'm doing now. I'm sorry you have to get to work, don't you?"

She'd been standing there, transfixed by the utter joy on his face when he talked about his daughter. Phoebe thought he was good-looking before, but that was nothing compared to the way his face transformed when he mentioned Lolly, now she roused herself. There was no point in getting herself a crush on the sexy operative. Nothing was going to happen between them.

Nothing could.

Heartbreak was the last thing she needed while she was terrified she was being followed and was broken inside thanks to her ex.

"It's okay," she said shyly. Shy wasn't something she'd ever been before. Phoebe had always known what she wanted and went after it with a confidence she now found herself lacking. "And I'm glad Lolly is okay. I know with a father like you and so many people there for her she'll bounce back, she's one strong little girl."

"She is," Asher agreed. "She's not the only one who's strong. I can't ever thank you enough for what you did. You saved Lolly's life."

Phoebe shrugged, uncomfortable with the praise. If he knew that she'd allowed a man to control and assault her, he wouldn't think she was strong. "I did what anyone else would have done."

"No." He reached out and took her hand, cradling it in his much larger ones. "No one else *did* do what you did. No one even noticed Lolly was in trouble, and if they did, they didn't try to help her. You saved her life. I owe you everything." He paused and dragged in a breath like he was nervous. "Would you like to have dinner with me?"

"Dinner?" she echoed, sure she must have somehow misheard.

"A date," he clarified.

"A date?"

Asher huffed out an amused chuckle. "I didn't think it would be such a shocking idea that someone would ask a gorgeous woman like you out on a date."

Before her ex, she would have jumped at a chance to have dinner with a man like Asher, but now all the thought did was make her stomach churn with panic.

No, she couldn't go out with Asher.

He was too big.

Too strong.

All it would take was one blow, and he'd render her helpless, then he could do whatever he wanted to her.

There was no way she could take that chance.

Just because Asher seemed nice, noble, and loving, it didn't mean that he was. He could be hiding anything beneath the veneer of hero who protected the innocent and dedicated father.

How could she ever trust herself to see the truth again?

The panic inside her was growing, and before she did something completely stupid and embarrassed herself, she quickly shook her head. "I can't go out with you. I'm sorry. I have to get to work."

Without waiting for a response, she turned and hurried across the street and into her building. Far away from Asher and his too-perfect looks, his too-perfect personality, and his strength that scared her more than it should.

Was this her life now?

Would there ever be a time when she could look at a man and not wonder if he was going to beat her once they were alone?

This was no way to live, but she had no idea how to get herself out of the mess that was her life. Was it time to go to her cousin and ask if there was any way Prey could help her with her ex? Was she ready to admit to her cousin that she'd let a man beat her down until she didn't even know which way was up?

Was she ready for the world to know she was a pathetic loser?

CHAPTER FOUR

"Daddy, when are Grandma and Grandpa getting here?" Lolly asked as they walked into their apartment after he'd picked her up from school.

"They'll be here in time for you to help Grandma cook dinner." Despite the fact Mouse had told his parents they didn't need to drive into the city to see Lolly, that she was fine, they loved her like she was their own, and while they'd held back on coming yesterday, they had told him they'd be coming today. It wasn't like he could really complain, he loved that his parents loved his little girl, and they had been a godsend after Emily died. Without them, he didn't know what he would have done.

"Yay," Lolly cheered. She loved helping cook or bake, he wouldn't be surprised if he had a little chef in the making. "What are we having for dinner?"

"I don't know, bumblebee. Grandma said she was bringing everything with her."

"Can I have a snack?" she asked already heading for the kitchen.

The doorbell rang before he could answer, and Lolly changed direction to head to the door instead. Checking he was behind her, when he nodded to let her know that the door cam had told him who was there and that it was okay for her to let them in, she flung the door open.

"Uncle Surf." Lolly giggled as Surf picked her up and swung her around.

"Hey, cutie pie, how are you?"

"What's a cutie pie?" Lolly asked.

"You," Surf replied.

Lolly made a face. "Pie isn't cute though it's yummy."

"Can't argue with that." Surf laughed as he set her down on her feet.

"We brought donuts," Arrow said, holding up a box.

"Yay, are there ones with sprinkles?" Lolly asked. She was a little obsessed with sprinkles. She loved them on donuts, ice cream, waffles, pancakes, and French Toast. Basically, if he let her, she'd eat them on anything.

"You really have to ask, munchkin?" Arrow asked with a laugh.

Lolly took the box and skipped over to the couch where she plopped herself down, turned on the TV, and scrolled through Netflix to find one of her favorite shows, and Mouse knew she would settle in and watch until his parents showed up.

"Two donuts is all you can have," he told her.

"Okay, Daddy," she said, but her voice was distracted, he'd lost her to TV land.

Leading the guys through to the kitchen, he grabbed mugs and started making coffee while Arrow set a second box of donuts down on the table. Once they were all seated, Mouse looked around at the men he thought of as his brothers. They'd been through a lot together, watched each other's backs more times than he could count, and they'd been there for him yesterday when the bottom had fallen out of his world.

There was nobody he trusted more than the men on his team.

"Do we have anything?" Mouse asked. Nobody at Prey was prepared to let Lolly's attempted abduction slide. They would do whatever it took to identify the men who had tried to steal his daughter, and the van they'd been using. The cops had spoken with his former in-laws, but they had denied being involved. Since their last petition for custody had been denied they were no longer represented by the firm his gut said was shady, they had also denied involvement, citing they had no motive and that they did not conduct business that way.

"Nothing much yet," Bear replied.

"We did find out the dog they used to try to lure Lolly away was stolen," Domino informed him.

"A woman walking her dog in the park was mugged. They took her purse and her dog. Purse was found in a trash bin by the playground, and the dog was found wandering around the park not long after we found Lolly," Brick elaborated.

"Obviously, they were planning on using a dog to try to lure Lolly away, probably thought since she was a little girl it would be an easy sell," Arrow said.

"Only your smart little girl didn't fall for it," Bear said.

"No, she didn't," Mouse agreed. He was so proud of his daughter. She might be sweet and bubbly, but she was also smart. Growing up around him, his team, and Prey she had been taught how to be safe, aware of her surroundings, and had also been given self-defense classes from the time she could walk.

When she'd been approached at the playground yesterday afternoon by a man with a dog who asked her if she wanted to come and see the dog's puppies, Lolly had said no. Having their ruse fail one of the kidnappers had shown Lolly a gun and threatened to shoot her friends unless she went with them.

His heart ached for the choice his barely seven-year-old daughter had had to make, but so proud of her sweet little heart that hadn't wanted anyone else to be hurt. There was also a healthy dose of anger toward the people who had put his child in that position.

"Anything on the van?" They knew where the van had been parked thanks to Phoebe, and they knew what time it had taken off. Surely they could get a number plate and track down its owner.

"It was found abandoned a few streets over," Bear told him.

Frustration burned inside him. He wanted those men, wanted

them punished for what they'd done to Lolly. "So that was a dead end too?"

"Cameras caught three men getting out of the van but no clear shots of their faces, so we can't identify them," Surf told him.

"So, we have nothing." He huffed. He'd known it was a long shot that they'd be able to trace the kidnappers, but he felt an urgency to find them he couldn't explain. There was no way to know if her own grandparents were behind it, whether or not Lolly had been targeted, and if she had whether she had been targeted specifically because of him or just because she had met some set of arbitrary requirements when the kidnappers had seen her.

If she'd been targeted because of him, he would never forgive himself.

It wasn't like in his job they were usually targeted by anyone. Usually, no one even knew they were there, they went in, did what they had to do to rescue a victim or take down a high-value target, and then left. But there was always a chance that someone had a grudge against them, or him in particular.

If the attempt had been a targeted decision to destroy his team by taking his daughter, then Lolly wasn't the only one he was worried about. Phoebe had saved his daughter's life. There was no denying that, but she had also put herself on the kidnappers' radar by doing so.

Was she in danger now?

When he'd gone to ask her out this morning, she'd been edgy, looking around as though she expected the bogeyman to come jumping out to grab her at any second.

Had something happened?

"Did you go see her?" Bear asked, his brown gaze much too astute to even bother lying.

"Yeah."

"It didn't go well?" Arrow asked. Apparently, all the guys seemed to have figured out that he was a little infatuated with his daughter's savior. It was more than the fact Phoebe had saved Lolly though, it wasn't until last night when he was lying in bed not sleeping that he'd realized she was the jogger who had caught his attention when Lolly had disappeared. Something about her drew him in, but it didn't seem like she was interested in even giving him a chance.

"She turned me down flat when I asked her out to dinner," he admitted. Although he'd sensed that there was more to it than that. The look on her face was fear. He knew it, had seen it many times before. Pure unadulterated fear.

But of what?

"You know she used to work for the firm your former in-laws used. The one you have a bad feeling about," Bear said cautiously.

"I know, but she left months ago, before they hired the firm, so I don't think there's any way she could realistically be involved."

"So, you just giving up on her?" Brick asked.

Was he?

Phoebe had said no, and he wanted to respect that. If she wasn't interested in him then he didn't want to pressure her into doing something she didn't want to do. And yet, he couldn't deny that when he'd seen her today, touched her, that infatuation he'd felt had only grown.

"Maybe I should have given her a little time before asking her out," he admitted. "She went through a traumatic experience yesterday, she's probably still shaken up about it. I should have just thanked her and left it at that, gone back another time to ask her out. Or given her my number, talked to her a bit first, let her get to know me, it wasn't like I made the best first impression."

The problem was could he overcome that?

He knew Phoebe said she had forgiven him for hurting her, and he honestly believed that she had, but that didn't mean she was willing to trust him. Without trust there could be nothing between them.

And he wanted something with her.

For a guy who thought he'd had his one chance at love, it was a disconcerting feeling to find himself drawn to a woman again. Mouse had no idea if anything would ever happen between him and Phoebe, but he knew he couldn't just walk away without trying at least one more time to see if she would give him a chance.

What was the worst thing that could happen?

* * * * *

February 15th
6:54 P.M.

Her neck was aching, her head thumping with a persistent headache, and her eyes starting to blur after so long staring at a computer screen.

With a small moan of pain, Phoebe pushed back in her chair, lifting a hand to rub at the tight muscles in the back of her neck, and was surprised to see it was dark out her window. Glancing at the clock she saw it was almost seven.

Wow.

The last thing she remembered was running to her office after Asher had asked her out. She'd come straight in here, jumped right onto her computer, and started working on her cases. Burying herself in work was the only way not to melt into a puddle of embarrassment and shame, so she hadn't even stopped for lunch.

Not that she had much of an appetite.

Asher was everything she used to think she wanted in a man, but now he was everything she feared.

At least it was done now, over with. He'd asked and she'd said no, there was no reason for her to see him again or have to talk to him again. It meant no more going to any Prey functions with

Hope, but maybe that was for the best.

It was time she started rebuilding her life.

That meant putting a little distance between herself and her cousin. Not cutting Hope out of her life or anything like that, she'd never give up her best friend for anything, but she needed to find her own place, buy her own stuff, and maybe even look for a job that Hope didn't get Falcon to find for her.

She had to stand on her own two feet again.

With that plan firmly in her mind, Phoebe gathered up her things, slipped into her coat, put her purse strap over her shoulder, and shut down her computer. Tonight, she was going to clear her mind of everything and get herself a good night's sleep. Surely if she was well-rested everything would look better in the morning.

The building was quiet and dark, everyone else seemed to have gone home for the night, and it felt kind of spooky in here.

When she pressed the button for the elevator, she fidgeted nervously and couldn't help looking over her shoulder. Anyone could be hiding behind one of the closed doors, or behind one of the desks.

Paranoid.

She'd become completely paranoid, and it wasn't a good look on her. Maybe it would be a good idea to find a therapist and talk through everything that had happened with her ex. When she could afford it anyway.

The lift doors opened, and Phoebe stepped inside. When she'd left California, she'd taken only a suitcase of clothes and a couple of personal items she hadn't wanted to leave behind. Not that the apartment she'd lived in with her ex had much of her stuff anyway. When they'd moved in together, he'd told her they should have all new things to start their lives together, so most of her things were in storage in her parents' garage. At the time, she'd thought it was sweet, but then she hadn't known he was a psychopath.

Crossing the lobby, she stepped out into the cold evening and already felt exhausted by the thirty-minute walk back to her apartment, and she hadn't even started yet. When she spotted a cab pulling up and someone hopping out, she hurried over. It was a splurge she couldn't really afford but the walk home was just too daunting tonight.

Tomorrow. She'd be strong tomorrow. After a good night's sleep she'd be stronger, clearer, and then she was going to write down a plan to rebuild her life. Her ex might have hurt her, but he hadn't destroyed her. She wouldn't let him.

Even with traffic the taxi ride cut her journey in half, and fifteen minutes later, Phoebe paid and dragged herself into her building. Despite skipping lunch, she wasn't hungry. As soon as she got home, she'd jump straight in the shower and then climb into bed. Sleep was what she needed the most right now, everything else would be so much easier to deal with when she was well-rested.

Phoebe hummed in relief when she stepped out of the elevator and walked down the hall.

Almost there, she consoled herself.

Soon she'd be snuggling under the covers and shutting her mind down. It sounded like heaven. In fact, she was so busy dreaming about how lovely it would be to rest her head on the feather pillow, snuggled under luxurious expensive sheets that she didn't realize anyone was behind her until she unlocked her door and pushed it open.

The next thing she knew she was swung around and slammed up against the wall hard enough the air left her lungs.

"Miss me, *sweetheart*," a voice sneered.

Her ex.

Dexter Hunt in the flesh.

Six feet, two hundred pounds of pure muscle. He could bench press double her hundred- and ten-pound five-foot two-inch frame. Golden blond hair, eyes as bright blue as a summer's sky, and dimples, he looked like he just stepped off the set of a photo shoot. IQ of one hundred and thirty, he was genius-level smart, and a brilliant actor to boot. A lawyer who worked custody cases for Hollywood elite, he was everything she thought she had wanted.

Then turned it into a nightmare.

Now he was here.

In Manhattan.

In her apartment.

With his hand around her throat.

Of course she hadn't missed him. She'd lived in terror for the last eight weeks and two days constantly expecting him to show up. If she told him that he'd beat her to a bloody pulp, then probably drag her back to LA with him.

"I gave you time, sweetheart. Time for you to come to your senses and come home, now, I'm sick of waiting for you. I think I've been more than fair. I let you spend time with your cousin, allowed you this little running away from home tantrum, but enough is enough. Pack your things and let's go."

Go?

She wasn't going anywhere with him.

Going back to LA and allowing this man to resume controlling her would end only one way.

With her death.

Sooner or later, Dexter would snap and kill her.

"No."

His eyes widened in surprise at her declaration but quickly narrowed in irritation. "It's been a long day, I'm tired, and I want to go home. Pack and let's go."

"No," she said again. "I told you it was over between us. This is my home now."

"Fool," Dexter said, throwing back his head and laughing. Abruptly he stopped and backhanded her, splitting her lip in the process. "Do you have any idea what I had planned for you? You would have had everything. *Everything* your heart would have desired. You would have been richer than your wildest dreams, houses across the globe, and I would have been one of the most powerful men in the world."

She had no idea what he was talking about. He worked high-profile custody cases mostly for actors and those involved in the film and television industry. Sure, he was very well off, but he was hardly rich enough to own multiple houses, and what kind of power did he think he was going to get from ruthlessly attempting to cut out of a child's life one of their parents?

Phoebe had suspected Dexter had gotten himself involved in something shady after witnessing a meeting with a client about six months back, but she hadn't any idea what it might be. Obviously, whatever it was, Dexter thought he was going to get money and power out of it.

More reasons—as if she needed any—that she should stay as far away from him as possible.

"I don't want money and power, Dexter," she said, injecting confidence she didn't feel into her tone. "And I'm not going anywhere with you. I told you when I left that it was over between us and I wasn't coming back."

The look that came over his face was nothing short of pure evil, and she realized as much as she thought she knew how cruel and vicious he could be she had barely scratched the surface. There was a lot more to Dexter Hunt than she had realized, and she was in more danger than she could have imagined.

Dexter stepped closer, using his bigger body to press her against the wall. One of his hands circled her wrist, and he pulled her arm up above her head and pinned it there. It was the same arm that he'd dislocated her shoulder right before she left, and she knew from the mean glint in his eyes that he knew it too and was reminding her that if he wanted, he could pop the joint right back out of its socket.

"Let me make one thing clear, *sweetheart*. I chose you because you're gorgeous, and I've put eighteen months into training you, I'm not giving you up. Ever. So, we can do this the easy way or the hard way. The easy way being I teach you a lesson you won't forget then I pack your things and take you home. The hard way being I teach you a lesson you won't forget, take you home, and then let my friends take a turn at you as well."

Fear clawed at her, making her shiver, and tears of pain and terror burned the backs of her eyes. But she wasn't willingly going anywhere with Dexter. She was done being his doormat. If he wanted her, he was going to have to do exactly what he'd threatened, but she would fight him every step of the way.

CHAPTER FIVE

February 15th
7:40 P.M.

The unmistakable sound of flesh hitting flesh sent a bolt of anger through him.

Mouse was approaching Phoebe's apartment. His parents wanted to spend the week with him and spend more time with Lolly because they were as shaken up about the near abduction as he was. After cookies and hot chocolate, she'd asked Grandma to read to her and he'd taken that as a chance to come and see Phoebe.

He knew full well he could be sent packing as soon as she saw him at her door, but he was hoping that she'd at least give him a chance. For now, he'd even take being friends, let her get to know him, and Lolly before they jumped into anything. With his daughter to think about it wasn't like he was going to immediately launch into a serious relationship.

What he didn't expect to find when he got here was her door partially open and a man assaulting her.

"You're mine, sweetheart, and don't you forget it," the man sneered.

Protective rage roared through him, and he shoved the door further open to find Phoebe shoved up against the wall, with one of the man's hands around her throat, the other roughly gripping one of her breasts.

There was fear in Phoebe's blue eyes as she fought against the man, but there was determination too. The same fire he could imagine being there when she'd fought off two armed men to save his daughter's life.

The man was a little smaller than his six foot two, two-hundred-and-twenty-pound frame, but even if he wasn't, Mouse knew his superior training was enough to eliminate any threat. So busy taunting Phoebe, the intruder—who was obviously someone who knew her—didn't even realize that anyone else was there.

Phoebe also hadn't registered his appearance, too busy trying to fight the man off.

Mouse closed the distance between them and slammed a fist into the man's head. He grunted in pain and spun around, fury etched into his face. When he spied the weapon in Mouse's hand, he froze. The weapon was more for intimidation, he didn't plan to use it, didn't need to use it, but he knew that the sight of a man with a gun worked wonders in keeping someone under control.

"Who are you?" the man demanded in a haughty voice.

At the sight of him, Phoebe had sagged in relief and was now edging closer to him.

"A friend of Phoebe's," he said menacingly. "And you are?"

"I'm Phoebe's boyfriend."

"Ex," Phoebe added, coming to stand beside him. Mouse shifted so his body was between hers and the man who had assaulted her. The question of why she'd looked so afraid of him and his team at the park yesterday was now answered. She'd been abused by her ex, a big, muscled man. To have multiple big, muscled men manhandling her must have been terrifying for her. As soon as he got rid of the ex he'd apologize again.

The ex's eyes narrowed. "We're trying to work things out," the man said.

"Phoebe, do you want him to stick around?" Mouse asked, already knowing the answer but wanting to reiterate that she'd already told the man it was over between them.

"No." There was just the slightest wobble to the word, and she edged even closer to him. At least she wasn't afraid of him anymore.

"There, you heard her. She doesn't want you around."

"This isn't over, Phoebe," the man muttered, shooting daggers at both of them.

"It most certainly is," Mouse warned.

With a growl, the man wisely made the decision this wasn't the time to argue about it because he stomped around them toward the door.

"I see you around here again, and I won't be so nice next time," Mouse warned.

The man froze in the doorway. "You hit me again, and you won't like the consequences."

Mouse couldn't care less about the consequences, and if the man ever put his hands on Phoebe again, he'd do much more than hit him once. Men who hurt women were the lowest of the low, and neither he nor Prey would tolerate anyone messing with one of them. She might not realize it, but saving Lolly's life definitely made Phoebe part of the Prey family.

Once he'd closed and locked the door, he turned to find Phoebe standing in the middle of the room, her shoulders hunched, arms wrapped around her middle. She looked small and fragile, and he wanted nothing more than to gather her up and hold her, but given what she'd just been through he was sure a man's hands touching her in any way wasn't what she'd want.

"Did he hurt you?"

"Just pushed me around a little," she mumbled. "It's nothing. I'm fine."

How many times had she told herself that she was fine, that what her ex had done to her was nothing?

Too many.

"Is that why you moved here from California?"

Her head lifted and her tear-drenched eyes locked onto his. "Please don't tell anyone."

Her plea caught him by surprise. "Your cousin doesn't know?"

Phoebe shook her head.

Mouse had thought the two women told each other everything. From what he understood, they'd grown up more like sisters than cousins, and were best friends. Why wouldn't Phoebe have told Hope? Especially given that Hope was married to Falcon Oswald, co-owner of one of the best security companies in the world. She had to know that Prey would help her in whatever ways they could.

"What's his name?"

Her brow furrowed and she looked adorably confused. "Why does it matter?"

"What's his name?"

"I don't need you to …"

"His name, Phoebe," he demanded, keeping his voice calm but also authoritative.

"It's Dexter Hunt," she whispered, her head dropping down again. She looked so defeated, and he couldn't stand it for another second.

Not the man who his in-laws had hired, but he recognized the name from his research into the firm. Dexter was a highflyer who was quickly building a reputation as a man who fought for his clients as hard as he could to make sure they won. Mouse wondered just what that entailed.

Taking his time, moving slowly so as not to spook her, he crossed to her, gently took her elbow, and led her over to the couch. Once he had her seated, he found the kitchen and located an ice pack in the freezer. Then he boiled the kettle, made her a steaming cup of tea, generously sugary to help counter shock, and took everything back to the living room.

Phoebe was sitting right where he'd left her, looking so alone it cracked his heart. Mouse had always wondered if when the time came that he found himself interested in another woman if he'd feel guilt because he still loved Emily. Now, looking at Phoebe, he realized there was no guilt. Emily would always be his first love, the mother of his firstborn, but she was also part of his past. He knew she would want him to find happiness again and not pass up a second chance at love because of her. Emily was kind, and loving, had a big heart, and cared more about others than she did herself.

He had no idea what the future held, no idea if there could be anything between him and the woman huddled in on herself on the sofa, but he knew he wasn't walking away from this chance with the first woman to capture his attention in seven years.

"Here you go, honey," he said as he held out the cup of tea. She took it with shaking hands and took a sip. "Plenty of sugar to help with shock. Ice for your lip." While she settled back against the cushions, he grabbed a folded crochet blanket from the back of an armchair and spread it over her, then perched on the coffee table in front of her. "I need to know if he hurt you anywhere else."

There was hesitation there, but she finally answered. "Just my shoulder is a little sore."

She'd had a sore shoulder yesterday too, an old injury re-hurt not a new one. Her expression clearly showed that it wasn't something she wanted to talk about, so he let it go. For now. She'd had a rough night, on top of yesterday, on top of what she'd endured at her ex's hand.

"I'll get more ice."

When he stood, her hand shot out to grab his wrist, holding him in place. "Please don't tell anyone, Asher. Please. I'm begging you. I didn't want anyone to know."

"Why not, honey?"

"Why not? Because it's embarrassing. I let that man control me, let him hit me. Eighteen months. That's how long we were together. That's how long I let him hurt me."

Mouse hated the self-recrimination in her tone. That wasn't how domestic abuse worked. The victim didn't *let* the abuser do anything to them. Telling her she had nothing to be embarrassed about likely wouldn't help, but he still needed to say the words.

"It's not your fault, Phoebe. Not. Your. Fault. It's his. He is the only one to blame."

It was obvious she didn't believe him, didn't even bother commenting on what he'd said. "Don't tell anyone, Asher. Please? Promise me you won't."

That wasn't something he could do.

He already cared about her, wanted to get to know her better, and wanted to see if they could work as a couple. She needed time, he certainly understood that. But she also needed a friend, someone to be in her corner, he understood that too.

As much as he wanted to ease her mind, tell her what she wanted to hear, he couldn't do that. Phoebe was in trouble, her ex had followed her here, and made it clear he wasn't going to walk away, so neither was Mouse. Unfortunately, part of helping Phoebe meant building her a support system, and that meant he couldn't agree to keep her secret, even if she ended up hating him for it.

* * * * *

February 16th
11:16 A.M.

So much for her get a good night's sleep and everything will look clearer in the morning plan.

That had failed.

Big time.

Instead of taking her hot shower, sliding under the covers, and going right off to sleep, Phoebe had arrived home to be assaulted by her ex and then taken care of by a man who was too sweet for his own good.

No, too sweet for *her* good.

Asher was all wrong for her, she knew that, believed it with all her heart. If she let him, he had the power to destroy whatever

50

remnants of her remained after Dexter's year and a half of torture.

She hated that he knew about Dexter. If she decided to tell anyone it should have been her decision when and how she broke the news to a person of her choosing. Asher wouldn't have been the person she chose to tell. Would he?

Maybe it was better that he knew than Hope. At least he didn't know her, wouldn't be disappointed in her. It was still embarrassing to have anyone know, but it could have been worse. Could have been her cousin who showed up after work to hang out. Hope did sometimes, and if her cousin tried to put herself between Phoebe and Dexter her ex wouldn't have hesitated to take her down.

Dexter might have been intimidated by Asher, but he wouldn't have been by an eight months pregnant woman. What if he'd hurt Hope? Made her lose the baby?

Phoebe's stomach churned as she realized for the first time that Dexter might actually be a threat to someone other than herself. He definitely would have lashed out at Hope if she'd been the one there last night, and never even given it a second thought.

"Mail," a voice at the door announced.

Sick to her stomach, Phoebe looked up, hoping she wasn't about to throw up in front of her colleagues. She was still the new girl here, having only started a few weeks ago, and while everyone had been nice and friendly, it was like they all knew she'd gotten this job only because Falcon had somehow arranged it for her. Or she was projecting her own fears onto them, she honestly didn't even know anymore.

"You okay? You're looking a little green." Marcia, another one of the younger lawyers in the office was looking at her with obvious concern.

Since there had been no way to hide the split lip, she'd told everyone that she'd walked into a door last night. Phoebe was pretty sure no one believed her, but she'd tried to sell it by saying she was still shaken up by the events of Valentine's Day, which they already knew about. Thankfully, no one had pressed her on it because the way she felt right now she would have spilled her guts.

"Umm, I'm okay, just a little upset stomach," she said, throwing in a wan smile for extra measure.

"Stress," Marcia said decisively. "You should go home. Take the rest of the week off."

"I can't. I just started here. Not a good way to make a good impression if I start taking time off before I've even been here two months." Besides where would she go? Hanging around her apartment wondering if Dexter would show up wasn't a relaxing way to spend her day.

"No one would mind after what you've just been through. You're a hero you know." Marcia smiled at her as she set a few envelopes down on Phoebe's desk.

A hero, yeah, some hero. She'd allowed a man to control her, hit her, then instead of standing up to him and going to the cops she'd run like a coward. Little good it had done though. Dexter had just followed her, and while she hoped he'd left last night and gone home she suspected he hadn't and wouldn't any time soon.

"Thanks, Marcia, I'll think about going home early." Hoping to get the other woman to leave, she picked up one of the envelopes and started opening it.

"All right, good. Call out if you need anything."

Once she was alone, Phoebe skimmed through the letters. Evidence from a PI tailing the spouse of a client desperate to get custody of his kids back from his ex who he believed was involved in money laundering. The next letter was just a monthly circular from her old law school. When she opened the third envelope, she felt the ball of fear that had settled in her stomach the first time Dexter hit her and never left, start to grow.

A blank sheet of paper, the same as the other letters she'd received over the last few weeks, was inside, only this time it wasn't the only thing in the envelope.

Nestled inside a small roll of cotton wool was a ring.

A diamond ring.

A diamond ring that looked far too much like an engagement ring.

Phoebe yelped when her cell phone began to ring.

Unknown caller.

She shouldn't answer, she knew that, but almost against her will she picked up the phone and accepted the call.

"H-hello?"

"Hello, *sweetheart*," Dexter sneered. She hated the way he used the endearment. It was always a clear way of mocking her and reminding her that he felt as though she belonged to him, but to the rest of the world he would seem to be a good-looking, successful, wealthy lawyer who cared about his woman.

"H-how did you get this n-number?" When she'd fled LA, she'd left behind everything but a suitcase of clothes and a few personal things, none of which were her cell phone. Claiming she'd accidentally lost the phone, Phoebe had accepted the offer from Hope and Falcon to add her to Prey's plan. She'd accepted not because she wanted the handout, but because she knew Hope believed she'd left the phone behind on purpose because it was a reminder of her cheating ex, and having her cousin believe that was better than her knowing the truth.

Dexter laughed. It wasn't a pleasant sound. "You think I haven't known your number the moment you started that job? You think I didn't know where you were heading the second I realized you'd left our home? You think I don't have contacts everywhere watching your every move? You're even stupider than I give you credit for."

Contacts everywhere?

The only people who had her new number were Prey and her job. No one at Prey would have reached out to her ex and given him her number which meant that someone at her job had. Someone here was secretly working for Dexter and keeping watch on her. It was likely how he'd gotten her address as well.

Who?

Marcia who had befriended her? The kind of geeky guy who had fumbled more than once to try to ask her out? Her boss who had let her jump right into things and handed her several cases?

It could be any one of them. Could be the cleaner, the guy in the copy room, the older man who worked security at the front desk, the receptionist, any one of the other lawyers.

Panic and fear battled inside her, clawing up her insides until she had to press a hand to her mouth or she was afraid she really would throw up.

"You can put that ring on your finger, meet me at my hotel, and we can go back home, work on pretending this entire little tantrum of yours never happened, or you can become like that blank piece of paper. A nothing that doesn't exist anymore."

Her heart tried to batter its way out of her chest.

He was threatening to have her killed.

Why? Just because she left? It felt like there was more going on than she comprehended, but she had no idea what.

All she had to do was go to Prey, they'd help her, find out what Dexter was really into and find a way to stop him. Or she could go to Asher. He'd given her his number last night. She hadn't intended to ever call him, but he already knew about her ex, and she was sure he would help her if she asked.

But asking for help meant exposing her greatest shame. Was she ready to do that? Did it even matter? It was either expose her shame or wind up either Dexter's prisoner again or dead. When she put it like that was it even a choice? Did she really want to let her pride wind up getting her killed? Or worse.

Somehow, winding up as Dexter's toy for the rest of her life seemed worse than being dead.

She had to get out of there. Hanging up the phone, Phoebe grabbed her things and hurried out the door, very aware of the fact that Dexter's spy was likely watching her every move, reporting back to him.

Phoebe felt trapped. How had developing a crush on a man who worked at her firm turned into a nightmare that seemed to have no end in sight?

CHAPTER SIX

February 16th
12:31 P.M.

She was going to hate him for this.

Mouse knew he might be ruining beyond repair any chance he had of convincing Phoebe to give him a chance, but he also knew this was absolutely the right thing to do.

Even if she hated him at least she'd still be alive, which was definitely better than the alternative. His gut was screaming at him that Dexter Hunt wasn't just your average abuser. There was something darker, more sinister in his eyes. Something evil. The sooner he got Phoebe away from him the better, and if this was the only way to do that and keep her safe then he was happy to do it.

Well, not happy, he did feel bad betraying her trust, but he never had agreed to keep her secret, and keeping her secret would wind up with her dead or back with Hunt.

"I'm here to see Hope Oswald," he told the doorman as he entered the building where Hope and Falcon lived.

"Of course, sir. May I have your name? I'll call up to let Mrs. Oswald know she has a visitor."

Mouse gave his name and waited for the doorman to make the call. Hope and Falcon lived in the penthouse, the only way to access it was with a special code to use in the lift. He'd never been to her place before, never been to any of the Oswalds' personal residences except the place Eagle used to live. After someone tracked him and his now wife Olivia there back when they just got together, Eagle had needed people he could trust, and Alpha team had come in and secured the place. Prey was a family, and they'd had numerous get-togethers over the years, but those usually happened at the office building. It felt odd being here, but he wasn't here on Prey business, this was personal.

"She said to go on up," the doorman informed him.

A couple of minutes later, he was stepping out of the lift and into the penthouse foyer. Hope was there to greet him, her long red hair pulled into a ponytail, her gray-green eyes curious, and a hand resting on her eight months pregnant belly.

"Mouse, what a surprise," she said. "I hope everything is okay with Lolly?"

"Lolly is doing fine, better than I could have hoped for," he assured her, stepping forward to kiss her cheek. "I brought pretzels. I hear they're your favorite at the moment," he announced, holding up a bag.

Hope's eyes lit up. "Gimme, gimme," she said eagerly, taking the bag and making him laugh. He remembered pregnancy cravings from when Emily was pregnant with Lolly. Scrambled eggs with peanut butter had been Emily's favorite and the combination was still enough to make him gag and smile.

He followed Hope through to the living room, and when she dropped down onto one end of the sofa he took the other end. Although he knew this was the right move—perhaps the only move he could make given the circumstances—it didn't mean it was easy to do. Hope was going to be upset, and she was pregnant. The last thing he wanted to do was cause her stress, but he suspected Hope was the only person Phoebe would listen to.

The idea of Phoebe hurt made his gut clench, he'd given her his number and told her to call if she needed him, but he knew she wouldn't. She needed to hear from someone she loved that she wasn't to blame for what her ex had done to her. Maybe then she could accept that it wasn't her fault.

"You want one?" Phoebe asked, holding up one of the five giant pretzels he'd bought for her.

"Nope, all for you."

"So," she said slowly as she nibbled at one of the treats. "What's up? Not that it's not nice to see you, but this is the first time I've ever gotten a house call from any of you guys. If it's not Lolly, then what? It has to do with Phoebe, doesn't it?" she answered her own question.

"Yes, but not the way you think. It's not to do with what happened in the park."

"You like her, right? Is that what this is about? Because I have no problem with you asking her out if that's what you're worried about. I think you'd be a great couple, and I know you wouldn't hurt her like her lying, cheating ex did."

So, Hope thought Dexter Hunt was a cheater. He wished that was all the man had done to Phoebe. But it wasn't. Dexter had hurt her much worse than that. "I *do* like her," he confirmed. "In fact, I wanted to ask her out, so I went around to her place last night."

"Did she turn you down flat? She asked me not to play matchmaker, but if you're here to ask for my help winning over my cousin then you got it," Hope said with a grin.

He hated he was about to wipe that sweet smile off her face. "It's not that, Hope. I hate that I'm the one to tell you this, but I don't think Phoebe is going to do it on her own. When I went to see her last night, she wasn't alone. There was a man in her apartment. He had his hand around her neck and had her shoved up against the wall."

Hope gasped. "She was attacked last night? Why didn't she call? Is she okay? Is she at the hospital? Do the cops know who he is?"

"She knows who he is."

All the color drained from Hope's face making the smattering of freckles across her nose and cheeks stand out in stark contrast. "It's Dexter, isn't it? Her ex wasn't cheating on her, he was abusing her."

"I'm sorry."

Tears filled her gray-green eyes. "Why didn't she tell me?"

"I think she feels embarrassed. No, I know she does, that's what she said. She said she was embarrassed that she let a man hit her and control her for eighteen months and that she didn't want anyone to know."

"*Let* him hit her and control her?" Hope fumed, setting the pretzel down and staggering to her feet. "You don't *let* anyone do that to you, that's not how abusers work. They trap you in their web until you feel like you can't escape."

Mouse's lips quirked into a small smile. "That's what I told her. Well, not the web part, but I told her it wasn't her fault. I don't think she believes me, actually I know she doesn't. She wanted me to promise that I wouldn't tell anyone, begged me to keep it secret, but I couldn't do that, I'm sorry."

"I'm not." Hope paused in her pacing and planted her hands on her hips. "I'm glad you told me, although I wish Phoebe had told me herself."

Feeling the need to defend Phoebe, he might not agree with her decision to keep it to herself, but he understood she wasn't in a good place mentally and emotionally right now and it was clouding her judgment. "She said they'd been together for eighteen months which was right around the time Falcon found you and brought you home. She knew how much you were dealing with, you were her focus back then, and when the abuse started she probably didn't want to add extra stress to you."

Hope grinned. "I'm not mad at her, but I love that you jumped in to defend her. I wasn't sure you were looking for another relationship after losing your wife."

"I wasn't either. Then along came Phoebe, jumping into danger to save my daughter, and things changed."

Her eyes narrowed. "So long as that's not all it is. Phoebe has been through enough, and it looks like her ex doesn't want to let her go without a fight. I don't want her getting hurt because you're just grateful that she saved Lolly. Everyone thinks Falcon is the scary one, but trust me, you mess with my cousin's heart, and I'll make you wish you hadn't."

The threat was adorable and sweet, and he had no doubt genuine. "I don't want to hurt her. I promise. And it's not just because of what she did for Lolly, although that is a big part of it. I love that she was fierce, and willing to put her life on the line to save a child she didn't even know. It's even more impressive now I know what she's dealing with. I can't promise that I can even convince her to give me a chance, let alone that things will work out between us if she does. But I can promise you that I will never ever deliberately do anything to cause Phoebe pain."

After studying him for a moment, she nodded and dropped back down into her seat, picking up her pretzel again. "Good enough for me. Once we make sure she's safe from her ex I'll do my best to convince her to give you a chance."

Mouse appreciated the fact that he had Hope on his side because he had a feeling it wasn't going to be easy to convince Phoebe to go on a date with him. Not only had she lost her trust in men, but she'd lost her trust in herself, and that was often the hardest kind of trust to rebuild.

* * * * *

February 16th
4:54 P.M.

Even though she didn't feel safe in her apartment anymore it wasn't like she had anywhere else to go.

Phoebe traipsed up the stairs, she'd been walking around the city all afternoon, and although her feet were tired, she hadn't felt like taking the elevator. The walking had helped, kept her mind occupied, and she wasn't looking forward to hanging around her place with nothing to do. If it wasn't winter and already starting to get dark, she might have stayed out longer, but knowing she might be being watched, she hadn't wanted to give Dexter the advantage of the dark if he wanted to try to snatch her.

As she opened the door to her floor, she peered cautiously through it, but the hallway was empty, no signs of her ex anywhere.

Not feeling any safer she hurried down the hall, opened her door, then screamed when she saw the lights were on and someone sitting on her couch.

"Whoa, Pheebs, it's fine, it's only me."

Slowly her racing heart slowed, and the fear receded. "Hope."

"Sorry, I didn't mean to scare you."

Hope tried to get up off the couch, but Phoebe set her purse on the small table by the door and went to join her cousin. "No, it's fine, I'm just a little on edge." Phoebe prayed her cousin thought it was just because of what happened at the park and not that anything else was wrong.

"I tried calling you several times and sent a few texts telling you I was here waiting for you, but you didn't answer."

Because she'd left the phone behind at her office. She wouldn't have put it past Dexter to have somehow put a tracker on her cell, so he knew where she was at all times. He was controlling enough to do it, which meant she'd never use that phone again. "Oh, I, uh, must have left it at the office."

The look her cousin gave her was far too penetrating. "Mouse called you too, left several messages."

Her heart felt like it had stopped beating.

No.

He wouldn't, would he?

No.

Of course not.

He'd promised to keep her secret.

"I lost the phone," Phoebe muttered. "I'll pay you back for it."

"Phoebe, you think I care about the phone? Falcon is a

billionaire, the phone is the least of my concerns. I'm worried about you."

Oh no, oh no, oh no.

Asher had told Hope.

She knew it but clung to denial. "You want to stay for dinner?"

"Falcon's in the kitchen cooking."

"Falcon is here?" More proof that Hope knew about Dexter. Falcon wasn't here to play chef, he was here to play bodyguard. After Asher had left last night, she'd been so afraid Dexter would turn back up. The Prey operative had told her not to worry, that he had it covered, but he hadn't given her details and she had worried.

"Don't worry, he won't get to you. Mouse called in Raven and asked that the cameras Prey have set up in the building and your apartment be turned on and monitored. You know this apartment is sometimes used as a safehouse, but when you moved in Falcon made sure no one would invade your privacy. Now your safety trumps privacy."

All hopes of denial shot down, Phoebe dropped her head into her hands. "You know."

"Yes. Why didn't *you* tell me?"

Phoebe just shrugged, she didn't want to be having this conversation again, especially after having it with Asher last night. And he had no right to go and tell her cousin. If she wanted Hope to know then it should be her choice when and how she shared.

Twice now she'd had that choice taken away from her.

While she expected nothing less from Dexter than him ruining everything he touched, she'd thought Asher was better than that. She'd trusted him. Despite all her self-talk about never trusting another man, and certainly not another tough alpha, she *had* trusted Asher. He'd saved her from Dexter last night, he'd apologized for hurting her at the park, and he'd been sweet and gentle when he took care of her.

Stupid.

How many times did she have to be betrayed before she realized that people—men—couldn't be trusted?

"Didn't you trust me?" Hope asked softly.

Lifting her head, she shook it emphatically. "It wasn't that at all. It had nothing to do with you. It was me. I didn't want anyone to know."

"We're not talking about anyone, though, Phoebe. We're talking about me. Your cousin. The woman who grew up more like your sister. Your best friend. We share everything, no secrets, at least that's what I thought. When Falcon left me after Colombia *you* were the one who convinced him to give us a chance. If you hadn't, I probably would have died when they attacked my house."

"I didn't do any of that because I wanted you to owe me," Phoebe snapped. Is that truly what her cousin thought? That she'd convinced Falcon to come to California for Hope just because then Hope would owe her something?

"I know, sweetie." Hope reached out hesitantly then placed a hand on her shoulder. "That's not what I meant. What I meant was that you've *always* been there for me. No questions asked. Because you love me. Don't you know that I would have been there for you too? Because I love you?"

"It wasn't about that. I know you love me, Hope. I was ... I *am* ... ashamed. You fought human traffickers and never gave up, I let a man control me, isolate me, and physically assault me. Don't you see?" Phoebe begged imploringly. "I was embarrassed for you to find out that I'm not strong like you."

Growing up they'd never really compared themselves to one another, they'd just loved and supported each other. When Hope was rescued and came back home, Phoebe had been so proud of her cousin. Not only was Hope a survivor, but she'd somehow managed to remain sweet, and kind, and caring. What had happened to her had of course changed her, but Hope was essentially still the same sassy, strong woman she'd always been.

Yet when push came to shove and Phoebe was thrust into her own version of Hell, it had shown her she wasn't strong.

"Oh, sweetie, no, just absolute no. It just doesn't work that way. When someone abuses you, you don't *let them*. You were crazy about Dexter, I remember you had a huge crush on him, and you were so excited when he asked you out. He's more than a decade older than you, was your boss, is double your size, and used his power to his advantage."

"I should have left the first time he hit me," she admitted softly. "I did. I packed a bag and went back to my apartment. But then he came around, apologized, and promised me it would never happen again. I believed him."

"Men like him can be convincing when they have to be."

"I felt trapped, and so alone. You were dealing with so much, and everything with Falcon's family, and then you moved away, and I wanted to replace you and the closeness we had. I let myself believe that I could have what you had with Falcon with Dexter, and by the time I realized he was evil it was too late. I was stuck."

"No," Hope said fiercely. "You weren't stuck. You knew you were in a bad situation and you were scared, but you ran. You came here because you knew you would be safe with me and Falcon."

"I'm not safe. Dexter followed me here, he said he's not letting me go."

"You think that Falcon and I, and all of Prey, are going to let him touch you again? Do you think Mouse is going to let him touch you again?"

Her cheeks heated at the mention of the sexy operative. Phoebe could admit that she was wildly attracted to Asher, but she was barely out of an abusive relationship and jumping into something with a man who scared her a little wasn't a good idea. Especially when the man had a daughter.

Especially when the man had broken her trust and lied to her.

"Hope, Asher is … what?" she asked when her cousin grinned

at her.

"You call him Asher?"

"So? It's his name, isn't it?"

"Yeah, but nobody calls him that. Everyone else calls him Mouse. Everyone except you apparently."

Phoebe narrowed her eyes. "It doesn't mean anything."

"Sure it doesn't," Hope said smugly like she had already decided that there was going to be something between the two of them.

"Hope, I'm not ready for another relationship right now."

"That's okay, Mouse gets that, he's prepared to wait."

"Well, I'm glad you two decided that behind my back." She huffed, her anger at Asher for blabbing about her personal life returning. Anger was a whole lot easier to deal with than fear. "You know what?"

"What?"

"I think I'm going to go over to Asher—Mouse's—house and give him a piece of my mind." Righteous anger was taking hold and Phoebe didn't even realize that while she thought Asher intimidated her, she wasn't the least bit afraid to go and tell him off for blabbing.

CHAPTER SEVEN

The chime of his doorbell drew Mouse's attention away from his laptop.

A quick glance at the clock said it was after eighteen thirty, and his parents and Lolly had been gone for over an hour. Although they'd invited him to go with them for dinner and ice cream he'd declined, wanting to dig deeper into Dexter Hunt.

After receiving a text from Falcon around seventeen hundred, he'd finally been able to stop worrying about Phoebe and do something productive to help her get free of her ex. All his texts and calls to her today had gone unanswered. While he might have just thought she was ignoring him, Phoebe also hadn't returned any of her cousin's texts or calls either. Ignoring him was one thing, ignoring her cousin was another.

She was in trouble, and he wasn't there to help her.

He hated that.

Phoebe had dealt with enough on her own, it was time for her to realize she wasn't fighting this battle by herself anymore. She had him, Alpha team, Hope and Falcon, and the entire might of Prey Security at her back. All she had to do was accept their help.

Well, he was helping her whether she wanted it or not, but it would be easier if she leaned on them all for support.

Leaned on him for support.

Bringing up the app on his phone for the doorbell camera, a huge grin spread across his face when he saw who was standing there.

The lady of the hour, Phoebe herself.

And she looked mad.

Good. It was nice to see something other than fear and defeat in her eyes. If she wanted to be angry with him for sharing her secret that was fine, he'd apologize for upsetting her but not for telling Hope what was going on.

Stretching his back, he shut down the laptop and sauntered over to the door. "Hey, beautiful," he said as he opened the door.

Phoebe rolled her eyes at the endearment, but he noticed some of the tension eased out of her, which had been his intention. "You had no right to tell Hope. You promised you wouldn't," she blurted out.

"Come on in." It seemed like the most natural thing in the world to reach out and take her hand. She tugged against his hold, but when he swept the pad of his thumb across the sensitive skin on the inside of her wrist she stilled, and he felt a shiver ripple through her.

"Don't, Mouse, don't try to mess with my head," she said once he had her seated on the couch.

His gaze narrowed. "Asher."

"What does it matter what I call you?"

It shouldn't, but for some reason it did. He'd been Mouse ever since he was eleven and he'd caught a mouse that escaped from the science lab at school. The poor thing was terrified, and once he'd caught it, it had curled up in his palm and gone to sleep as though knowing it was safe.

The nickname had stuck, followed him to bootcamp, then the Army, to Delta Force, and then to Prey. Everyone called him that, including his parents. Even Emily had called him Mouse. But it seemed important that to Phoebe he was Asher. Maybe it was because a lot of the guys he knew, active or retired from the military, seemed to be called by their first name by their wives or girlfriends.

Whatever, it didn't matter, he just knew that to Phoebe he was

Asher. "You call me Asher," he repeated.

"Fine," she huffed.

"And I'm not trying to mess with your head," he clarified. "I care about you and what happens to you, and that's why I told your cousin what was going on."

"It was up to me to tell her when I was ready."

"You weren't going to tell her," he reminded her.

She huffed again. It was cute, she kind of blew a breath of air up and the soft locks of blonde hair that curled across her temples and down beside her cheeks wafted gently. "I told you why I didn't want her to know."

"Yeah, you told me. And I told *you* that you had nothing to be embarrassed about. What did Hope say? Did she think you should be ashamed about what Dexter did to you?"

The question was of course rhetorical, they both knew what Hope had told her, but still Phoebe shook her head. "Still, you promised you wouldn't say anything."

"No, sweetheart, I didn't." Mouse still held her hand, and he brushed his thumb lightly across her knuckles. "I'm going to tell you a really important lesson I learned after Emily died. I thought I knew what it was to be part of a team. I was in the army, joined Delta, I trusted my team with everything, and knew they had my back no matter what. Then I lost my wife and was the sole parent to a newborn. Lolly was my responsibility, and I took that seriously. I tried to juggle everything myself. Funeral arrangements, caring for Lolly, taking care of the house, laundry, cleaning, grocery shopping, midnight feeds, and a colicky baby. I thought I had to do it all and didn't want to accept help from anyone. You know what eventually happened?"

"What?"

"I crashed. Two months after Lolly was born, I was cooking dinner, lay down for just a moment, and woke up an hour later to someone hammering on my apartment door. Dinner burned which set off the smoke detectors, the fire department came, and

I realized that raising my daughter wasn't a mission I could undertake without my team. I needed my parents, needed Bear and the rest of Alpha team, needed Prey and the Oswalds. So, I reached out for help. That's why we have family and friends, to be there when we need them, and to do the same for them in return. Everyone needs help sometimes, it's not a weakness. Phoebe, you have a team here to watch your back, to support you, to help you. Don't turn your back on that."

He could see her processing his words, and he fought the urge to hold his breath as he waited to see if she was ready to accept the help she desperately needed. All of them would be there for her regardless, but he knew from personal experience it would be a weight off her mind if she accepted that she wasn't alone in this.

"Okay," she said softly.

"Okay?"

"I ... I do need help, and ... maybe ... maybe I'm not completely to blame for what Dexter did to me."

The completely part broke his heart, but he was still calling this a win. "You won't regret this, honey." Her gaze found his and clung to it, and he lifted a hand to palm her cheek, letting his fingers caress her soft skin. When his thumb stopped at the corner of her lips her eyes widened, and he could see her pulse fluttering wildly in the hollow of her neck. He wanted to kiss her so badly, but he also knew that it would be taking advantage. So instead, he leaned down and pressed his lips to her forehead, holding them there for a long moment.

When his front door suddenly slammed open Phoebe jerked back, scrambling to the other side of the couch to put some space between them.

"Daddy, we decided to make ice cream sundaes at home instead ..." Lolly trailed off when she obviously realized he wasn't alone. "Phoebe!" she squealed in delight and flew across the room and onto Phoebe's lap, locking her arms around her neck.

"Oh, ah, hi, Lolly," Phoebe said, shooting him a look that

begged for help. Mouse merely smiled back at her. He hadn't pretended he wasn't interested in Phoebe, but if there was going to be anything between them, she had to know that he and Lolly were a package deal. Not that he had any doubts that Lolly and Phoebe would hit it off, if he had he wouldn't want to kiss her so badly.

"Is your head better?" Lolly asked, touching a finger right beneath the lump on Phoebe's temple.

"It's fine," Phoebe assured his daughter. "How are you doing?"

Lolly glanced around the room, first to him, then to her grandparents, then him again, before leaning up to whisper in Phoebe's ear. "I'm okay, but I'm still a little scared."

Mouse opened his mouth to reassure his daughter, hating that she had been traumatized and wanting to use his powers as her daddy to make it better, but before he could say anything Phoebe spoke.

"I'm still a little scared too," she whispered to Lolly.

"You are?" Lolly's eyes widened.

"Mmhmm." Phoebe nodded. "Those men were scary."

"I cuddled Mrs. Fuzzy real close in bed last night. She reminds me of you because she has pretty gold fur just like your hair, and you saved me, so when I was cuddling her I pretended it was you there in my bedroom, and I knew no scary men would get me."

"Oh, baby." Phoebe hugged Lolly hard, and Mouse felt his heart swell.

"Did you have someone to hold at night?" Lolly asked.

"No, sweetie."

Lolly's brow furrowed. "I don't want you to be alone. Come to my room." Lolly jumped to her feet, took Phoebe's hand, and pulled her along after her.

Before they disappeared down the hall, Phoebe's gaze met his, it was softer, warmer, and tears sparkled like diamonds in the blue depths. He could read her like a book, Lolly's stuffed cat had made her feel safe, but he had been the one to make Phoebe feel safe because he'd saved her from her ex last night.

"I like her," his mom said when the two disappeared.

His mom's approval meant a lot, but not as much as Lolly's. Once he got Dexter Hunt out of her life Mouse was going to show Phoebe how a real man treated his woman.

* * * * *

February 17th
9:11 A.M.

"You want us to come up with you?"

Phoebe turned to Hope who was standing with Falcon behind her, his large hands on her shoulders, gently kneading. After she'd had ice cream with Asher and his family, he had insisted that she wasn't going to her apartment alone, so he'd taken her to Falcon and Hope's place. This morning he'd texted the new phone that had appeared on the nightstand of the guest room and asked her to come over to his friend Bear's place.

As much as she truly appreciated everything her cousin and Falcon had done for her, she also knew it was time to start standing on her own two feet again.

No more letting her life be ruled by fear.

She was taking back control of her life and that started by handling her problems and not hiding from them.

"I'll be fine," she replied.

"If you need …"

"She'll be fine," Falcon cut off his wife. "Mouse is a great guy, and so are the rest of Alpha team. Completely trustworthy." Although his words were said to Hope, Phoebe knew he was really talking to her. Reminding her that while her ex might have hurt her, the men she was going to see this morning wouldn't.

Shockingly, she believed it.

Phoebe wasn't quite sure when it had happened. Perhaps when Asher apologized for hurting her before he knew she'd been the one to save Lolly, perhaps it was when he saved her from Dexter, or when she learned he made sure she was protected in her apartment by having someone watch over her. Or it could have been when he made them all chocolate sundaes and laughed with his daughter.

"Completely trustworthy," she echoed, and Falcon nodded encouragingly. When she'd first met the man, she hadn't liked him. He'd broken her cousin's heart when he'd left her behind, but then she'd gotten to know him, understand him, and now she barely noticed how gruff and standoffish he could be.

"Call when you're done and we'll pick you up," Hope said.

"Yes, *Mom*," she said with an eye roll and a laugh. It felt so good to laugh again. A weight had been taken off her shoulders now that she was no longer keeping such a dark secret. Who would have thought she'd be grateful to Asher for blabbing?

Hope laughed and hugged her, not an easy thing to do with her huge pregnant stomach between them. Impulsively she turned to Falcon next and hugged him too, appreciating his unquestioning support. Awkwardly he patted her back, but he did give her a little squeeze before releasing her.

Since she knew the two would wait until she was safely inside, she headed into the building where Asher's friend lived. She didn't quite know why she'd been summoned this morning, but when Asher had asked her to come, she hadn't been able to say no.

What was with that?

Why the attraction to a man who, while she might know would never hurt her the way Dexter had, posed an even greater risk?

Phoebe had thought she loved Dexter, but in reality, she'd been infatuated with him. She'd fallen in love with who she thought Dexter was not the man himself. Lesson learned. One she wouldn't forget anytime soon.

Taking the stairs up to the tenth floor, Phoebe knocked on the door to apartment ten, a moment later it was flung open and a pretty woman with smooth cocoa skin, warm brown eyes, and corkscrew curls greeted her.

"Hi, I'm Mackenzie, you must be Phoebe. I'm so excited to meet you," the woman said. She had a small baby bump, and from the way a large, gruff-looking man appeared behind her and rested his hand on her shoulder, she assumed he was the baby's father.

"You're scaring her," the man said, his voice all growly, reminding her of a bear, and she assumed he was the man with the nickname Bear.

"Oh, sorry." Mackenzie gave her a sheepish smile. "I'm just so excited to have another girl in the group. All the guys except for Luca are single, so I get testosterone overload when we hang out."

"Umm, I'm not ... it's just ..." she stammered. Had Asher given them all the impression that they were a couple? Is that why he'd called her today, to try to guilt her into saying yes if he asked her out again?

"Kenz, leave her be. We're not together, but we are friends, and Phoebe needs some friends right now. How did you sleep?" Asher asked, turning his attention to her. When he reached out and kissed her cheek, she felt a pleasant warmth flush through her. Whether she wanted to be or not she couldn't deny that she liked Asher despite their odd meeting.

"Actually, I slept well," she replied.

"Good, I'm glad."

"It was actually a relief to have Hope and Falcon know. Maybe it was a good thing that you ... you know." Casting a glance at Bear and Mackenzie as Asher led her into the apartment, she asked, "Did you tell them."

Asher grinned. "I think you know the answer to that."

"Sorry, Phoebe, the guy is a blabbermouth, no wonder his kid can't keep a secret to save her sweet little life." Mackenzie laughed, and Phoebe decided she liked the woman. There was no judgment in Mackenzie's eyes, Bear's either. She had expected her cousin to tell her that what Dexter had done wasn't her fault, Hope loved her, but she didn't even know these people. If they thought she wasn't weak and stupid, then maybe it meant she wasn't.

"I brought Baby Kitty," she told Asher, pulling the stuffed animal from her bag. Lolly had insisted that since she had Mrs. Fuzzy to keep her safe at night, Phoebe had to take Baby Kitty home with her to cuddle in bed. When she'd agreed—only because the little girl had seemed so serious—she had intended to just leave it in her purse. But when it was time to get into bed, she found herself bringing it with her.

In the end the toy had soothed her. It made her think of Lolly, which made her think of Asher, which somehow made her feel safe enough to let go and finally get the rest her body so badly needed.

"Lolly wants you to keep it until you're not scared anymore. Are you still scared?" Asher asked.

As much as she wanted to say she wasn't, she couldn't. "Yes."

"Then you hold onto it. I don't think you got to properly meet everyone the other day," he said as they entered the kitchen where four other men were sitting around the table. She recognized three of them from the park. "This is Domino, Arrow, Brick, and Surf, and you met Bear and his fiancée, Mackenzie, at the door."

Everyone smiled warmly at her, and she got this feeling of home. It was crazy because just a few days ago these men had hated her and thought she was a child kidnapper. Now they seemed ready to welcome her into the fold.

"Hi," she said awkwardly. Never before had she been a shy, awkward person. Phoebe had always been confident, a people person, she loved to go out with friends, have fun, but Dexter had changed everything. Stripped from her not only her confidence but her joy as well.

She wanted it back.

Forcing herself to relax, she smiled at the men. "Thanks for giving me a second chance."

"Darlin', thanks for giving *us* a second chance," Surf said.

Her smile became more genuine. "I'm glad everything worked out, and I hope the men who tried to kidnap Lolly are found and punished."

"We're looking for them," Asher told her as he pulled out a chair for her, then sat beside her. "But right now, we need to focus on your problem."

Phoebe grimaced. "You mean Dexter?"

"I've been checking up on him, but we need to know anything you can add to it before we go and see him," Asher said.

"Before you what now?"

"Before we go see him, make sure he knows you're off-limits."

"You can't go see Dexter and threaten him." While she thought it was actually incredibly sweet that Asher and his friends wanted to help her, she couldn't ask them to fix her problems for her.

"Yes, I can, and it's not up for discussion," Asher said firmly.

Phoebe narrowed her eyes at him. He really could be bossy, and yet somehow, it felt different than when Dexter had ordered her around.

So far, she'd been trying to deal with everything on her own and all that had accomplished was getting her mired further and deeper into the quicksand that was her relationship with Dexter. If she wanted her life back maybe it was time to take a different approach.

Asher had told her that it wasn't a weakness to ask for help when you needed it. She might not know these people, but they were offering to put themselves on the line for her. It would be stupid to refuse.

All eyes were on her, silently offering support, all she had to do was reach out and take it.

One by one she met each of their gazes directly before settling on Asher's. He placed his hand on the table between them, palm up, and waited.

In what felt like perhaps one of the biggest steps of her life, she reached out and placed her hand on his.

Immediately his fingers curled around hers, warm and strong.

She soaked up that strength, needed it so badly. She had always believed that she was strong enough to handle anything, smart enough to make good decisions, and loving enough to trust anyone. This whole thing with Dexter was humbling, but it wouldn't break her.

Phoebe hadn't realized it at the time, but she had taken several steps to free herself from Dexter's clutches. She'd left, come somewhere safe, refused to be threatened into going back, and now she was accepting the help she needed.

This could either be a really good idea, and scare her ex off, or it could wind up being a disaster. Putting her in more danger than she was already in, *and* putting everyone she loved and cared about in danger along with her.

CHAPTER EIGHT

February 17th
10:44 A.M.

His hands had been curled into fists ever since Phoebe had hesitantly told them what her ex had put her through.

Mouse was more than ready to issue a threat to Dexter Hunt that he hoped was enough to keep Phoebe safe so she could finally move forward. He knew he wasn't being entirely selfless. Once Phoebe felt safe, she could begin to process the trauma she'd been through, and then maybe she'd be ready and willing to give him a chance.

When he had to be he could be patient. It was one of the things he'd had to learn when he joined the military. Before that, it definitely was something he struggled with, he'd been impulsive since toddlerhood, but he'd learned the value of waiting, assessing, and figuring out a plan to get his desired outcome.

Right now, that outcome was protecting the woman who had risked her life for his daughter. Then it would shift to convincing her to go out on a date with him. There was no way to explain this possessiveness he felt toward her, maybe it was because she was strong, but he saw the cracks in her armor she was trying desperately to patch up.

All he knew was that if he was looking for another woman to share his life with it had to be someone who he would trust with his daughter, and Phoebe had proved that she would put Lolly first before she even knew them.

"You think this will work?" Surf asked from the driver's seat.

"No. But I hope it will," Mouse replied.

"Guy is used to getting his own way," Brick said.

That he was. Dexter had been the only child of middle-class parents who spoiled him rotten. He'd inherited their money and home when they died in a freak water accident and used it to pay his way through law school. Along the way, he'd found just the right people to schmooze and upon graduating had been taken on as a junior partner at a prestigious law firm that dealt primarily in custody battles of the Hollywood elite.

By the time Phoebe had been offered a job at the same law firm, he'd worked his way up to one of the senior partners. Handsome, fit, wealthy, and intelligent it wasn't hard to see why Phoebe had fallen for him.

But that was all surface stuff. What had really shown them the man underneath was hearing how Phoebe talked about him.

The man beneath the mask was nothing like the veneer he wore every day.

They hadn't pressed her for details, there was no need for her to share her deepest pain with a room full of people she barely knew, but Mouse intended to earn her trust so she would feel free to share anything and everything she needed to get off her chest.

"He's in for a surprise," Mouse said as they pulled up outside the hotel where Dexter was staying. "Because we're used to getting our way too."

"Damn straight," Bear said fiercely. "Especially when someone messes with our family." Bear and Mackenzie had gone through hell a few months back, but they'd come out the other side, and there was a light in his friend's eyes he couldn't ever remember seeing before.

He and Bear had been friends since childhood, although they'd had wildly different upbringings. He'd had a loving family, but Bear had the opposite. Thankfully, things between Bear and his parents were finally starting to improve, and it had a lot to do with the gorgeous woman his friend had proposed to. Mackenzie had breathed life back into not only Bear but his whole family.

While he was happy with his daughter and his parents, Mouse was starting to find he was lonely. He wanted a partner again.

He wanted Phoebe.

In so many ways she reminded him of Emily, but in other ways she was completely different. She was exactly the kind of woman he wanted to spend his life with.

"I appreciate you guys coming with me," he said as they all climbed out of the car. While this was something he could definitely handle on his own, it was good for Dexter to know that this wasn't just about Phoebe, or him. Phoebe had an entire team of people at her back, he should cut his losses and walk away. If he didn't, he wouldn't like the consequences.

"We all owe Phoebe," Arrow said. "We all love Lolly, and your girl saved her life."

"Besides that, none of us would tolerate a man hurting a woman," Domino added.

As much as he loved his family, and the sacrifices his parents had made to help him with Lolly, he loved his Alpha team family just as much. He trusted these men with everything and knew they would always have his back no questions asked.

Dexter Hunt was staying in a suite on the eighth floor, and that was where they headed. Nobody stopped them although the sight of six large men striding through the hotel drew a few curious glances.

They heard the man's raised voice when they approached Dexter's room. Since there were no other detectable voices, he assumed the man was on the phone, and whoever he was talking to he wasn't happy.

Mouse hammered on the door. Dexter's voice dropped right down, and then a moment later he flung the door open.

His brows drew into a deep V when he saw who was there. "You're not room service," Dexter muttered.

Without giving him a chance to protest, Mouse shoved his way into the room, his team at his back. Dexter took a few stumbling steps backward and beneath the veil of arrogance he could see that the man was intimidated by them.

"You," Dexter sneered at Mouse. "You were at Phoebe's the other day. I really should have you sued for putting your hands on me."

Mouse approached the man, who backed up until his back was flat against the wall. "And I should have you arrested for putting your hands on Phoebe," he growled as he leaned in close.

"It was just a misunderstanding," Dexter muttered, but he'd gone pale.

"Well, we're here to straighten out that misunderstanding," he said. "Phoebe told you to leave her alone. I don't think sending her threatening letters and calling to tell her you have a mole at her office who's watching her is leaving her alone. I told you if you didn't back off you wouldn't like the consequences." At least he knew why his calls to Phoebe the day before had gone unanswered. After receiving a letter with an engagement ring and then a phone call from Dexter telling her he had her watched, Phoebe had panicked and left the phone at her office.

"My relationship with Phoebe is none of your business." Dexter huffed, but since he was pressed against the wall, straining to get as far away from Mouse he knew the man was afraid. "You were at her place and you've tracked me down here. Are you sleeping with her?" he sneered.

"My relationship with Phoebe isn't why I'm here. Let me make myself perfectly clear, you go near her again and it's over."

"Over? You threatening that you'll have me killed?" Dexter sneered, but there was a flare of fear in his eyes.

"No. I don't need anyone to do my dirty work for me. If you remain a problem for Phoebe, I'll eliminate you myself. And let me assure you that if I decide you need to disappear nobody will ever find your body."

Dexter swallowed. "You can't threaten me like that. I could have you arrested."

"Try it." Mouse had no doubt that Eagle and Prey would make sure they were covered, besides, if Dexter went to the cops, it would come out that he had been abusing his girlfriend. He suspected that would ruin the man's reputation and that wasn't something Dexter would risk. For men like him appearances were everything.

"You can't talk to me like this. You have no idea who I am," Dexter spluttered.

"I don't care who you are. You mess with someone I care about—someone we care about," he added, gesturing at his team behind him, "and there are consequences. Go home, Dexter, and forget about Phoebe, she's off-limits."

Turning his back on the man, he headed for the door, his team followed, and Brick let the door slam closed behind them. Mouse had no idea if the threat would work, he couldn't shake the feeling that there was more to Dexter Hunt than abusing his girlfriend, but he hoped it was enough heat for the man to back away.

Phoebe deserved a chance to find the woman she'd been before she met Dexter, she deserved to find happiness and peace. Both he and Lolly liked her, cared about her, and wanted to get to know her better.

Whether he and Phoebe ever got together as a couple, or whether things worked out between them, he would make sure that she was safe. She had singlehandedly saved his daughter's life. He owed her everything.

* * * * *

February 17th
1:04 P.M.

"Ugh, I'm never going to get it." Phoebe sighed as the ball of wool rolled off her lap and onto the floor, rolling until it went under the coffee table.

Mackenzie just laughed. "Practice makes perfect."

"Practice doesn't make a scarf anyone can wear," Phoebe shot back, but she found that she was grinning. She didn't really care that knitting was way harder than it looked when Mackenzie did it, she was having fun and felt normal again. Sitting here in Mackenzie and Bear's living room, trying to learn to knit, she wasn't an abused woman trying to get out from under her violent ex's control and rebuild her life. She was just a woman hanging out with a friend. Mackenzie already felt like a friend even though they'd only known each other for a couple of hours, they'd talked non-stop since the guys left, and she had learned a lot about Asher in that time.

Every new thing she learned about him made her like him so much more. There was attraction there, there was even the beginnings of trust, but bottom line was she wasn't ready to jump into a new relationship so soon. Especially when there was a child involved. Asher would want them to be at least committed to seeing if things would work because he wouldn't want Lolly hurt and she couldn't make that kind of commitment, not when Dexter was still circling around.

What if Asher and the guys were successful in getting Dexter to back off?

Would that change anything?

Phoebe honestly didn't know, and right now, she was too tired to make that kind of decision. What she needed was time to find herself again and get back the woman she'd been before Dexter broke her down piece by piece.

"You'll get there. I mean if you want to, if you're not having fun you don't have to keep trying," Mackenzie said. Mackenzie ran her own business called Made by Mackenzie, where she knitted, crotched, and sewed toys and clothes for children.

Smiling at her new friend, she reached down under the coffee table to retrieve the ball of wool. "I don't want to make a career out of it, but I'm having fun. Actually, I'm having lots of fun.

Thanks for hanging with me."

"Anytime. It's nice to have a new friend here. I only moved here from Virginia a few months ago, and since I work from home it's kind of hard to make friends. Pretty much the only people I know here are Bear and his team, and some of the other people from Prey. I keep meaning to get back out there, do the things I used to do, but I guess I'm not ready yet," Mackenzie admitted.

Phoebe knew something bad had gone down with the woman last year, but she had no idea of the details and didn't want to pry. Just because Mackenzie knew about Dexter didn't mean the woman owed her and had to spill her secrets. "When you're ready you'll know it," she said, "and it seems to me like you have plenty of friends."

"Hey." Mackenzie set aside her knitting and reached over to squeeze her hand. "You have a lot of people in your corner too. You know the best thing about these guys?"

"What?"

"They're not just friends, they're family."

That was nice, but they weren't *her* family. Dexter had isolated her from her friends to the point she'd lost them, and even her relationship with her parents had changed. They hadn't understood why she was pulling away from them.

"It's not true you know."

"What isn't?" Phoebe asked, she hadn't said anything.

"You are part of our family. You saved Lolly, that makes you one of us."

"How did you know that's what I was thinking?"

"Because it's how I felt when I first met them. I couldn't understand why they were all being so nice to me when I met them. Luca saved my life and then I kind of saved his. That's what these guys are like, their bond was formed in blood and once you're in you're in for life. So, you can now enjoy having five big brothers."

"Six," she corrected.

"Five," Mackenzie repeated.

The last thing she needed was another person trying to play matchmaker. Hope couldn't stop talking about how wonderful Asher was, and now it seemed Mackenzie was also trying to push them together. It wasn't that she didn't agree with both women, Asher was a great guy, but that didn't mean they could be a couple.

"You know what you told me just a moment ago? That when I was ready to get back to my old life I'd know, you'll do the same. Asher would never pressure you for something you don't want to or aren't ready to give, but maybe one day you will be ready."

"Yeah, maybe." Right now, it was hard to see that she could ever be ready to trust another man with her heart. Then again, six months ago it was hard to see that she could ever be free from Dexter's wicked clutches. Now she was here in New York, she'd made new friends, had a new job, and didn't have to live constantly in pain and fear. Maybe one day she might be ready for a relationship, but it wasn't fair to expect Asher to wait.

The door opened and the guys filed in. Quickly she scanned all six of them, but she didn't see any blood or bruises. Phoebe hadn't even realized how afraid she'd been that Dexter would hurt Asher or one of their friends until relief knocked the breath from her lungs.

Bear headed straight for Mackenzie, grabbed her, and pulled her into his arms, kissing her thoroughly with no concerns for the fact that they had an audience. The way Mackenzie melted into his arms was so sweet, and Phoebe felt a pang in her chest.

She wanted that.

Someone who loved her so much he had to have a taste of her the moment he saw her. Dexter had never been that way with her. Sure, when they were with his friends, he was all sweet and over-the-top nice with her, but it wasn't real, it was just part of his act.

While Bear kissed Mackenzie, Asher headed in her direction.

She set down the knitting and stood. "Are you okay?" she asked.

"Fine, honey."

"Dexter didn't hurt you? Any of you?" she asked, including the others in the question. Just because she couldn't see any injuries didn't mean they didn't exist.

"We're fine," he assured her.

"Is he going to leave me alone?" Phoebe wasn't sure their plan to threaten Dexter into backing off would work, but she appreciated they wanted to try.

"I don't know, but I think we scared him enough that he'll at least consider it before he harasses you again," Asher replied.

"Prey is monitoring airlines so if he books a ticket to go back to California we'll know about it," Arrow added.

Could it be that easy?

Would Dexter realize that coming after her now meant taking on a bunch of highly trained former special forces operatives and back away?

She desperately wanted to believe that he would. It would be so much easier to move on, find the Phoebe that had gotten lost along the way, and get back to living her life on her own terms if Dexter was permanently out of the picture. But as much as she wanted to believe it, there was that niggling little bit of doubt whispering to her from the back of her mind that it would never be that easy, that Dexter would never let her go.

"Thank you," she said, placing her hands on Asher's forearms and standing on tiptoes to kiss his cheek.

A flare of heated desire turned his eyes the same color as molten chocolate, and Phoebe found her body responding. What would it be like to make out with Asher? He'd be a skilled lover, of that she had zero doubt, those hands of his were bound to be magic, and heat pooled between her legs as she imagined what his tongue would feel like sweeping through her most intimate area.

Quickly she took a step back.

He was making her feel too much too soon.

They'd only just met, she shouldn't feel anything for him. Yet she did feel things, and it wasn't just attraction. He was putting himself on the line for her. Sure, she'd saved his daughter, but she hadn't done that so he would owe her. He was helping her because he wanted to, because he wanted her to be safe. How could that not touch her heart?

Yet despite the tug she felt, she still knew the time wasn't right, she wasn't ready to date again.

As though sensing her internal turmoil, he curled an arm around her waist and tugged her against his side. Leaning down, he kissed her temple and whispered, "It's okay, honey, you don't have to solve all the world's problems today. You don't even have to solve all your own problems today."

Instead of reassuring her, his words only made her more confused. How was it possible to both crave this man and fear him all at the same time?

CHAPTER NINE

February 17th
4:50 P.M.

"You didn't have to see me home," Phoebe said softly as they walked down the hall toward her apartment. She'd been quiet since they left Bear and Mackenzie's place. They hadn't exchanged more than a handful of words on the cab ride to her building, yet the silence hadn't been uncomfortable or awkward. On the contrary, he'd felt like she finally trusted him.

Mouse was also getting better at reading her body language and he was sure that something was bothering her. While she might trust him now, that didn't mean she was going to open up about whatever it was, and although he would love to push to get answers so he could fix whatever it was he'd vowed to be patient.

A vow he was currently regretting.

It was hard being this close to her and not being able to do what he wanted, which was shove her up against the wall, claim her mouth in a kiss that would leave both of them burning, and then chase away all her bad memories by giving her all the pleasure she deserved.

Since he couldn't do that, he took her hand and turned her to face him. "When you're with me I will always make sure you're home safe."

A cute pink blush tinted her cheeks. "But we're not ... you know."

"No, we're not together," he said deliberately, letting the *yet* hang in the air between them. Phoebe needed time. Her self-confidence had taken a battering and he didn't even know much about what Dexter Hunt had done to her, but he had already made up his mind he was prepared to wait as long as it took. Something primal inside him told him this woman would be more than worth the wait.

"Thank you for what you did for me, I can't believe it worked."

Before they'd left, they'd gotten word from Raven Oswald that Dexter Hunt had booked himself a first-class ticket back to San Diego. The flight left in an hour, and he was already checked in and at the airport. Phoebe was free now, she could rebuild her life, learn to trust herself again, and then maybe she'd be willing to give him a chance.

"Honey, it was my absolute pleasure to kick that man out of your life. Although I wouldn't have minded a chance to beat him to a bloody pulp for everything he put you through." Above the lump on her temple from when he'd knocked her down the other day there was a pale pink scar. A scar he guessed was a mark left behind by the monster who thought he owned her. With a featherlight touch, he brushed a fingertip across the mark. He wished he could erase them all, make it so that Phoebe had never been hurt, or been touched by the darkness that lurked in their world.

She sucked in a breath at his touch, and her tongue darted out to sweep across her bottom lip. His body responded by sending blood south and he felt himself start to harden. It would be so easy to bow his head, kiss her, perhaps take her inside for more. Mouse had a feeling she wouldn't resist, but it wouldn't change the fact that he'd be taking advantage, and that was something he wasn't prepared to do.

When he took a step back, Phoebe looked startled. "I guess we're even now," she said nervously, and he got what was bothering her. Phoebe thought he was being nice to her to pay her back for saving his daughter's life and now that he had—in her mind, in his that was a debt that could never be repaid in full—he would lose interest in her.

Hooking an arm around her waist, he pulled her up against his body, allowing her to feel how badly he wanted her. "Let me assure you of one important thing, butterfly. This isn't about me repaying you. I couldn't. Lolly is everything to me. I helped you because the thought of you in danger makes my blood feel like it's turned to acid and is eating away at me. I like you, I've already asked you out, I'm not going to change my mind on that, I just don't want to pressure you."

"Butterfly?" she asked on a hint of a whisper.

"You're about to rebuild yourself into something more beautiful, and stronger, than you were before. Dexter didn't destroy you, he couldn't, it's not possible, and you're about to show the entire world how amazing you are, I know it."

"I'm not ready to date again." Her tone said it as though it were a fault on her part. "What if I'm not ever ready?"

"You will be."

"How can you be so sure?"

"Because you've forgotten how strong you are, but you'll remember, I'll make sure of it." Leaning down he kissed her forehead. "Now go inside, enjoy knowing you're safe tonight. Cameras in the apartment are off, but the ones in the hall are on, just so you don't have to worry about anything."

Since he knew if he didn't leave now, he might not be able to resist the stunning blonde temptation, he released her and strode down the hall back toward the elevators. Mouse could feel her eyes on him, and while he waited for the elevator to arrive, he said, "Head on inside now, butterfly."

"How did you know I was still here?"

"Can feel you when you're close."

He heard her gasp, felt her smile, and then heard the soft click of her door as she went into her apartment and closed it behind her. He was smiling like an idiot as he stepped into the lift. Lolly was his bumblebee, Phoebe was his butterfly, and they were both important to him.

Outside he didn't bother calling a cab, he'd jog home, use the time to work off the sexual energy coursing through his body. Just being around Phoebe had him growing hard, but it was more than physical attraction. It wasn't anything he could explain. The connection had been almost instantaneous, he would have thought it wasn't possible, but it had been that way when he met Emily too.

It was like his soul recognized hers, and now it recognized Phoebe's.

"Daddy!" Lolly squealed and threw herself at him when he walked through his door.

There were paints on the coffee table and sheets of paper, his mom and daughter must have been painting after school, it was one of their favorite things to do together. "Hey, bumblebee. How was school today?" he asked as he lifted her up into his arms.

"It was *great*! We're learning about what makes rainbows in science class!"

"Sounds like fun, sweetie." Science had been his least favorite class as a kid, but his daughter loved everything.

"Did you see Phoebe today?" Lolly asked. His daughter had really taken to Phoebe even more after they'd had ice cream the other night.

"Yeah, honey, I did."

"Is she still scared?"

"Actually, she said that Baby Kitty helped."

Lolly grinned. "I knew Baby Kitty would help because Mrs. Fuzzy helped me."

"She said to tell you thank you."

"Daddy?"

"Yeah, baby girl?"

"I want to tell her you're welcome. Can I go and visit her?"

Mouse caught his mom's eye. The woman merely raised an

eyebrow and smiled, obviously not wanting to intrude, although both his parents had been singing Phoebe's praises. It wasn't like he had to worry about Phoebe winning over his parents or his daughter, the problem was convincing her that she didn't have to be afraid of him. Trusting him as a friend was one thing, trusting him as a boyfriend was quite another.

The last thing he wanted to do was spook Phoebe by moving too fast, but maybe hanging with Lolly would help her see him as someone other than the man who had knocked her down that first day. While he knew she knew he'd never do that again, that there had been extenuating circumstances, given what she'd just been through it was hard for her to be around a man who was so much bigger and stronger than her. But he wasn't just Mouse the former Delta special operative, he was also Asher Whitman, Lolly's dad.

"I guess that would be okay," he said slowly.

"Can we bake her cupcakes?" Lolly asked.

"Sure."

"With purple buttercream frosting? Purple is Phoebe's favorite color."

"How do you know that?"

"She told me. Ooh, Daddy, can we dip the frosting in chocolate? I saw a video of that on TikTok and it looked really easy," Lolly added.

"We can try it out." One thing he'd learned being a parent was that messes could always be cleaned up, and everything could be a learning experience for his kid.

"Thanks, Dad." She squiggled out of his arms and skipped off to the kitchen.

"You sure you know what you're doing, son?" his dad asked.

"I hope so. Phoebe has …" How could he explain it without betraying her confidence?

"Your girl is cautious, and it has more to do with something else than what happened with Lolly," his mom said.

"Yeah, cautious, and she has every reason to be. I feel like I'm walking a tightrope," he admitted. "I feel like if I push too hard, I could lose her, but if I don't let her know how I feel then I could lose her anyway."

* * * * *

February 18th
4:22 P.M.

This was the first time she'd been out jogging since the incident.

As terrifying as it had been, when she'd realized she was watching a kidnapping in progress, it had turned out to be the catalyst for getting her own life sorted out.

Phoebe smiled as she looked at the spot where she'd managed to take down the two armed men. It was the same place where Asher had knocked her down. At the time she'd been so scared, but now she knew that Asher was a good man, one who would never intentionally hurt someone.

He'd done so much for her. Dexter was back in LA, she'd quit her job, there was no way she could go back there knowing someone was a spy for her ex, and she finally felt like she was beginning to find herself again.

It all started here.

When she realized Dexter hadn't broken her, that she could still be strong. Now her strength was returning bit by bit and it was an amazing feeling.

Deliberately, she walked past the spot that had changed her life and started jogging. She was so very grateful that Asher had come into her life. What would have happened to her if he hadn't?

She knew the answer to that.

Dexter would have beaten her up, raped her, then dragged her back to LA with him.

But that hadn't happened. She was safe for the first time in eighteen months, and she relished her newfound freedom.

What she'd told Asher yesterday was true. Phoebe didn't know if she would ever be ready to give her heart to another man, but that didn't mean she couldn't daydream about how nice it would be to have a man like him love her. He'd be sweet and attentive, would always make sure she was okay and had what she needed, would be protective, bossy too, but she would always know that when things were down, he'd be there to lift her up.

The smile slipped from her face as that old familiar feeling came back.

Someone was watching her.

The spy Dexter had claimed he had at her old job?

Cool it, Pheebs, she coached herself. *It's nothing, just stress, lingering fear from living under Dexter's thumb for so long.*

Phoebe hoped with every fiber of her being that was all it was because if Dexter was still determined to get to her even after Asher and the guys had threatened him, then he truly was never going to let her go.

If she hadn't been preoccupied with her no doubt irrational fears, she would have seen the man coming toward her before she plowed into him sending them both down to the hard ground.

Panic gripped her.

This time she wasn't letting anyone hurt her.

Dexter, one of his minions, or someone else entirely, Phoebe didn't care, she just knew she was never going to let someone do anything to her against her will ever again.

"Relax, butterfly."

The amused voice melted the panic away and she blinked and looked into Asher's brown eyes. They were crinkled at the corners, and he had a grin he was trying to hide, and Phoebe felt her cheeks flame in embarrassment.

"Asher, I didn't see you," she admitted.

"You were in the zone," he said as he stood and offered her

his hand.

"Phoebe, are you okay?" Lolly asked, bouncing from foot to foot beside them. At least she hadn't knocked the little girl down along with her dad.

"Fine," she assured the girl.

Asher raised a brow, silently asking if she really was all right or if she just didn't want to worry Lolly.

"Really, I'm good, just embarrassed." Still, at least she knew that the only ones watching her had been Asher and Lolly. There was not a doubt in her mind that the two weren't here by accident. They were here because Asher thought if he used his daughter then he could make inroads in convincing her to date him. It would be more annoying if she didn't actually like the little girl.

And Asher.

Damn him for being so sexy, and for getting Dexter out of her life, and for being sweet, and funny, and smart, and … none of that changed the fact that she wasn't ready to date again so soon after escaping Dexter.

"Phoebe, guess what we made?" Lolly shouted, still bouncing about excitedly.

The little girl's excitement was contagious, and Phoebe found herself relaxing in a way she hadn't in so long. "What did you make, peanut?" The nickname just slipped out, it was what her dad always called her, and she quickly darted her gaze to Asher, trying to convey her apology without making it a big deal in front of Lolly. It was completely inappropriate to be making up nicknames for Asher's daughter, and a really bad idea.

The last thing she needed was another excuse to get any closer to Asher and Lolly.

Already she was a whole lot more invested in them than she should be.

Lolly didn't seem to notice, or care if she did, and plowed on. "We made cupcakes. For you! They're chocolate, and they have purple buttercream frosting because purple is your favorite color. And Daddy let me try dipping the frosting in chocolate because I saw it on TikTok. We made a big mess, but they look perfect, and they're super yummy, Daddy let me have one."

"You made me cupcakes?" Phoebe asked. Why did the thought of Lolly and Asher baking her cupcakes make her heart tighten in her chest and her vision go watery? It was so sweet. It was *too* sweet. Much more of this and she'd give in and say yes if Asher asked her out again.

"It was Lolly's idea," Asher said, smiling down at his daughter. The tenderness in his expression didn't change when he shifted his gaze from Lolly to her.

"It's the sweetest thing anyone has ever done for me," she said.

Lolly's brow furrowed in concern. "Then why are you crying?"

"Happy tears, sweetheart," she assured the child.

"Oh, okay," Lolly said. "Is it okay that we came to the park to see you?"

Phoebe glanced at Asher and saw the sheepishness in his eyes. They both knew he was shamelessly using his kid, but she couldn't seem to find it in her to care. Asher was a great dad, and she was honored that she was someone he wanted around his daughter, even though she disagreed. Right now, she wasn't the kind of role model she'd want for her own kid let alone anyone else's.

"It's okay, I'm glad to see you," she told Lolly.

"You are?" Lolly looked delighted. "See, Dad, I told you Phoebe would be happy to see me."

"Never disagreed with that, bumblebee." From the look he gave her, she knew it was him she would likely not want to see, but that wasn't true. It wasn't that she didn't like Asher, it was that she was starting to like him *too* much.

"Can you come play with us at the playground?" There was a tiny wobble in the little girl's voice and she suspected Lolly was a little apprehensive about going back to the playground where she had been abducted.

"I sure can. Hey, Lolly, you like the monkey bars?"

"I love them. Daddy always gets worried when I get right up on top." The child shot her father a rebuking frown.

"You scared of the monkey bars, tough guy?" Phoebe snickered.

Asher held up his hands, palms out. "Hey, there's something about seeing your baby girl hanging upside down that curls your stomach."

Both she and Lolly laughed. "You know, peanut, I used to do gymnastics when I was your age, and my favorite was the uneven bars. They're different than monkey bars, but I used to love to spin and flip over them. I could teach you a few tricks. If it's okay with your dad?" She looked to Asher for permission.

"Please, Daddy, can she? Pretty please with sprinkles, and fudge, and chocolate chips, and a cherry on top?" Lolly begged.

"Sure she can, bumblebee."

"Yay," Lolly cheered. The little girl grabbed Phoebe's hand and started running toward the playground, her earlier apprehension completely disappeared.

Phoebe ran alongside Lolly, feeling Asher's eyes on them, although he didn't hurry along after them. It seemed Asher trusted her completely when it came to his daughter, and she wasn't quite sure how she felt about that.

Well, she knew it made her feel all warm and gooey inside, like a fresh from the oven cookie, but he knew about her past. Knew that she had allowed a man to control and abuse her.

Okay, so he would tell her that what Dexter had done wasn't her fault, not that she quite believed it. Still, even if he thought that he hardly knew her. How could he trust her with the most precious thing he had?

Right now, Phoebe didn't even trust herself to look after herself, let alone a child. A child that she was already attached to, that she was falling in love with.

A child that sooner or later she was going to have to walk away from.

CHAPTER TEN

February 18th
5:08 P.M.

The stupid woman thought it was over.

Thought just because he had gotten on a plane and returned to California that he was no longer a threat to her.

She'd learn.

Dexter watched in amusement as Phoebe played at the playground with the man and his daughter.

It didn't seem like she had any idea that someone was watching her. That someone had eyes on her from the moment he realized she was gone and had fled to her cousin in New York. Just because he had waited to see if she was going to come to her senses and return home didn't mean he hadn't been watching her the entire time.

Watching and waiting, looking forward to punishing her when he got her back.

Phoebe might disagree, but she was his and he had no intentions of letting her go. Dexter was very possessive when it came to his belongings, and Phoebe had been his from the moment he laid eyes on her and decided he wanted her.

He always got what he wanted.

Always.

And the gorgeous blonde was everything he wanted in a partner. He needed someone who was beautiful and elegantly graceful, Phoebe was both of those things. He also needed a woman who was smart and could engage in intelligent conversation, Phoebe was that as well. She had also broken beautifully for him, and he had been in the process of molding her into the perfect wife.

At least he'd thought she was broken.

Obviously, he hadn't done as good a job at that as he thought he had. Not his fault though, Phoebe had likely been pretending so she could lull him into a false sense of security. If that had been her game, he was hip to her now. Apparently, he needed to be harder on her, no more taking things easy because the woman was so pretty it seemed a shame to mar her smooth ivory skin.

When he took her back, he would teach her a lesson that would leave an impression she would never forget. There was plenty of milky white skin he could play with that he could still keep hidden behind clothes when he took her out.

Phoebe was like a gorgeous pet, one he would take care of and reward for good behavior. At social functions he would trot her out and she would perform like he'd taught her. Then when it was just the two of them, he could have a little fun with her.

As he watched, Phoebe played with the child and made her laugh. Dexter smiled despite his anger at her for leaving and refusing to come back. He liked seeing her with a child, children were something he definitely wanted, it was part of the reason his last relationship had ended.

The woman had lied to him, told him she wanted kids, and when he'd chosen her to be his and invested time and money into the relationship, he had been livid to learn that in fact due to a freak accident when she was a child the woman could no longer conceive.

But his beautiful Phoebe could give him the heir he craved. He'd had her thoroughly checked out when he'd first started dating her. Bringing her back to his apartment after one of their first dates, he'd given her a sedative in her drink, and while she was unconscious had a doctor he trusted run tests. Unfortunately, his timing had been bad and that same night someone had set fire to Phoebe's cousin's place and Hope had tried to desperately track her cousin down. Thankfully, by the time they realized she was at his place, Phoebe had woken up and everything was all right.

The cousin was likely the reason for his pet's rebellion.

If the woman wasn't married to Falcon Oswald, he might teach her a lesson about sticking her nose into other people's business. But taking on the Oswald family and the might of Prey Security wasn't something he was prepared to do. Especially since they were already interested in his associates.

Phoebe had no idea how lucky she was to have been chosen by someone within the New Order. It meant that when the time was right, she would be married to one of the most powerful people in the world. She would have all the money she could dream of and have everything her heart desired. She'd be treated like a queen, and while she herself might not have any power she would reap all the benefits of his.

Yet she had thrown it all away. Run away like a cry baby because she didn't like him putting his hands on her. How else did she think she was going to learn what was expected of her?

Once he got her back, he'd work her over harder. Phoebe needed to learn she was one hundred percent reliant on him. He had merged their bank accounts. and restricted her access. He'd isolated her from family and friends, he'd made her leave her job so she could be home taking care of the house all day, he'd thrown away most of her belongings except the things he had bought for her, but obviously that hadn't been enough.

Things would change when they got home. They'd be married almost immediately, she'd be sequestered in his house, he'd get her pregnant, and then he'd always have a way to keep her under control.

Perhaps he'd take the little girl too. Threats to the child would help motivate Phoebe to learn her lessons quickly, and he kind of liked the idea of punishing the man who was obviously having sex with his woman.

Something to ponder on.

For now though, he wanted to check in with the man he had hired to tail Phoebe. Closing the video stream down, he called the number for today's disposable cell phone.

The man answered almost immediately. "Hey, boss."

"Does she know you're watching her?" Dexter asked.

"No idea. Thought she might have clued on earlier when she was jogging, she got that panicked look on her face and she was looking all around. But then she ran into the goon and his kid and must have assumed it was them watching her."

Dexter smirked at the term goon. It was so appropriate. Asher Whitman was all brawn and no brain just like all the rest of those military types. They were good when you needed something taken care of and didn't want to get your well-manicured hands dirty, but not for much else.

"You want me to move in?"

"No, not yet," Dexter replied. "For now, I want her to think that it's over, that I've backed off. The goon is Prey, and we know how they get. If we lay low for a few weeks, they'll assume the threat has been handled and move on. That's when we pounce." One of the first rules of war was that sometimes it was important to temporarily retreat in order to gain the upper hand. That was something Dexter had no problem doing. He was in this for the long haul, and if that meant he had to be patient and wait a little before getting his woman back then that was what he would do.

"Want me to keep the pressure up in the meantime?"

The man took great pleasure in other people's fear. It was why he was Dexter's favorite mercenary to work with. He didn't just take care of problems, and procure packages, he also liked to play with his game first. The man had always reminded Dexter of Scar from The Lion King and was no doubt where he'd gotten his name from. Dexter didn't know who he really was, but Scar was always who he called when he was in a bind.

"No, let's ease up completely. Keep tracking her, make sure we have eyes on her whenever she's out of her apartment, but don't make contact. I want her to think that everything is over and that I've given up. That way when it's time for you to move in she won't see it coming."

Scar didn't need to know, but that was one of the things Dexter intended to use in his training of the woman he had chosen to be his. He wanted her to know that everything in her life was because of him, good and bad alike.

Their relationship didn't have to be confrontational. Once she learned her place, knew how to play the role of wife and mother to his children to perfection, then she had nothing to fear from him. Yes, he may put his hands on her from time to time, and yes, he'd take her in the bedroom any way he chose, but she could be the pampered, spoilt wife as well.

It was her choice.

"Okay, boss. Let me know when you're ready for me to make a move," Scar said before disconnecting.

Dexter immediately brought the live video feed back up. "Soon, my love, very soon you'll be back with me, and once you are you will never escape again."

CHAPTER ELEVEN

February 18th
6:21 P.M.

"Daddy?"

"Yeah, Lolly?"

"When can we see Phoebe again?"

Mouse looked over at his daughter who was standing on her step stool stirring the pasta. Since Lolly loved to cook, he always let her help out. He might not know a lot about kids, about when they met milestones, and what was too much responsibility, or what they were capable of doing at what ages, but he knew his daughter loved to be treated like she was smart and capable so that was what he did.

Didn't mean he didn't stay right by her side when she was stirring a pot of boiling water. The last thing he would ever do was hurt his daughter.

"Eyes on the pot, Lolly," he reminded her.

"Sorry, Daddy."

Once she had dutifully turned her attention back to the pot of spaghetti, he answered. "I don't know, sweetie. We don't want to pressure Phoebe."

Although no one had said anything directly to her, Lolly seemed to have sensed that there was something big and bad that Phoebe was dealing with. Something that had nothing to do with the bad men in the park who had tried to kidnap her. Mouse loved that his little girl was so perceptive of other people's feelings, her mom had been too, another thing Lolly had gotten from Emily.

"But Phoebe had fun with me, she told me she did." There was a slight pout on his daughter's face and a whine in her tone. That was something he didn't tolerate. Life was going to throw you a whole lot of curve balls, some of which were going to hurt when they hit. If you spent your time looking for things to complain about, you'd find them. But what kind of life was that?

"Of course she did, bumblebee, but we have to be respectful of Phoebe's time." Even though she'd known he was using Lolly as an excuse to spend time with her, Phoebe hadn't called him on it, instead she'd embraced hanging out with his daughter. Watching her on those monkey bars had been amazing. She'd looked so carefree and happy, showing Lolly, and a bunch of other kids who'd come to watch, how to swing up and down, weaving between the rungs. She really was his butterfly. She'd looked like an adorable caterpillar moving along the bars, then at the end she'd somersaulted off the last bar, flying through the air, and landing perfectly on her feet.

That was the Phoebe he wanted her to find again. The one who wasn't scared and beaten down, the one who hadn't experienced first-hand how evil some people could be. He wanted her to be free to soar through life, stronger and more spirited than she'd already been, bringing joy and happiness to those around her because she was beautiful and sweet and funny, and a joy to be around.

"Can we at least call her then?" Lolly asked.

Was that too much of an intrusion?

It had been on the tip of his tongue to ask her to come home and have dinner with him, Lolly, and his parents, but he was trying really hard not to push too hard too soon. It was enough that she'd spent time with them in the park, getting to know him and Lolly better, having fun, then eating cupcakes.

"Daddy? Can we call her?"

"Not tonight, sweetie."

"Tomorrow then?"

"Maybe," he hedged. Honestly, he had no idea how he was supposed to handle this. Never before had he chased a woman like this. In high school he'd been a good-looking jock and girls had been falling all over themselves to go out with him. Then he'd met Emily in boot camp, she might have dropped out, deciding the military wasn't for her, but by then they'd already fallen in love. With Phoebe, he wanted her to know he cared without making her feel like she had to give more than she was ready to.

"Is maybe, yes or no?"

"It's maybe, bumblebee," he said with an amused smile. "Hop down and let me drain the spaghetti, then you can stir in the sauce."

While he carried the pot to the sink and drained out the water, Lolly moved her step stool over to the counter and got the sauce. It was some cheesy tomato thing that she and his mom had cooked up together a while back. Since it was Lolly's favorite, they often kept extra on hand in the freezer so they could have it if they needed a quick dinner.

When he set the pot in front of her, Lolly added the sauce and stirred just as his phone began to ring. As soon as he saw whose name was on the screen, the smile he'd been wearing since he saw Phoebe at the park fell from his face.

"Sorry, Lolly, I have to take this," he told her.

"Can I spoon the spaghetti into bowls?"

"Sure, then go call Grandma and Grandpa and tell them dinner's ready." A dinner he wouldn't be eating with his family. "Hey, Bear," he said when he answered.

"We're heading out," his friend said without preamble. Although Bear never complained, and he never turned down an assignment Prey handed them, Mouse knew that ever since Mackenzie had come into his life leaving on a job wasn't as easy. Especially now that Mackenzie was pregnant. Leaving loved ones behind always sucked, but it was the life they had signed up for, and a part of themselves they couldn't turn off. For men like him and Bear, this wasn't a job it was a part of who they were. A part of themselves they couldn't turn off not even for the people they loved.

"When?"

"Wheels up in sixty, debrief on the plane," Bear replied.

"See you then." Hanging up, Mouse looked down at his daughter who was carefully carrying bowls of spaghetti to the table. After eating ice cream in here with Phoebe the other night he couldn't not picture her here with him and his daughter every time he entered the kitchen.

Should he tell her he was heading out and didn't know when he'd be back?

They weren't together, but they were friends and he had made his intentions clear. Surely, she had to know he was dead serious about wanting to date her because he was letting her spend time with Lolly and bond with her.

Still, she had also been clear that she wasn't ready for any commitments right now, and that she wasn't sure she ever would be. Calling her to tell her he was heading out definitely felt like a coupley thing to do, and that would no doubt add pressure that Phoebe didn't need right now.

Besides, it wasn't like she wouldn't find out from Hope that he was on a mission. Hope was firmly in the matchmaking corner and would likely mention sooner or later that he and his team had been called out.

Decision made, it was time to tell Lolly that Daddy wouldn't be tucking her in tonight. "Hey, baby girl," he started slowly.

When his daughter looked up at him, he knew she already knew. She was growing up, and this was a routine they'd been through dozens of times before. Although Lolly never complained, this was the first time he was leaving since the kidnapping. His team was supposed to be grounded so whatever this mission was it was something important, something he assumed was related to everything that went down with Storm

Gallagher.

"You're leaving," Lolly said.

"I'm sorry, bumblebee, I know I promised that I wouldn't leave for a while but this is really important."

Lolly sighed but gave him a brave smile. "I know. It's okay. I'll be okay with Grandma and Grandpa. And I have Mrs. Fuzzy to sleep in my bed with me at night."

"I'm so proud of you, do you know that?"

"You are?"

"Absolutely. You are one brave, strong little girl. I know it's hard for you when I have to leave, but you never complain."

"You save people like Phoebe saved me." Lolly knew a little of what he did, but she didn't know that in saving people he often had to kill other people. Bad people, but it still wasn't something he wanted his daughter thinking about at this age.

"Yeah, baby girl, just like Phoebe saved you. Come here and give me a great big squeezy hug."

Lolly flew into his arms, and he held her tightly. These days would be coming to an end much sooner than he was ready for. In just a few years Lolly would be a teenager, she wouldn't want to hug her dad anymore, might start giving him attitude because he couldn't be around as much as he'd like. Before then, he'd love to have a more stable home for her so she didn't have to keep going between their apartment and his parents' house.

When he pictured that home, he saw Phoebe standing beside them, kissing him goodbye, with her arm around his daughter as he walked out the front door.

"Tighter, baby girl, this hug has to last me until I come home," he said. For now, it was just him and Lolly. That family might change in time but even if it didn't, Mouse knew he was one very lucky man.

* * * * *

March 4th
2:42 P.M.

"Do you think we have everything we need?" Hope asked.

Phoebe shot her cousin an amused smile. "I think you have everything an entire hospital would need to care for a baby." With oldest Oswald sibling Eagle and his wife Olivia and their sixteen-month-old daughter Luna, Raven Oswald and her husband Max and their fourteen-year-old daughter Cleo and fourteen-month-old son Roman, and youngest Oswald son Hawk and his fiancée Maddie's ten-month-old son Louie, she had assumed that Hope and Falcon wouldn't be as nervous about the arrival of their baby.

But her cousin's panicking as the weeks ticked down toward the birth of her baby was the only thing stopping her from obsessing over the fact that she hadn't heard from Asher in two whole weeks, so at least there was that.

"This is our first baby, I want to make sure we're prepared," Hope said, tossing her red ponytail over her shoulder.

Taking Hope's hand, she guided her cousin out of the nursery and through into the living room, sitting her down on the couch. "You're prepared, I promise. This little bitty almost here baby is going to be the luckiest baby of all time to have you and Falcon as its Mommy and Daddy."

"Thanks, Phoebe, I needed to hear that. I don't know why I'm freaking out. We've had the nursery all set up since about a week after I found out I was pregnant. And we've bought new stuff almost every week since. Plus, Olivia, Raven, and Maddie all offered us their old baby things that Luna, Roman, and Louie have outgrown depending on if we have a boy or a girl. We have everything we need, and yet I still have this panicky feeling in my stomach that won't go away."

"Because your baby is about to become real. You know what I mean," she added quickly. "Obviously it's always been real, but now it's about to be here."

"I'm scared."

There was more going on here than Hope was letting on, and Phoebe had a feeling she knew exactly what it was. "Are you getting scared about giving birth?"

Hope's gray-green eyes filled with tears, and she nodded. "What if the same thing that happened to my mom happens to me? What if it's hereditary? What if I'm going to leave Falcon a widower with a newborn? Or worse, what if my baby dies with me the same way my twin sister died with Mom while she was giving birth to me?"

"Oh, honey." Phoebe moved and wrapped up her cousin in her arms. Their moms had been sisters, and she and Hope were only a couple of months apart in age. Her mom had taken Hope under her wing, stepping into the role of mom and helping with the things Hope's dad couldn't do. She and Hope had always been more sisters in her mind, and this was her absolute best friend in the whole world. There wasn't anything she wouldn't do for Hope, and it killed her she couldn't take away this fear, this pain.

If she hadn't been so wrapped up in her own problems, trying to find herself again after Dexter had broken her down, and moping because she hadn't heard from Asher, even though he had no reason to keep reaching out when she kept telling him nothing could happen, then she would have known Hope was struggling.

"I'm sorry, I haven't been a very good best friend lately," she said, hugging her cousin tighter.

"That's not true. At all. You've been by to see me every day. You've helped me out with things, done laundry so I wouldn't have to, cooked for us, made the bed, you've even painted my toenails for me. And you've done it all while trying to pretend you're not suffering from a broken heart."

"I didn't love, Dexter. At first I thought I did, I'll admit that, but I fell for the façade not the man behind it."

Hope gave her a gentle smile. "I wasn't talking about Dexter."

"Then who?"

Calling her on the lie, Hope kept hold of her hands as she settled back against the couch cushions. "I think you know the answer to that."

"Asher?"

"Bingo."

"But I'm not in love with Asher, so I can't have a broken heart." Although even as she said the words, she was forced to admit to herself that while she didn't love the man, she was falling for him. How could she not when he had taken time to help her with her problems when his own daughter had just been through a traumatic event?

"You might not be in love with him, but you do like him," Hope said, echoing Phoebe's thoughts. "No point in denying it, I remember the look on your face when I told you Mouse and his team had been called out."

After a week of radio silence, her mind running into overdrive thinking of all the reasons why he might have decided to stop contacting her, she'd finally broken down and tried to ask vague questions of her cousin. Despite the fact she'd tried not to be obvious, she'd failed. Hope had grinned, said she'd wondered how long Phoebe could hold out before asking about Mouse, and told her that he and his team had been sent out on a mission.

He hadn't told her he was leaving.

It was a stupid thing to be upset about, Phoebe absolutely acknowledged that. He'd asked her out several times and she'd turned him down each one of them. She'd told him several times that she wasn't ready for a relationship, even going so far as to say she never might be, so it wasn't like she could blame him for believing her.

Asher owed her absolutely nothing, certainly not keeping her apprised of his comings and goings. So why did she have this ache in her chest every time she thought about him?

"It won't get any easier, but you will get used to it," Hope said.

"What won't get easier?"

"Knowing he's in danger. That he's risking his life for strangers when he has people at home who care about him. Knowing that one day he might not come back to you. Or he might come back but not be the man you knew. You get used to living with the ball of fear in the pit of your stomach, can function, but it's not easy. Is this something you're going to be able to handle? No judgment if you can't, but this is who Mouse is. If you can't deal, you're better to walk now."

To be honest, she hadn't even really considered anything that far ahead. For now, it was hard enough just learning to do all the things she'd once taken for granted. "I respect Asher and what he does, I would never expect him to give that up for me. And if anything were to happen with us then I would learn to deal with it." Was that why she'd felt so anxious these last two weeks? Was some of it fear that Asher wouldn't come home?

"So, you're admitting you like him and want to be with him?" Hope asked, looking delighted, the earlier fear and pain washed away. If talking about Asher was helping her cousin, then she'd do it even if she was uncomfortable about it.

"I didn't say I didn't," she reminded Hope. "I just said I wasn't ready for a relationship."

"I hate Dexter Hunt for what he did to you. He took my bright, bubbly, outgoing cousin and turned her into someone who's afraid of everything, but it's not forever, okay? You'll work through it. You'll find your way back to the woman you used to be."

What if she didn't.

"No doubts," Hope said firmly, obviously reading the expression on her face. "You'll get there, just like I got there."

Still being abducted by human traffickers seemed a whole lot worse than dating a man who hurt her.

"Not a competition, Pheebs," Hope said.

"Stop reading my mind," Phoebe said with a smile.

"That's what best friend's do."

It was bad timing given Hope's fears, but she had to know. "If your dad had ... met a woman, do you think you ... would have been okay with that?"

"Thinking about Lolly?"

"Yeah. I don't know what's going to happen with me and Asher, but he and Lolly are a package deal. If anything did happen, I'd be getting an instant family, I'd be someone's stepmom. I'm ... scared I won't be a good role model for her. I wouldn't ever want her to be like me and let someone hurt her the way Dexter hurt me."

"First, we have to stop with this let talk, we'll work on that. Second, from what I hear, Lolly is already enamored with you. Third, Falcon and I talked and if anything happened to both of us, you're going to be our child's legal guardian."

Phoebe gasped, and tears blurred her eyes. "You would trust me to raise your child?"

"Of course. I'm sure Falcon's siblings would want to be involved, they're a nosy, intrusive bunch, but yeah, that's what we decided. Together, Falcon too, we both decided you were the best person to raise our child if we couldn't do it."

"I love you so much." Phoebe threw her arms around her cousin, a little piece of her confidence returned to her. "You are going to be the best mom. Everything is going to be okay, the birth is going to go smoothly, and in a week or two you're going to meet your baby. You need to tell Falcon about your fears."

"I will if you promise to work on believing you didn't let Dexter do anything to you. You left, you got yourself out, all on your own, you're stronger than you think you are."

She wanted to believe that so badly, but it was hard. Because she'd wanted to leave sooner but had stayed because she was scared. If she couldn't find a way to work through her fears then she would never be able to have anything with Asher, and that left her feeling like someone had carved out a piece of her heart.

CHAPTER TWELVE

March 4th
10:38 P.M.

Home.

As it always did, stepping through his front door gave Mouse the peace he needed to deal with the things he had to see and do. Without the love and support of his family he was sure he would have lost his mind a long time ago.

This mission had been hard. They'd rescued a dozen young girls and boys—the oldest was only eight, the youngest just eighteen months old—who had been abducted and trafficked. The children were traumatized, their tiny bodies ravished by the physical injuries from the abuse they had suffered.

It was heartbreaking.

And as it always happened when he dealt with little kids, he couldn't help but see his precious daughter as one of the victims. This time had been harder than usual because of Lolly's near abduction. Was that what his baby's future would have been if it wasn't for Phoebe.

Phoebe.

The woman he couldn't get out of his head.

Had things changed over the two weeks he'd been gone?

It could have gone either of two ways. Either Phoebe had decided he'd ghosted her and moved on and wouldn't give him a chance, or she'd been regaining her confidence and might be ready to go on a date with him.

He prayed it was the latter but was prepared for the former.

"Welcome home, my sweet baby boy."

Mouse couldn't not smile at his mom as she slipped into the living room and wrapped her arms around him. Even as a teen he'd had a good relationship with his parents, of course there had been those awkward years where his parents had embarrassed him just by existing, but other than that they'd been close. And after Emily's death, they had been an absolute godsend.

"Hey, Mom, I don't think I've been your baby boy in a long time though."

"You will *always* be my baby boy no matter how big you get. Just like when Lolly is thirty-five, she'll still be your baby girl." His mom kissed his cheek then went to the kitchen and turned on the kettle.

"Have I told you lately how much I appreciate your and Dad's support?" he asked as he followed her.

"We're happy to help you with Lolly," Mom said as she grabbed two mugs and set them on the counter.

"You go way beyond just helping me and you know it." Nudging his mom aside, he guided her into a kitchen chair and took over making coffee. "Helping is looking after Lolly while I'm away, but you always go the extra mile for both of us. You drove back into the city tonight so my daughter would be here at home in her own bed when I got here because you know I need to see her when I get home from a mission."

Not only had his parents helped shape Lolly into the warm, caring little girl she was, but if it wasn't for them and their help, he would have lost custody of her. They'd sacrificed so much for him and his daughter, he could never repay them, and he knew they wouldn't want him to. They'd done it out of love, that was what family did.

"Lolly's expecting you to go in and see her," Mom said as the kettle boiled, and he poured the boiling water into the two mugs.

"I will." Mouse wanted to broach the topic of Phoebe, and how his parents would feel about him being in a serious relationship. It wasn't that he didn't think they'd be happy for him, he knew they would, but he didn't want them to feel like once he had a woman in his life he wouldn't need them anymore. The last thing he wanted was for them to feel used after they'd give up so much to help him with Lolly.

"You thinking about your girl?" Mom was watching him with curious eyes as he sat down across from her at the table.

"She's not mine."

"Not yet."

"Maybe not ever." Although he hoped she wouldn't feel that way, Phoebe had warned him that she might never be ready to date again.

"She was hurt?"

"Yeah, she was. She's under the impression that makes her weak."

"She saved my granddaughter, she's the strongest woman I've ever had the pleasure of meeting," his mom said fiercely, making him smile.

He agreed. Whether she saw it or not, Phoebe had gotten herself out of an abusive relationship, and she hadn't hesitated to put her life on the line for his daughter. "If she decides to give us a chance, I have a feeling things could move pretty quickly."

His mother's smile was warm and genuine. "So, marriage might be in your future."

"I hope so." It was weird because a month ago marriage hadn't been on his radar. Not that he'd been opposed to it, he just hadn't been thinking about it at all. Then Phoebe blasted into his life and things had changed. The only other woman he'd ever felt this way about was Emily, and no way could it be a coincidence that Emily had given Lolly life, and so had Phoebe when she saved the girl from death or a fate worse than death.

"If that happens you won't need your dad and me so much."

"We will *always* need you," Mouse corrected.

Mom smiled again and reached over to cover his hand with hers. "I know you will, Asher. I'll always be your mom and I'll always be Lolly's grandma. But if you get married again you won't need as much help, you'll have a wife, maybe other kids someday."

"I don't want you to feel like I've just used you these last seven years," he admitted.

"Oh, my sweet baby boy." Mom stood and circled the table to stand beside his chair and wrap her arms around him. "I would never feel that way. If you never get married, then your dad and I will be happy to continue to help you with Lolly. And if you do get married then your dad and I will be happy just to be Grandma and Grandpa like we are with your sister's children. Bottom line is, we love you and Lolly so much and just want you both to be happy." Mom kissed his temple. "Phoebe makes you happy."

"I didn't know if I could find happiness with a woman again."

"Dad and I both really like her. She's beautiful, smart, sweet, and she gets along wonderfully with Lolly. When we had ice cream the other night, I saw the way she looked at you."

"We only just met, Mom," he reminded her.

"It only takes a split second to recognize your soulmate. I felt that way with your dad, your sister was that way too, and you were like that when you met Emily. I remember the letters you wrote home bragging about her, how smart she was, how strong, she could do no wrong in your eyes."

Emily had been so laid back, the two of them had rarely fought, they'd just clicked and everything had fallen into place. Things with Phoebe hadn't gone the same way, but he still felt that click.

"I do really like her," he admitted. "And so does Lolly."

"Then you know all you need to know." Mom kissed his temple again, then took her cup of coffee. "I'm going to head to bed, go give your daughter a kiss. Everything will work out the way it's supposed to, have faith, my sweet son."

Leaving his coffee, he'd come back and drink it and eat after he'd seen his daughter and taken a shower, he headed to Lolly's room. She was sleeping curled up on her side, Mrs. Fuzzy locked tight in her arms. Asleep she looked so small and sweet, so innocent, but someone had tainted that innocence, someone who had to pay for that.

Crouching beside her bed, Mouse swept a hand across his daughter's soft blonde locks. "Hey, bumblebee, wake up." Even though it was late, he *always* woke Lolly when he got home from a mission.

Lolly woke almost instantly. "Daddy!" she squealed, launching up and into his arms. "I missed you so much."

"Missed you too, baby girl."

"Daddy?"

"Yeah, sweetie?"

"Can we call Phoebe tomorrow?"

Mouse smiled. Seemed like he wasn't the only one who had been missing Phoebe. He'd given her time, but nothing had changed for him, he still wanted her so badly she had been constantly fluttering at the back of his mind no matter what he was doing. There was no way he and Lolly were giving up on Phoebe. Not ever.

Not when she meant so much to both of them.

Life didn't always hand out second chances at happiness, but he was going to grab hold of this one and never let go. He'd lost the love of his life—or one of them anyway—and she had been abused by a man she thought she loved. The darkness was in the past, behind them, and light was shining brightly in the future.

"Yeah, bumblebee, we can call her tomorrow."

* * * * *

March 5th
12:13 P.M.

For the first time since Dexter first put his hands on her,

Phoebe actually felt positive about her future.

The fear was still there, and the doubts, the lack of trust in herself and the uncertainty about the future, but there was also a little ray of positivity shining through all the darkness. A whisper that everything was going to be okay. That the hardest part had already been done when she made the decision to get herself out of that relationship, and that she had the strength and the will to clean up the mess Dexter's abuse had left behind.

She could do this.

It was an invigorating thought and one she clung to when the darkness wanted to creep back in.

The last few weeks had been quiet. No signs of Dexter, no feelings of being followed, and no creepy letters or threatening phone calls. To keep herself from going crazy obsessing over Asher she'd been busy. She'd found a new job, one she'd gotten all on her own and not because Falcon Oswald arranged it for her. It was a small firm, but she'd be doing family law which is what she'd always wanted to do. With a job she'd got by herself she'd felt her confidence returning, and now she was saving up with the determination to have moved out of the Prey apartment and into her own by the summer.

Phoebe was taking control of her life again.

At least that's what she thought until she heard a door open behind her and turned to see Asher and his team.

They were back.

And he hadn't called to tell her.

It annoyed her that she cared because he was only giving her the space she'd asked for, yet it did hurt. Made her doubt herself and her worth all over again. It was stupid, but it was what it was, and her therapist was helping her learn that instead of fighting against her emotions she should name them, accept them, and deal with them.

That was why she was here. Hope had suggested she speak to someone, and Falcon had offered Prey's on staff psychiatrist. At first, she'd felt silly going to see a woman who worked with men and women who literally put their lives on the line to make the world a safer place, but it had helped a lot.

If Asher was back and had chosen not to call her then she guessed that told her all she needed to know.

Quickly, she turned her back and resumed waiting for the elevator.

When it dinged and the doors swept open, she was about to hurry inside when a hand closed around her wrist. The hold was firm but gentle. "Oh, no you don't, butterfly."

Asher turned her around, and the rest of his team disappeared down the hall. He guided her into the room where he and his team had been, a small conference room with a large table in the center and a dozen chairs around it. Asher pulled out one of those chairs for her and once she was seated took the one beside hers, then he just stared at her.

"What?" Did she have something in her teeth? Toothpaste on her face? Why wasn't he saying anything?

"I forgot how beautiful you are."

What a line. And yet … it did give her a warm tingly feeling. Her hormones seemed to go into crazy overdrive when it came to Asher.

"You know I wasn't ghosting you, my team got called out."

"I know. Hope told me."

"We only got back last night, then this morning we had debriefings, I was going to come around and see you this afternoon."

"You were?" That warm tingly feeling grew. She'd told Asher over and over again that she didn't want to go out with him and yet here he was, still willing to give her a chance. Yet she knew that if she told him he was scaring her, or upsetting her, he would back off. Asher would always respect her, not like Dexter.

"Of course." He reached out and took her hands. "I've told you that I'm interested, and Lolly is desperate to see you again, we both want to spend more time with you. But …"

"But?" Buts were never good.

One side of his mouth quirked into a smile. "It's not a bad but. You've been honest with me too. You told me you weren't ready for a relationship, and I respect that. So, I want you to know that I won't ask you out again."

Her stomach dropped.

She had resisted when he'd asked because she had been afraid. Fear had ruled her life for eighteen months, it was hard to let go and see beyond it. Was that really how she wanted to spend the rest of her life? Too afraid to live it?

If she was still going to live in fear, she may as well be back with Dexter.

The whole reason for leaving was so she could be free, in charge of her own life, and have the life she'd always wanted.

She could see herself having that life with Asher and his daughter.

"I still want to be friends, hang out, but I'm not going to ask you on a date until you're ready. I hope that takes the pressure off you." Asher stood, then leaned down and kissed her forehead.

When he walked toward the door she knew she had to make a choice.

Fear or a future.

If she didn't break the hold fear had on her life now, she might never do it. She'd fall into a rut, it would be harder to get out of it, and she'd wind up trapped in a different kind of prison.

"Asher, wait."

He stopped and turned, eyebrows raised.

"When I didn't hear from you in weeks I realized something."

"I wanted to call or text, tell you we'd been called out, but we weren't together, and I wasn't sure it was appropriate." He returned to the chair he'd vacated and once again took her hands in his. "Sorry if I hurt your feelings."

"You didn't hurt my feelings … exactly," she added with a

smile. "Maybe the last couple of weeks not seeing you or hearing from you have been good. I've been seeing Piper a couple of times a week and it's helped a lot. I have a new job, and I'm planning on finding my own place by the end of spring. I've been doing a lot of thinking and I ... I like you."

Asher gave her that sexy smirk of his that made her toes curl. "I like you too, butterfly. And I still want to take you on a date, I was just worried that I was pushing too hard, adding more stress to what you're already dealing with."

"You're not," she assured him, suddenly feeling shy. She'd had plenty of boyfriends, and it wasn't just because of Dexter, it was that things felt different with Asher. They felt like maybe they could really go somewhere.

"Phoebe, would you like to go out to dinner with me tomorrow night?"

"A date?"

"A date."

"I would love to," she accepted, feeling a weight lift off her shoulders. She had just taken a really big step toward reclaiming her life and her self-worth. "But, Asher?"

"Yeah, sweetheart? You can tell me anything," he added when she didn't continue right away.

"Can we ... would it be okay if we took this slowly, no pressure, just let things develop however they do?"

"Come here." Asher tugged on her hand until she stood then pulled her closer, settling her on his lap. She'd never sat on a man's lap like this before. Straddling a guy's lap for sex was nothing like this, here on Asher's lap she felt safe, protected. There was no fear, and she knew she'd made the right choice. Something really special could develop between them. "We can take things as slow as you want to. And I have Lolly to think about, she already thinks you're her hero, but this will be the first relationship she's ever seen me in, and I don't know how she's going to react."

Phoebe relaxed further, another pressure off her mind. They could take things slow, hang out, have fun, maybe do a little making out, without feeling like they had to progress at any set timeline.

"So," Asher drew the word out. "No pressure, but if you want, we could go pick up Lolly from school and hang out, maybe have dinner?"

"I would love to."

"Yeah?"

"Absolutely. You aren't the only one I like."

The smile Asher gave her arrowed right through her heart. "I know. That's one of the things I like the most about you, that you really care about my daughter."

"I care about both of you." More than she should given how short a time she'd known them, but she wasn't going to overanalyze it. Name her feelings, accept them, and deal with them.

Her feelings for Asher were like quickly growing to more.

She'd accepted them by agreeing to go out with Asher.

And dealing with them would be the fun part because she got to spend time with two people she cared about.

CHAPTER THIRTEEN

March 5th
2:50 P.M.

"What made you decide to join the military?" Phoebe asked.

Mouse hadn't stopped smiling since their talk at the Prey offices a couple of hours ago. Phoebe was willing to give them a chance. She'd agreed to dinner just the two of them tomorrow, and today she'd agreed to pick up Lolly with him and spend time together the three of them.

It wasn't what he'd expected when he'd returned from this latest mission. He'd been worried whatever tenuous connection he and Phoebe had might have eroded over the weeks he was gone. So many times, he'd second guessed his decision not to text and tell her he was going. At the time, he hadn't wanted to pressure her, but he'd had no idea if he'd read the situation correctly.

But he'd doubted Phoebe's strength and determination.

Even though he'd told her that he believed in her and her strength and ability to rebuild her life, he'd underestimated her. She'd grabbed onto her new life and was working hard to make it the life she wanted. He was so proud of her. What she was doing wasn't easy, Dexter had systematically worked at dismantling her self-confidence. He'd broken her down so he could rebuild her the way he wanted her.

He'd failed.

Phoebe was going to fly high and have the last laugh by living her best life.

"I just always knew it was what I was supposed to do with my life," he said as he slung an arm around her shoulders and drew her close. It was hard to be around Phoebe and not touch her, but he watched carefully every time he did. The last thing he wanted to do was trigger any bad memories or do anything she wasn't ready for.

"Your parents owned and ran a restaurant, right?" she asked as she snuggled against his side, no hesitation, and he took that to mean she trusted him never to hurt her the way her ex had.

"Yep. My dad studied business and my mom was a chef. When they met and fell in love it seemed only natural they should open their own restaurant."

"So does that mean you're a good cook?"

"Unfortunately, no. Guess the cooking gene skipped a generation because Lolly *loves* spending time in the kitchen. Although I guess she's more of a baker—cookies, cupcakes, cakes, that's more her jam."

"The cupcakes she made for me were amazing, she's definitely got talent. The way she's bounced back after almost being kidnapped, you have one strong, determined, amazing little girl there."

"I couldn't agree more."

"Is it okay to ask about your wife?"

"Absolutely. Lolly and I talk about Emily a lot. It does hurt, but I want my daughter to know her mother because Emily loved her so much."

Phoebe pulled back so she could look up at him but, didn't break out of the circle of his arm. "I hope you know that I would never try to take Emily's place. She's always going to be Lolly's mom. If things get serious between us, I'd never try to take over as Lolly's mother. I'll be there to lead her and guide her, help her with anything, love her as though she were my own, but always respect that Lolly had a mom who loved her a lot."

Things were already serious between them as far as he was concerned, not that he said that out loud since they'd agreed to not force anything. "I know you would be an amazing stepmom. You're everything that I want in a role model for my daughter."

Darkness and pain filled Phoebe's beautiful blue eyes like storm clouds. "Even after ..."

"Don't say that, sweetheart." Mouse touched a finger to her lips, not wanting to hear her put herself down. "You're strong, and resilient, and a fighter. You care about other people and didn't hesitate to put your life on the line for my child. You're everything that I want in a role model for my daughter," he repeated.

The clouds didn't completely clear away, but she nodded. "Okay."

"Tell me about your parents."

"Well, my dad owns a construction company, and my mom was an electrician before she retired about three years ago."

"That's cool. I bet you learned a lot from them."

Phoebe grimaced. "You know what you said about cooking skipping a generation, well, building and electrical skills can do the same. I'm terrible at anything handy, you should have seen me when I moved into my last place, I couldn't put together any of the furniture, Hope laughed at me for a week before she finally helped."

Mouse laughed. "It's nice you and Hope have each other."

"My parents wanted more kids after me, but they kept having miscarriages. Eventually they decided they had me and they looked after Hope a lot too. My mom made sure she was home for us every day after school, and during term breaks and over the summer. She was there for all the important things in our lives. She might have been Hope's aunt, but she stepped up and into the mom role when needed. I spoke to Hope about Lolly, I hope that's okay. It's just Hope lost her mom the same way Lolly did, and I wanted to understand things the way Lolly might see them."

Which was exactly why he knew she would be a great mother to his daughter and any other children they might have one day.

Instead of saying anything he pulled her closer, dipped his head, and captured her lips in a soft kiss. His first taste of her and already he was hooked.

"Daddy?"

He broke away when he heard Lolly's voice. Despite the fact that the kiss had been sweet, chaste, he was breathing heavily, deeply affected by this small taste of a woman he already knew was his. "Hey, bumblebee, how was school?"

"Phoebe!" Lolly threw herself at Phoebe who laughed and caught her.

"How was school, peanut?" Phoebe asked.

It was the most adorable thing when she called his daughter peanut. At first, she'd seemed embarrassed about it, and he had no doubt the word had just slipped out, but when he hadn't said anything about it she must have assumed he didn't mind. He didn't mind, he wanted the two of them to bond. If he played his cards right then one day—hopefully not too far away—they'd be a family, he wanted her to be comfortable being a parent to Lolly.

"School was great," Lolly replied enthusiastically. "We got to write our own stories. I love telling stories. Daddy tells great ones."

"He does, does he? Guess he hasn't shown me that superpower yet." The grin she shot him was sassy and flirty, a hint of the Phoebe he suspected lurked beneath the damage inflicted on her by Dexter.

"I have a lot of superpowers," he said with a wink. When she was ready, he intended to show her every single one of them, lavishing attention on every part of her body, replacing her bad memories with good ones.

"I have a few of my own," she said, throwing a wink right back at him.

"Are you having dinner with us, Phoebe?" Lolly asked, taking Phoebe's hand.

"Well, your daddy invited me to, so yeah, if it's okay with you,

I'd love to have dinner with you two."

"Yay! Can we play too? Are you going to stay for dessert? Can you read me a story before I go to bed?"

"Whoa, bumblebee, that's a lot of questions."

"I could stay for dessert, and read to you, if it's okay with your dad." Phoebe looked to him, seeking his permission. He had no problem with her spending time with them and participating in their family rituals.

"We're reading The Babysitters Club," he said as he took Lolly's other hand and started walking his girls down the street. His girls. He loved the sound of that. There had been plenty of important women in his life, his mom, sister, grandmothers, aunts, cousins, his wife, his daughter, and now Phoebe. The woman who had breathed new life into his world.

"I loved The Babysitters Club when I was in elementary school," Phoebe said.

"So, you'll stay and read to me tonight?"

"Wouldn't miss it for the world."

"When we get home can we do makeovers? Grandma and I do them, and sometimes Daddy even lets me give him a makeover."

"Oh, I would pay good money to see photos of that," Phoebe said with a grin.

Since there wasn't anything he wouldn't do to keep that smile on her face he said, "I'll do you one better. How about we all do makeovers when we get home, then we can cook dinner, eat ice cream sundaes, then we can tuck Lolly in together." If he was lucky after that he'd get another chance to kiss Phoebe's sweet lips.

"Swing me," Lolly said, tugging on their hands.

As he and Phoebe swung Lolly between them, he didn't think anything could be more perfect.

* * * * *

March 6th
8:59 P.M.

Phoebe giggled as Asher finished a hilarious story about one of the many times he and Bear and their friends had gotten up to mischief when they were boys. Some of the things they'd done certainly rivalled some of the crazy things she and Hope had done when they were little girls.

"What's the most embarrassing thing that's ever happened to you?" she asked. They were having a great time on their first official date. Asher had taken her out for a nice dinner, they'd asked each other all sorts of questions, and she'd learned so much about Asher as well as shared a lot about herself. Now they were strolling hand in hand through the streets of Manhattan.

"Well." Asher grimaced as he drew out the word. "When Bear and I were in boot camp we were pretty cocky. We were young, had been jocks and popular in school, we were used to people thinking we were hot stuff, our egos were way bigger than our muscles. One day we were talking ourselves up, bragging, our training officers decided to make us put our money where our mouths were. Pushed us so hard I ended up puking up my guts out in front of everyone. Never lived that down."

She giggled again. She could see that, men like Asher thought they were bulletproof, they likely had to in order to do what they did, but she could see it biting them in the behind sometimes. "I'm surprised your nickname isn't something to do with that."

"I think it would have been if the name Mouse hadn't already been established."

"You going to tell me how you got the nickname?"

"It's nothing exciting. When I was a kid a mouse escaped from the science lab at school, it was terrified. I caught it in our classroom, it curled up in my hand and went to sleep. I wouldn't let it go back to the lab, took it home and kept it as a pet. Kids started calling me the mouse man, eventually it got shortened to mouse, even my sister and my dad call me Mouse. Only ones who don't are my mom, Lolly, and you."

She shivered, a delightful little shudder that seemed to heat her blood. Phoebe knew what Asher was really saying. She was special. That was how she felt about him too. It was the weirdest thing because she'd thought she'd been in love before, but how she felt about Asher already told her she'd never even come close. The feelings she was developing were already stronger than anything else she'd ever felt.

"You're such a softie inside. Caring about that little mouse, the way you are with Lolly, you're this alpha tough guy on the outside and this big marshmallow on the inside."

"Shh," he whispered in her ear, nuzzling her neck. "We don't want everyone to know."

She laughed, but it was a breathy sound as his lips kissed and nibbled their way down her neck. Although she'd been the one to say she wanted to take things slow, if he kept this up she was more than ready to do something. Maybe not sex, but they could still have plenty of fun without it.

When he straightened it took everything she had not to beg him to put his lips back on her, might have done it if they weren't out on the street.

"So, what's your most embarrassing moment?" Asher asked.

For a moment the euphoria she'd been feeling ebbed away. "Dexter."

Asher muttered a curse. "Sorry, honey. I didn't think. Last thing I wanted to do was ruin tonight by bringing those bad memories up."

Slowly she drew in a breath. It was up to her whether those memories had the power to ruin what had so far been the best date she'd ever been on. She was starting to remember that her emotions didn't have to control her, she could be the one to control them. This was her life, no one but her was in charge of it.

"No," she said firmly. "It's not going to ruin tonight. Dexter is my most embarrassing moment because I wasn't smart, and I wasn't strong when it came to him. But I'm being smart and strong now, and I think saying yes to going out with you tonight might just be the smartest decision I've ever made."

Asher growled, grabbed her, and dragged her up against his body. His mouth crushed down on hers and he kissed her with a fiery passion that left her entire body burning for more. His tongue swept into her mouth, and a throbbing need took up residence between her legs.

She wanted him.

Badly.

More than she'd ever wanted a man.

"Can we go back to your place?" she asked. It was closer than the Prey apartment she was staying in.

His gaze was tender as he looked down at her, one of his hands curled around the back of her neck, the other brushed a lock of hair off her face and tucked it behind her ear, letting his fingertips linger on her cheek. "Are you sure? We agreed no pressure."

"I don't feel pressured. But it's okay if you're not ready, I can wait." She knew that Lolly was spending the night at her grandparents but that didn't mean Asher wanted to make out with her.

A growl rumbled through him. "Not ready? Babe, I look at you and I'm ready, but I want you to be sure. We haven't known each other long and you wanted to go slow. I don't want you to do anything you'll regret."

"I won't regret this," she said with absolute confidence. There was no way she was going to able to go to sleep tonight if she didn't do something to ease the desire pulsing through her. She could take care of things herself once he dropped her off, but she would so much rather have Asher's hands on her.

"All right, sweetheart." The same need she felt was reflected in his gaze as he took her hand and they headed for his place.

The walk passed in a blur, all she could think about was how much she wanted to touch him, how much she wanted him to touch her. There was no darkness to her thoughts, no fear, no worries, just a need so deep she wasn't sure it could ever be quenched.

By the time Asher was opening his front door and guiding her inside, she felt like she was about to combust if they didn't do something to douse the fire burning inside her.

"I want you so badly," Asher said as he dropped onto the sofa and pulled her down to straddle his lap.

"Me too, I think I'm going to die if you don't hurry up and touch me now," Phoebe said as she fumbled with his zipper.

"I don't think anyone ever died from lack of orgasm." Asher smirked.

"You want to risk it?"

"No way. Better safe than sorry." He shoved her skirt up and pushed her panties aside "Soaked," he moaned as he swiped a finger along her center. "You're so wet for me, butterfly."

Her hips rocked, trying to seek more as she shoved his boxers down and his impressive length sprung free. "Need you so much."

"You've got me, babe." A finger slipped inside her as hers curled around his hard length which quivered at her touch.

The finger inside her pressed against a spot and she gasped as amazing sensations bubbled inside her. "Oh, wow," she gasped.

"You like that, honey?" A smile that was pure sex spread across his lips, Asher slid another finger into her and brushed against that same spot making her internal muscles clench and pleasure bubbled further.

"I've never felt that before," she admitted as she gasped again and pressed down to take his fingers deeper inside her.

As his fingers stroked inside her and his thumb found her throbbing little bundle of nerves, Phoebe felt pleasure building. She'd forgotten what it was like, it had been so long since she'd come from sex, all Dexter had cared about was making her do things the way he wanted and getting himself off.

But Asher was all about making her feel good.

Not wanting to be left out, she stroked her hand up and down Asher's shaft as intense sensations began to crescendo, she tightened her hand, increased her speed. Asher's mouth found hers, kissing her thoroughly, and when his thumb pressed against her hard little bud, that bubbling crescendo burst and pleasure spiked through her body.

Phoebe cried out her pleasure into Asher's mouth and felt him come in her hand.

When the pleasure bubbles finally died down to a low simmer, she rested her forehead against Asher's. "That was something else," she whispered.

"More than something else, it was earth-shattering."

She huffed a chuckle, pleasantly relaxed and sated. "Definitely shattered my earth," she agreed.

"Let me go get something to clean you up then we can have coffee, maybe go for round two." He waggled his eyebrows, making her giggle.

Asher slid her off his lap and while he disappeared down the hall she stood and righted her panties and skirt. As she did, her gaze fell on a stack of papers on the coffee table. Amongst them was a photo.

Phoebe gasped as she recognized the man in the photo.

She'd seen him before.

In Dexter's office.

About six months ago she'd seen that man in Dexter's office. The man had been brandishing a gun and ranting something about needing custody of a baby that didn't even exist yet.

Her heart was hammering so hard in her chest she could hardly breathe.

Panic scratched and clawed inside her.

Dexter said he had people watching her. Dexter knew this man and apparently Asher did too. Were Asher and his team the men her ex had sent to watch over her? Was it all a set up from the beginning? Was Asher only being nice to her to keep her close so he could get paid for the job?

Tears blurred her eyes, and she ran for the door.

Had she made out with a man who was merely playing her?

Worse, was she falling for a man who was really in bed with her abusive ex?

CHAPTER FOURTEEN

March 6th
10:31 P.M.

Phoebe was gone.

Mouse frowned as he looked around the now empty living room. He'd just been in the bathroom grabbing a warm, wet towel to clean Phoebe up, so he knew she hadn't been in there. If she'd gone to his bathroom, she would have had to pass the second bathroom and she hadn't done that. The kitchen door was closed, and he might have thought she was in there, but the front door was slightly ajar.

She'd left.

Why?

Everything had been going perfectly. Dinner had been fun, asking one another get to know you questions, and then they'd made out which hadn't been on his agenda for the night. Mouse hadn't wanted to do anything that would make her feel pressured, but she'd been clear that it was what she wanted.

At least he'd thought she wanted it.

Phoebe had seemed happy, relaxed, had that floating down from an orgasm fueled high look in her eyes. How could things have changed in the sixty or so seconds he'd been gone?

What was going on?

He spun in a circle, examining the room as though the answers he sought might be hiding somewhere. Then his gaze landed on the coffee table. After taking Lolly to school, he'd spent most of the day working on trying to find leads on the men who had tried to abduct Lolly, then alternating to looking into the man who had been pulling Storm Gallagher's strings.

That case was personal to Prey and his whole team specifically. Storm had had Dove Oswald and her now husband Isaac abducted and almost killed, then after he'd escaped, he'd abducted his sister Mackenzie. It was on a raid of his compound that Bear had found Mackenzie, weak and injured and imprisoned. After fighting for their lives, sparks had ignited between the pair and eventually they got together. Not before Storm abducted his sister and they found out that his plans of a utopia where there was no government, no money, and people lived off the land, were being used by someone to manipulate him. They just had no idea who that person—or persons—was.

His gaze narrowed as he stepped closer. Had Phoebe seen the picture of Storm? Was that why she ran?

No.

That made no sense.

How would she even know who the man was?

Storm had believed he would produce an heir who would usher in a new world, Phoebe was involved in family law. Had Storm sought legal advice?

If he had, it was unlikely to have been from Phoebe, but Dexter was a high flyer at one of the most prestigious family law firms in the country. It was conceivable that Storm had spoken to Dexter about getting legal custody of the baby he wanted to create.

But if that had happened, how would Phoebe know Storm?

Could Storm and whoever had been pulling his strings been involved in Lolly's near kidnapping?

Could he have threatened or blackmailed Phoebe into being part of it?

No.

That was utterly crazy.

If Phoebe had run it was much more likely because she'd freaked because the two of them had made out. That made a whole lot more sense. She was already uncertain about the two of them dating, that she would have doubts was almost a given, especially when they'd gone from zero to sixty in one night.

Yet …

His gut screamed that the reason she had run was because she'd seen this photo of Storm and it had freaked her out.

Why else would she leave so abruptly? If she was just having second thoughts about the two of them then she probably would have made some lame excuse to leave once he came back.

Pulling out his cell phone, he sent out a group text to his team. He needed their opinions on this before he did something stupid.

By the time his team responded to his SOS and turned up at his apartment thirty minutes later, he was no closer to figuring out what was going on.

"What's up?" Arrow asked as his team settled into his living room.

"I don't know," he said slowly.

"Don't think you asked us over here to hang out for nothing, brother," Surf said as he lounged in the armchair.

"Spit it out," Brick added.

Bear just watched him with an unreadable expression on his face, his gaze moving between Mouse and the papers on the table.

"Something to do with Storm?" Domino asked.

"Thought you were on a date with Phoebe," Surf said. "Your first date."

"Something happen with her?" Brick asked.

"Maybe. I'm not sure." How did he explain his fear without sounding like he was paranoid or insane? It made no sense that Phoebe would have anything to do with Storm Gallagher, no sense that she even knew who he was, yet everything had been going so well, then he left her alone in a room with pictures of him and she'd suddenly disappeared.

What was he supposed to think?

"You called us to talk whatever it is out," Arrow reminded

him. "What's going on?"

"Phoebe and I came back here after dinner, we didn't have sex, but we did make out," he told the guys.

"She run?" Brick asked.

"Yeah, but not how you're thinking. She was happy after, at least I thought she was. I left the room for a moment then we were going to have coffee only I came back a minute later and she was gone," he explained.

"So, if it wasn't because she was upset you two made out, why would she run?" Surf asked.

When his gaze dropped to the papers, he felt Bear tense. "You think she knows Storm?" his friend demanded.

"It's crazy, right?" he asked, needing someone to reassure him. It made no sense yet his gut was tingling.

"What other reason could there be for her to run?" Bear growled.

"Maybe that she's just out of an abusive relationship and a man touching her was too much for her," he suggested.

"Or she knows something about who was working with Storm," Bear said.

Perhaps sharing his fears with his team wasn't a good idea. He'd just painted a pretty large bullseye on Phoebe's back. Prey and his team were desperate for answers, and if they thought Phoebe had them they wouldn't stop until they got out of her what she knew.

By any means necessary.

While none of them took any pleasure in interrogations, sometimes they were a necessary part of their jobs. No way could he put Phoebe through something like that, not until he was sure she actually knew anything.

There was every chance he was blowing this way out of proportion.

"We don't know that she knows Storm," he cautioned.

"We don't know that she doesn't," Bear countered.

"One way to find out," Arrow said.

"We should call in Prey," Brick added.

"No. Not yet. Not until we're sure," he said firmly. The Phoebe he had been getting to know wasn't someone who would be involved in a plan to kill military vets, bankrupt the government, and blow up several buildings aiming for maximum casualties. The Phoebe he knew was sweet, caring, strong, brave, and had risked her life for his little girl. "We go easy on her until we know if she's involved. No one hurts her, that's non-negotiable."

No one disagreed. Since this was Phoebe they would take his lead, do things his way, unless they found out she was involved. Then all bets would be off. He wouldn't like it, but if she was involved in something dangerous and messed up then they had to use whatever she knew to stop it before anyone was hurt.

A misunderstanding.

That was all this was.

All it could be.

Because the alternative was that he was falling for a woman who had no soul and was prepared to kill innocent people for money and power.

Worse, he'd let a woman like that spend time with his daughter.

"She's staying in one of Prey's apartments, we should be able to get in easily enough," Bear said. "We question her find out what she knows. If she doesn't know anything, then we apologize."

Yeah, as if it would be that easy.

There was no way his tiny little fledgling relationship with Phoebe could withstand him being wrong.

However this played out, either way he lost.

Either Phoebe was in cahoots with the men who had played Storm and encouraged him to abduct his sister, helped him try to start a war, in which case she would be spending a lot of time in prison, or best-case scenario, she could turn on them, make a deal, and maybe get herself placed in witness protection. Or he was about to further traumatize her in which case she would never trust him again or want anything to do with him.

Tonight had gone from perfect to awful real quick.

* * * * *

March 7th
1:22 A.M.

Someone was hammering on her door.

Phoebe sprung awake, terror gripping her in a vice.

Was it Dexter?

Things with her ex had been quiet, and she'd assumed he'd been outmuscled and moved on. But what if he hadn't?

Since she was in one of Prey's safehouses someone would come for her if they saw Dexter break in here.

Right?

She'd been told that even though the cameras in the apartment wouldn't be turned on to give her privacy, the ones outside would be just in case Dexter came back for her. Were those cameras still on?

Was anyone watching those cameras?

Would they know she was in trouble?

As she climbed out of bed her knees were shaking so badly she could hardly stand up. The hammering on her door hadn't stopped, and she didn't think it was going to.

Should she rely on Prey noticing someone was there or call the cops?

At least she should see who was there first. Maybe it was just a neighbor who needed help, she'd look stupid calling the cops if they weren't needed.

Creeping through the apartment like she expected the

bogeyman to jump out at her at any moment—which part of her did—she went to the front door and stood on tiptoes to see through the peephole.

It was Asher's team.

What were they doing here?

Had something happened to Asher?

Panicking for a whole different reason now, Phoebe through open the door. "What's wrong? Is Asher—"

Five large, intimidating men shoved their way past her, backing her up until she was pressed against the living room wall.

Were they here because of the picture she'd seen in Asher's apartment?

Was it possible they really were in cahoots with Dexter?

Tears filled her eyes. She was still terrified, but she was more heartbroken at the moment. It was clear Asher had thrown her to the wolves, hadn't even bothered to come with his team. Why did she keep picking men who only wanted to use and abuse her? Why couldn't she find a good, honorable man like Hope had?

"Sit," Bear ordered, gesturing at the couch.

Afraid to comply.

Afraid to disobey.

In the end she decided that doing as they told her was the best option, so she scurried towards the couch, trying to keep as much distance between as possible. Not that it did much good, these men were big and they seemed to fill the apartment with their presence.

Phoebe felt trapped.

Helpless.

There was no way she was getting past five former special forces operatives.

"So it's true," she whispered through her tears.

"What's true, Phoebe?" Brick asked.

"You work for *him*," she spat.

"Who is him?" Arrow asked.

Like they didn't know. Still if they thought she was so stupid and wouldn't figure it out then she'd spell it out for them. "Dexter."

"Huh?" Surf said, sounding surprised. Apparently, they hadn't thought she was smart enough to catch on to their game.

"You need to tell us what's going on," Bear demanded. He sounded angry and there was no use in pretending she wasn't wildly intimidated by the large man. Right now, he was nothing like the guy who had kissed Mackenzie like she was the most precious thing in the world.

When her apartment door slammed open all their attention snapped towards it.

Asher stormed through, a handcuff dangling off one of his wrists.

"Back off," he growled at his friends. "Think I wouldn't get free?" He wiggled his arm at his team, the handcuff jingling. Giving his friends one last glare he stormed over to her, dropping to his knees before her.

Phoebe wanted to throw herself into his arms, but she didn't. She still wasn't quite sure what was going on. It was hard for her to trust Asher given her recent history, harder to trust herself. Just because it looked like Asher had been left behind on purpose didn't mean that he *wasn't* working with the rest of his team with or for Dexter.

Even though she was still scared out of her mind, anger was leaking in too. She'd done nothing wrong. *Asher* was the one playing games, using her, working with the man who had beaten her, and raped her, and controlled her every move.

"Does Prey know?" she asked. There was no way Falcon would allow men like this to work for him. Somehow, they'd fooled their bosses into thinking they were honorable men, but if they took contract work for people like Dexter then they weren't good men at all.

"No. Since Hope is your cousin, we wanted to give you a

chance to explain before Prey stepped in," Asher replied. His hands were clenched in fists and resting on his knees, she got the feeling he wanted to reach out and touch her but was restraining himself.

Her mouth dropped open. "*You* think you're doing *me* a favor?"

Asher's brow furrowed. "Why do I get the feeling we're talking at cross purposes here?" He looked over his shoulder at Bear who studied her for a long moment before nodding.

When Asher leaned closer she tried to shrink away from him but there was nowhere to go.

No escape.

Trapped.

Air began to saw in and out of her chest as panic surged. How many times had Dexter tied her up so he could do whatever he wanted with her? Was Asher going to hurt her? Whatever trust she'd had in him had been obliterated when his team came barging in here.

Scrambling to her feet she scampered to the other side of the room, pressing herself into the corner, attempting to make herself as small a target as possible, like an animal hiding from a predator.

Six predators.

"Easy, honey," Asher said, hands held up, palms out, trying to put her at ease.

It wasn't working.

"Look," he said as he very slowly removed his weapon.

He was going to shoot her.

White spots danced in her vision as she hyperventilated.

Her chest hurt from the thousand micro breaths she was taking.

"See," Asher said as he set the weapon down on the coffee table. "I'm not armed, I'm not going to hurt you."

Yeah.

Right.

It was too late for that.

Tonight had broken what pieces she had left after Dexter.

"Why do you think we're working for Dexter?" Asher asked, his voice not unkind, but no way was she getting played again.

"Because you have a photo in your apartment of a man I saw in Dexter's office," she replied, not sure why they were still pretending they weren't Dexter's spies.

"She has no idea who he is," Arrow announced.

"Agreed," Bear said. "Sit down, Phoebe, we need to talk."

She shook her head so hard her neck hurt. No way was she getting any closer to these crazy men than she already was.

"Hey," Asher said softly, drawing her attention back to him. As he took a step towards her she was hit hard by the regret and pain in his dark eyes. "I'm sorry. We messed up. When I saw you were gone, I thought you'd run because of the picture you saw."

"I did," she whispered. Who was the man in the photo? And why did them thinking she knew who he was give them the idea they had to barge in here and interrogate her?

"Not in the way I thought. I'm so sorry." His tone sounded defeated like he already knew that whatever had been growing between them was ruined now. "Sit, please. We need to know why you were afraid enough of the man you saw to think I was working for your ex, why you had to run."

He held out a hand and she eyed it, wanting so badly to take it, have him protect her, care for her, but she no longer trusted him.

Wrapping her arms around her waist, she skirted around him and sat down on the couch, perching on the edge, ready to spring away if they came at her. It likely wouldn't work, there were six of them to her one, and they were highly trained and so much bigger than her, but she wouldn't ever be an easy target again.

Not ever.

Pointless or not, she would fight for her life with everything she had.

"What did you see that day?" Arrow asked as all six men also took seats. She'd noted that they had all removed their weapons as well, all six now sat on the coffee table. If it was meant to put her at ease it didn't, she wasn't stupid enough to think they all weren't still armed. Or that they weren't just as deadly with their bare hands.

It was obvious this man was a dangerous person. If he was involved with Dexter then her ex was a whole lot more dangerous than she'd realized. Even though she didn't trust Asher or his men, she'd tell them what she knew. "You aren't working with Dexter?"

"No, honey," Asher said. He was sitting beside her on the couch but had been careful to keep some distance between them.

She wanted to believe him so badly, but she didn't trust her judgment. Her recent track record with men was awful to say the least. "It was a few months before I ran. Dexter called me to his office one day, I got there early, that man was in there with him. He had a gun, and he was yelling something about needing to get custody of a baby. That's all I know." Mostly. All she'd heard that day anyway.

"The baby was the one he wanted to make with Mackenzie," Bear growled.

"What?" Phoebe asked. Mackenzie was somehow connected to this man? That was why the guys had come here tonight, they thought she knew something about a man who was connected to their family.

That was nice. For Mackenzie. She had a family who cared about her enough to do this, but it also served to remind Phoebe that she wasn't part of their family. While it seemed Asher hadn't been onboard with his team's plans, he still had to have called them in and told them he suspected her of working with a man who had hurt the team.

"I'll fill you in later. Do you know something else about the man?" Asher asked.

Keeping secrets was only going to wind up getting her in

trouble, wasn't like she knew much anyway so they may as well get it all out. "There was something about the man that scared me. I knew he was bad news. I asked around about him, I didn't learn anything, but Dexter obviously found out. He was angry." Really angry, but she wasn't telling them about that last night before she'd run. The night she'd realized that she was involved with a sociopath. "I knew that whatever Dexter was messed up in was bad. I wanted out, that was when I decided I had to leave."

It had taken her a few more months to get up the courage to actually walk out the door. She might have left, but it didn't seem to matter where she was or what she did, Dexter and his mess tainted everything.

She was never going to be safe.

Never going to be free.

And the new start she'd thought she had here in Manhattan had just gone up in smoke.

CHAPTER FIFTEEN

March 7th
2:02 A.M.

Mouse had made a terrible mistake.

One there would be no coming back from.

Phoebe sat beside him on the couch, arms wrapped around her middle, devastation and betrayal in her eyes. Every time he or one of his team moved, she flinched, her gaze circling the room, seeking an escape.

He'd handled things badly tonight. What he should have done was come over himself and asked her why she'd run. Instead, he'd called in his team, and taken a potentially bad situation and made it a whole lot worse. In theory, if she had been working with Storm Gallagher, then he'd handled things the right way, but his gut had told him she didn't have it in her to be in any way involved in a plot to overthrow the government.

Should have listened to his gut.

When his team had decided to ambush Phoebe he'd refused to do that to her. They'd thought cuffing him to his fridge would keep him away long enough for them to get answers from her.

They'd been wrong.

He'd need a new fridge but he'd made it here before too much damage had been done.

At least that's what he was hoping.

"We need to know everything you do about Dexter," Bear growled, and Mouse shot his friend a glare. He knew this case was personal for Bear—for all of them really—because of what had happened to Mackenzie. But taking it out on Phoebe was only going to make things worse.

"I … I don't know much. Anything really," she said as she shrank further in on herself.

Whatever progress he'd made in earning her trust over the last few weeks was now decimated. Phoebe would never trust him again. One wrong judgment call was all it had taken to ruin the best thing to happen to him in years.

"We'll talk more in the morning," he said, she'd been through enough tonight. "You need to go pack a bag and we'll take you to stay with Hope and Falcon."

Red stained her cheeks and he saw a flare of anger in her eyes. Good. Anger was much easier to deal with than her pain. Pain he had caused.

"I haven't done anything wrong. I don't need to be watched like some criminal," she snapped.

Mouse fought a smile that wanted to quirk up his lips, he didn't think she'd be pleased that he found her anger amusingly adorable. She still had a lot of fight left in her, fight she was going to need because this had moved from her running from an abusive ex to something a whole lot more complicated.

If Dexter Hunt knew Storm Gallagher, then he was in some way involved in the man's plans. They knew someone had been pulling Storm's strings, could it be Phoebe's ex?

"You're not going there to be watched because we think you'll run, honey. You're going there so we know you're safe," he told her.

"Your ex just got a whole lot more dangerous, darlin'," Surf said.

"I don't understand." Phoebe lifted a hand to her head and rubbed at her temples. She had a headache, what he wouldn't give to massage it away for her.

"I know, and we'll explain everything, I promise, but right now you need to get some rest."

"Dexter has backed off," she protested.

"I don't think he has. More like he strategically retreated," he said. If they'd known the man was more than just abusive, he never would have left Phoebe alone and unprotected. It was sheer luck that Dexter hadn't made a play for her while Mouse and his team were out of the country.

Her eyes widened. "You think he's going to come back?"

"He won't touch you again," Mouse vowed.

The doubt in her big blue eyes was all on him. Of course she no longer trusted him.

"I'll go pack," she said softly. It didn't go unnoticed that she edged around the room, trying to keep as much distance between herself and him and his team as she could.

Once she was gone, he shoved to his feet and raked his fingers through his hair as he paced around the room. He had no one to blame but himself for screwing up what they'd been building.

Just a couple of hours ago he'd had her in his arms, pleasure etched into every line of her face, and now she hated him.

"We'll apologize to her. We'll get everything sorted out," Arrow told him.

"Yeah, right. She hates me, and I deserve it. All I wanted was to be someone she could trust, someone she knew would never hurt her like her ex did. Instead, all I've been is a man who's hurt her over and over again."

"You haven't," Brick said. "Tonight was a mistake. We shouldn't have handled things the way we did but we all care about Mackenzie, and we want everyone involved in what happened to her to pay."

"Only that's not what happened. That day, when I saw her with Lolly, I was purposefully rough with her. If my daughter hadn't been there, I probably would have beaten her up first and asked questions later."

"You thought the woman had abducted your kid," Domino said.

"No excuse. And tonight, I let myself believe that she could be mixed up in the Storm mess even though I knew better. It's like all I do is hurt her."

"So, you'll apologize, make it up to her, earn her trust back," Surf said like it was no big deal at all. "We all do."

"If you were her, would you ever trust me again?"

"If I was her, I would understand that we're talking about some very dangerous men with very dangerous plans, and that while we didn't approach this as we should have, emotions were running high. I would also understand that you have a handcuff hanging from your wrist, its clear you weren't on board with how we chose to handle things," Surf said.

That was no excuse.

Emotions could still be running high while you made sound, logical decisions.

"I'm sorry, man," Bear said, looking truly remorseful. "This is on me. I'm the one that couldn't wait, that needed to know if she knew anything about who was working with Storm. I'll make sure Phoebe knows that."

"I'm ready to go," Phoebe said quietly as she stepped back into the hall, a suitcase beside her.

The woman looked so defeated, so alone, it was hell not being able to go to her, sweep her up into his arms, rain kisses down on her face, and undo all the damage he'd caused. She'd be lucky to ever trust a man again at this point. He had vowed to protect her, never hurt her, and yet he'd failed at every turn.

"Phoebe." Her name fell from his lips in a ragged plea. It was so wrong of him to ask her for another chance when she'd already given him one. Yet how could he just let her walk out of his life like she wasn't already important to him?

"I know, you're sorry," she said, her gaze fixed on the floor.

"You'll never know how much." If she gave him even one little indication that there was hope for them, he would jump all over that, but she couldn't even look at him. "I'll take you to Falcon and Hope's."

She nodded and didn't protest when he took the suitcase from her hand. In silence, they headed downstairs and out to the vehicle. As he drove through the quiet streets, he searched his mind for something to say that would convey just how bad he felt but came up empty.

When he pulled up outside Falcon's building he reached out and took her hand to stop her getting out of the vehicle. Cradling her small hand in his, he brushed his thumb across her knuckles. This could be the last time he ever got to touch her, and if it was, he wanted to drag it out for as long as possible.

"I'm so sorry, I should have come over on my own to ask questions. I shouldn't have brought in my team, and I shouldn't have allowed them to barge into your home in the middle of the night and intimidate you like that."

"I should have stayed and confronted you, but I panicked. Thought you were working with Dexter."

His gaze snapped up at the smallest of indications that maybe things weren't completely hopeless. Phoebe's eyes were watching his thumb as it continued to caress her hand. "What happened tonight was on me. I hate that I broke the promise I made to you that I wouldn't ever hurt you."

Slowly she lifted her eyes to look up at him. "It doesn't matter who's fault it is. If I really was working with this Storm man, then I guess I understand why your team came in like that did. You thought I was dangerous and had information that would help your friend."

What she hadn't said rang through as clearly as what she had. Everyone's focus tonight—*his* focus tonight—had been on Mackenzie and not on her. Mouse wished he could argue the point, but she was right. He'd let finding the men responsible for Mackenzie almost dying take priority over a woman he could have seen himself sharing his life with.

"I messed up, didn't have your back. It won't ever happen again."

"Asher," she drew the word out. "We can't … we aren't … I don't … I don't think I want to see you again."

The words were what he'd expected and yet still they scored a direct hit.

Phoebe wanted nothing to do with him.

How could he earn her trust back if she didn't give him a chance?

"I told you I wouldn't give up on you and I won't. Even if you can't forgive me and give me a second chance, I promise I will make Dexter pay for what he did to you. Whether he's involved in Storm's scheme or not, he deserves to pay for hurting you."

Leaning over, he touched his lips to her forehead, much too aware that this could be the last time he ever kissed her.

* * * * *

March 7th
2:33 A.M.

Walking away from that car felt like walking away from her heart.

But Phoebe did it.

What else could she do?

Asher had proved over and over again that he wasn't someone she could count on. That if someone else was in jeopardy, he would hurt her.

Okay, so she understood why he'd been rough with her that day in the park, and why he'd been suspicious of her tonight, but that didn't mean she could keep herself in a situation where she would continue to be hurt.

She felt his eyes watching her as she walked inside the building. She wanted to turn around and go running back to the car, extract whatever promises she could from him that he wouldn't hurt her again, but they'd be promises she wouldn't believe.

The trust between them had been tentative at best, she wasn't in a good place, although she was doing her best to climb out of the dark hole she'd been trapped in, and what trust had existed had now evaporated like smoke.

"They're expecting you," the doorman said, and she gave him a weary nod and mustered a small smile as she trudged toward the lifts.

As she waited for the doors to open, she made the mistake of turning and looking back outside. Asher's truck was still there, she could feel him still watching her.

All she had to do was go running out there, tell him it was okay what had happened tonight, and let him take care of her. But that felt too much like letting herself get stuck in another situation too similar to the one she'd just escaped.

So, she forced her feet to remain still.

Deliberately turned her back so she didn't have to stare temptation in the face and prayed the lift would hurry up and get there.

A ding announced it was coming, and when the doors opened and she stepped inside, she felt like the last tie to Asher snapped when those doors closed.

It was done.

Over.

Time to face reality.

By the time the lift doors opened again at the penthouse, Phoebe was about a second away from losing it.

Instead of her cousin being there to greet her, Falcon was standing in the foyer, dressed in sweatpants and nothing else. He was big, gruff, intimidating, yet there was a softness there that she wasn't used to seeing.

A softness that cracked through the last of her barriers.

When he stepped forward and opened his arms, she threw herself into them.

"You okay?"

"No," she wept, not bothering to lie or to hide the tears that were flowing freely now. Tears she should have shed a long time ago, allowing herself to vent the emotions that she'd held back because she felt like she was partly to blame for what Dexter had done to her.

If she was stronger, she would have left.

If she was smarter, she never would have been there in the first place.

"Come here, sweetie." Hope's arms replaced Falcon's and she was guided through into the living room and down onto the sofa.

She shouldn't be here, bringing her problems to her cousin's doorstep. Not when Hope had already been through so much, not when she was just a week or so away from giving birth. It was selfish of her to have agreed to come and stay here.

"I'm s-sorry," she sobbed.

"For what?" Hope asked as she stroked Phoebe's hair.

"You don't need my mess right now."

Behind them Falcon growled, and Hope's arms tightened around her.

"Don't say that. We're family, this is exactly where you should be right now. Here, with the people who love and care about you. The people you can trust to have your back and help you through this," Hope said.

"Bear called, told me what happened. All of Alpha team will face disciplinary actions," Falcon told her.

The announcement startled her enough that she pulled away from Hope's embrace and stared at Falcon in shock. "What?"

"They know better than to go after my wife's cousin like that. If they had come to me, I would have set them straight and we would have brought you in to Prey, asked about what you knew, in a way that wouldn't have traumatized you in the process."

Warmth spread throughout her. For the last eighteen months she'd felt so very alone, trapped in a hell she couldn't see a way out of. Shame had her withdrawing from her support system when she'd needed them the most, but this morning that support system was out in full force.

"Asher told me that this man, Storm, hurt Mackenzie. I understand why they reacted the way they did. They were protecting their family," she said. Phoebe thought that was the crux of her issue. She could understand why they had reacted the way they had, but it reminded her that she was an outsider in Asher's little family. He hadn't believed in her, his priority had been Mackenzie because she was important to Bear, while Phoebe was … nothing.

"They know better than to go after *my* family," Falcon growled.

Phoebe huffed a chuckle despite everything going on. Falcon's protectiveness of her was sweet. "They didn't hurt me."

As she said the words, she realized they were true.

Even though he thought she might be working with a man who had hurt someone he loved and cared about, Asher hadn't wanted his team to go rushing over to her apartment to confront her. In fact they 'd had to handcuff him to keep him from interfering. His team had terrified her, but they hadn't laid a hand on her.

The only permanent reminders of tonight would be in her mind not on her body.

"You keep defending him," Hope noted, reaching out to brush a lock of hair off Phoebe's wet cheek.

She shrugged. When Asher first asked her out, she said no because the man reminded her too much of Dexter. His size and his ability to be ruthless when he wanted to be. She'd thought she might just be trading one toxic relationship for another.

Tonight had proved Asher and Dexter were nothing alike.

In the months they'd been together, Dexter had taken great pleasure in inflicting pain on her. Her pain had been his pleasure, but that wasn't the case with Asher. Her pain had been echoed in his deep, soulful eyes.

He was hurting because she was hurting.

Put like that the two men couldn't be more different.

"You look like you just had an epiphany," Hope said.

"Maybe I did," she said thoughtfully. "Who is this Storm man?" Perhaps if she could understand more about the situation, it would help her to better understand what had happened tonight.

"He's Mackenzie's half-brother," Falcon replied. "He took control of a couple of survivalist communities, turned the men and women there into his own personal army to bring in a revolution. He intended to abduct military vets then use them as hostages to bankrupt the government, then he wanted to do away with money and have everyone go back to living off the land. His version of a utopia."

"He also had a list of targets he intended to blow up," Hope added.

"Wow." So the man was crazy and dangerous. "What does that have to do with Dexter?"

"We don't know yet, but we'll find out," Falcon promised. "What we do know is that Storm was just being used by someone more powerful."

"Dexter knows a lot of powerful and wealthy men," she said. Was that how her ex was tied up in all of this? "I found out that Dexter was taking money from people to pay off witnesses to help his clients get custody of their kids. He was blackmailing them, they either paid up or they lost their kids. Maybe one of those men was the one pulling the strings on Storm."

"We'll figure it out, I promise," Falcon assured her.

"You don't need to punish Asher and his team. I think they thought they were doing me a favor by handling it themselves." Phoebe couldn't deny that Hope was right, the need to defend Asher ran deep. Even though she'd been terrified her tonight, she didn't want him or his team to be punished because of it.

Her feelings for Asher were still there, she didn't have a switch where she could just turn them off and on, but she also didn't have a switch that would allow her to just trust him again.

She wasn't sure she would ever trust a man again.

Yet was she ready to just walk away? To forget about how Asher made her feel and about Lolly and the little family they could have become?

But how did you get past something like this?

And what would happen next time Asher suspected she could be involved in something?

Could she trust that he if he and his team had questions they would just ask them like a normal person?

Could she trust herself and her judgment or would she wind up making another mistake? Perhaps this time one there would be no coming back from?

CHAPTER SIXTEEN

March 7th
7:47 P.M.

That had to be a mirage because no way was he that lucky.

Mouse knew good luck was the last thing he deserved right now. Yet when he set his phone down and went to the front door, he saw the same thing he'd seen on the door cam.

Phoebe.

At his apartment.

Looking up at him with a tentative smile.

"May I come in?" she asked. Her voice was soft, but there was a determination there that said she'd come here for a specific purpose and likely wouldn't leave until she'd achieved it.

"Of course." He stepped back and curled his hands into fists at his sides to stop himself from reaching for her. "Are you okay."

She shrugged. "I've been better, but I'm all right."

"I'm so sorry for what went down this morning. I panicked when I found you gone, didn't want to believe it was because I'd done something to scare you by mauling you like a hormone ravaged teenager. When I saw the photos I couldn't not wonder if you knew Storm. From there things snowballed. I know I should have trusted you, gone to you myself, and I definitely shouldn't have allowed my team to terrify you. I'm so sorry." The words tumbled out of him, he'd apologized already but this wasn't the kind of thing that was a one and done situation.

All day he'd obsessed over what had happened, desperate for a chance to make it right. He'd debated and debated on whether or not to call or track her down, but decided the least he could do was give her space.

At least for a couple of days.

If he could hold out that long.

The smile she gave him was encouraging. It gave him hope he wasn't sure he should be cultivating. Forgiving him and giving him a second chance were two completely different things.

"I accept your apology, and I'm sorry I didn't stay and talk it out with you. I should have known that you wouldn't work for a man like Dexter. I'm sorry I doubted you, guess I panicked too," she said wryly.

"Can I?" Mouse asked as he opened his arms and took a step toward her.

Without hesitation she stepped toward him, into his embrace. His heart seemed to shudder in his chest as he closed his arms around her and pulled her full up against him. Mouse had been so sure he would never get a chance to hold her again. Touching his lips to the top of her head, he held them there for a moment, breathing in her sweet scent.

When she went to pull back, he reluctantly released her, that determination was still gleaming in her eyes and she moved a few steps back, putting a bit of distance between them.

This time his heart shuddered in his chest for an entirely different reason. Fear. She'd forgiven him but had said nothing about the future.

"Earlier today I went to Prey's offices with Falcon and Hope. I didn't know a lot, but I told them everything I could about Dexter, his job, his friends, I don't know if it will help but it felt good. Like I was doing something. Taking charge of my life again. I figure if it helped to purge all that information to them, even if it doesn't lead anywhere, then maybe purging other stuff will help too."

Despite her obvious determination to do this it was clear she was nervous. She kept curling her fingers into fists then stretching them out, and she was moving nervously from foot to foot.

"Come, sit." Mouse reached for her hand and guided her to the sofa, sitting beside her, keeping hold of her hand. "You can tell me anything, you know that, right? I might have messed up today, but I care about you, and I would never intentionally hurt you."

"I know. You thought you were protecting me by dealing with it yourselves rather than calling in Prey. Falcon wanted you guys punished," she said with a smirk.

"I know, he told us, also told us you fought for us, didn't want there to be any fallout. Thank you." This woman was everything, even when she had every right to demand they be fired she'd done the opposite and fought for them. "Falcon is protective of you, cares about you, sees you as a little sister. You have a support system, Phoebe. People who are there for you, who have your back. Hope and Falcon, Falcon's family, me."

Phoebe drew in a long, controlled breath, then her fingers tightened around his as she started talking. "At first it started with just the occasional slap, when we were arguing or something. I walked away the first time, but he apologized, seemed so sincere, so remorseful, I got lured back in. I don't even remember things getting worse, it happened so slowly. Before I knew it, he'd moved me into a new apartment, isolated me from my friends and family, closed down my bank accounts and opened joint ones I barely had access to, and he'd progressed past the occasional slap."

Mouse's chest tightened, but he controlled the anger burning inside him. Phoebe needed support, not anger that could be interpreted as being aimed at her.

It wasn't though, it was aimed squarely at the man who had dared to put his hands on a beautiful, spunky, kind woman and twist her into his idea of what she should be. Dexter had tried to break Phoebe, but he'd failed. Phoebe wasn't broken, just a little banged up.

"I'm so sorry that you had to go through that," he said,

smoothing the pad of his thumb across her knuckles.

"He was always careful not to hurt me where anyone could see. He liked that I was smart, that I worked at the same firm as him, he used to show me off like I was a dog performing in a show. At least until he learned I was asking around about him. Then he made me quit. That last night was the worst, it was when I finally realized if I didn't leave then I never would, and sooner or later he'd kill me."

"What happened, that night, baby?" he asked when she didn't continue.

The haunted look in her eyes was one he wished he could wipe away, it killed him that he couldn't, all he could do was be here, hold her hand, and offer her comfort and reassurance.

"Even after he made me quit I tried to find out how dangerous he was. Maybe in my head it was one thing for him to hurt me— by then I almost believed his lies that I deserved it—but it he was hurting other people then me leaving was justified. I tried to be careful, but it must have gotten back to him. He told me I was his and he could do whatever he wanted with me. He dislocated my shoulder." Her hand moved—likely subconsciously—to rub at her right shoulder, the one he'd noted had been sore that very first day at the park.

"What else did he do, honey?" he prodded gently. Phoebe was right, she needed to get this out so she could deal with it and begin to move forward.

When she spoke, her voice trembled. "He made me use that arm to give him a hand job, then he shoved his penis in my mouth, and then he tied me to the bed and raped me. It wasn't the first time, but it was the roughest. When he was done, he yanked on my arm until it went back in." Tear-drenched eyes met his. "The pain was … I can't even describe it. It's been hurting ever since, I didn't want to go to a doctor because I didn't know how to explain the injury without telling the truth, and I wasn't ready to share that with anyone."

"You left the next day."

Phoebe nodded, the jerk of her head enough to send tears tumbling down her cheeks. "As soon as he left for work I called Hope, told her my credit card was hacked, and asked her to buy me a ticket to New York. I packed a bag with a few clothes and some personal things, left behind my wallet, phone, and everything else, drove to the airport, left my car there, and got on that plane. I knew Hope thought Dexter had cheated on me and that's why I left, I never corrected her because that felt better than her knowing the truth."

"Aww, baby." Tugging gently on her hands, he drew her over and into his lap, cocooning her in an embrace, curling himself around as much of her body as he could so she would feel protected, safe. He hadn't been there to protect her from her ex, but now that she was his, he would protect her from ever being hurt like that again. "You're so brave, do you know that?"

Her head shook against his shoulder. "Didn't feel very brave when I was on my knees in front of him trying to get him off with an arm that would barely move."

"That's exactly why you're brave, sweetheart. You survived that, you got yourself out, and you're starting over."

Tears still shimmered in her eyes when she lifted her head to look up at him, but there was a small smile on her lips. "Thank you for saying that. Thank you for listening and letting me get that out."

"Thank you for trusting me with it."

"I figured it was only fair that you know everything since we're together."

A combination of relief, joy, and gratefulness hit him hard. "We're still together?"

Picking up his wrist, she traced her fingertips along the bruises left behind from the handcuffs. "You fought enough to stop your team from coming to my apartment they cuffed you and left you behind. You might not have trusted me completely but you didn't want to scare me or hurt me either. So unless what I just told you changes things."

The doubt in her eyes was something he had to deal with immediately, so he did it the only way he knew would convince her that she was the smartest, most beautiful, and brave woman he'd ever met.

* * * * *

March 7th
8:24 P.M.

The second his lips touched hers, the last of her anxiety melted away.

Asher knew.

Knew and was still here, holding her on his lap, his lips on hers in a kiss that went from sweet to scorching almost instantaneously.

Today might have started out terrifying, she might have been punched in the gut with betrayal, but it didn't have to end that way. She'd shed the last of the hold Dexter had on her when she stopped hiding what he'd done.

Now she was free.

Free to face her future.

A future she still wanted to share with Asher.

Would it take time for the trust between them to be rebuilt? It definitely would. But she wanted to rebuild that trust, wanted to forgive and move forward. It might have hurt that he hadn't trusted her, but she hadn't trusted him either, and he'd fought to get to her, wanted to protect her from his team.

"More, Asher, I want more," she murmured against his lips.

"You said you wanted to take things slow."

"I thought I did, but I changed my mind. I want you. All of you."

His large hands framed her face, his touch gentle as his fingertips swept across her cheeks in a series of soft caresses. While his expression was tender, she could see the fire shining brightly in his dark eyes. "Are you sure?"

"Never been more sure of anything in my whole life. I want you. I *need* you. And this time I want to fall asleep afterward cuddled up in your arms." She'd laid her cards on the table, now it was time for him to do the same. It might take time to rebuild the broken trust between them, but that didn't mean they couldn't be together while they worked on fixing it.

"I want you too, butterfly. I want to bury myself in your tight, wet, heat, imprint myself on your soul so you forget everything that man did to you. I want to watch your gorgeous, expressive face as you come, remembering what it feels like for a man to bring you pleasure and not pain. I want to wrap my arms around you and be your guard dog protecting you from all your nightmares, the ones while you're asleep and the ones while you're awake."

Asher's words stoked a fire inside her, heat pooled between her legs, and she could feel herself growing wet. It had been so long since her body had responded positively to anything a man said or did. Last night with Asher was the first time a man's touch had made her come since those first weeks of her relationship with Dexter.

She should have realized he wasn't the man for her when he stopped caring if she got off when they had sex. He'd always apologize afterward, tell her he thought she'd come, then made her feel like it was her fault she hadn't.

Dexter hadn't cared about giving her what she needed, only taking what he wanted. But Asher was the opposite. He wouldn't hold back, he'd give her everything she needed and more.

"We need a bed for what I have planned for you," he said as he stood with her in his arms, a sexy grin on his face.

As he carried her through the apartment, Phoebe trailed a line of kisses down his neck, licking and nibbling as she went. The groan that rumbled through his chest made her smile. She'd lost her confidence along the way with Dexter, but now she was getting it back.

Piece by piece she was going to rebuild her life.

In the bedroom, Asher set her on her feet and ran his hands from her shoulders down to her wrists as he kissed her again. Then moved his hands across to her stomach. His fingers traced lazy circles on her stomach, making a rush of goosebumps prickle her skin.

Slowly his fingers drifted higher. She would have urged him on, begged him to hurry up, but she was enjoying his slow seduction, the brush of his fingertips on her bare skin, the sweep of his tongue inside her mouth, it all made the ache between her legs grow.

When he finally grazed a finger over one of her nipples, she had to clench her legs together so she didn't explode just from the simple contact. Never before had her body been this sensitive, but Asher made her hyperaware of every touch, every breath, every sweet sensation.

He dropped to his knees in front of her, grabbed the hem of her sweater and pushed it up. Phoebe pulled it over her head and let it drop to the floor beside them.

"Purple lace," Asher groaned as he took in the bra she'd bought today with him in mind.

"Purple is my favorite ... oh ..." her words ended on a gasp when his lips closed around one of her nipples, drawing it into the heat of his mouth.

Asher suckled first one breast then the other, and she found her fingers curling into his short dark hair almost of their own accord.

A mewed protest fell from her lips as he left her breasts to trail a line of kisses down her stomach, making him chuckle.

"Don't worry, butterfly, I intend to put that mouth to good use on other parts of your delectable body."

The heat pooled between her legs turned to a raging inferno as he unsnapped her jeans and pushed them down her legs.

"Matching lace," he groaned again.

"I chose them for you," she whispered.

"Oh, baby." His hands curled around her bottom, and he drew her close, burying his nose between her legs and inhaling.

She'd always liked when a man went down on her, but Dexter had never done it, telling her it was too disgusting. Not that he ever cared about shoving his thing down her throat. Double standards for everything with him.

With excruciatingly pleasurable slowness, he drew the panties down her legs, his fingers never breaking contact with her skin, and when she stepped out of them he returned his hands to her backside.

"Open up, sweetheart," he said, nudging her legs apart.

"Asher, you don't have to if you don't want to," she cautioned even as she spread her legs.

"Oh, baby, I want to."

That first swipe of his tongue was pure heaven. While his tongue worked its magic, and he used one of his hands to slip two fingers inside her, opening her further, his other hand remained on her backside, an anchor of sorts.

She knew what he was doing. Trying to heal one of her hurts. She'd been forced to her knees before Dexter, injured and made to perform sexual acts against her will, now he was willingly on his knees before her touching her because he wanted to.

In this moment, the first tendrils of love took hold inside her heart.

His tongue did some sort of swirling thing inside her, and she felt an earth-shattering orgasm rush toward her. Asher must have felt it coming because his fingers stayed inside her, stroking and pumping, while his mouth moved to capture her pulsing little bundle of nerves.

It hit with the power of a tornado, sweeping her up into its path and flinging her into space. Phoebe felt like she was taking a ride on a shooting star as pleasure more intense than anything she had ever experienced swept through her.

Before it had faded, Asher had picked her up, laid her down on the bed, sheathed himself, and plunged into her. As he pumped, his fingers found her still tingling bud and he set off a second orgasm so close on the heels of the first that it felt like one endless, powerful stream of pleasure that consumed her.

"I think that was pretty good for a first try," Asher teased as they both floated back down to earth.

"Pretty darn good," she agreed with a sleepy, sated smile. "We can definitely practice as much as you want though."

Asher's laugh was like the icing on the cake of the most amazing and intimate connection she'd felt. "I'm going to go get a towel, you going to be here when I come back?"

Although his tone was light, there was a shadow of doubt in his eyes that she didn't like knowing she had placed there. "Right here," she promised.

After touching a quick kiss to her lips, he headed into his bathroom returning a moment later with a warm towel to clean her up. It was the sweetest thing, she'd never had a guy do that for her before. Her previous boyfriends had never bothered, and Dexter had liked looking at her with his cum on her thighs, sometimes mixed with blood because he'd taken her so hard.

But not Asher.

He was a protector down to the smallest of details. He wanted to take care of her, and she wondered how she'd lucked out with him. Telling him everything about Dexter hadn't been easy but she was glad she'd done it. Now the air was clean, nothing standing between them.

"Come here, my sweet, brave butterfly," Asher said as he lifted her, pulled the covers back, then lay with her snuggled against his side and tucked them in.

Phoebe rested her head on the planes of his chest and gave a content sigh as his arms tightened around her. She was so happy. Perfectly so. But at the very back of her mind, in the dark recesses where worries lived, there was the fear that a man as dangerous and possessive as Dexter Hunt would never truly let her go.

CHAPTER SEVENTEEN

March 8th
8:44 A.M.

"Sorry," Phoebe said as she sneezed again and reached for a tissue.

"Sorry for what, honey? Being sick? You can't help that," Mouse soothed as he took the tissue and tossed it in the wastepaper basket he'd set beside her bed. Phoebe had woken around midnight with a cough, running nose, and fever. He'd got some meds into her, was making sure she kept up with the fluids, and was keeping her in bed where she could rest.

"No, not for being sick, because you had to reschedule your whole day because I'm sick," she corrected then erupted into a coughing fit.

"I'm happy to rearrange my day so I can stay here and take care of you." It was absolutely the truth, it was no trouble for his team to come here for a meeting rather than to Prey's offices, and this was part of being a couple. "I *want* to take care of you, butterfly."

"Thank you. It's been a long time since someone took care of me like this. Not since my mom when I was a kid."

"Well, get used to it." He helped her lie back against the pillows and smoothed a lock of hair off her red fever-stained cheek. "You want some more water?"

"I'm good," she said sleepily as she snuggled into the pillows.

"All right then, call out if you need anything and I'll be right here." Mouse tucked the covers up around her chin, then touched a kiss to her forehead. It was still hot with fever, but he loved the content little sigh she gave and the slight quirk of her lips.

Leaving her to get the rest she needed, he closed the bedroom door and headed down the hall to the living room. His phone buzzed to alert him his team had arrived, and he had the apartment door open before they had a chance to knock.

"How's our girl?" Surf asked as the guys trailed into the room.

"Stuffed up and coughing, but she'll be okay, she's getting the rest she needs," he replied.

"So, you guys are good?" Brick asked as he dropped into one of the armchairs.

"Yeah, we're good." Mouse knew he was grinning like a love-struck fool as he took the other armchair. "Sorted everything out last night. She talked through everything she knew about Dexter with Falcon and Eagle, then she talked through some more personal things with me. *You* guys might have some groveling to do though."

"Whatever it takes," Surf said. "I like her, and she's good for you. Lolly too. Time you found a good woman so you can be happy again."

"We need to do some groveling to you as well?" Arrow asked.

Did they?

Mouse couldn't say he didn't feel a little betrayed that they'd taken his concerns and run with them, terrifying Phoebe in the process. He got that Mackenzie was part of their family, but they'd known that Phoebe was important to him, and they'd still gone in hard. Not as hard as they could, he knew none of the men on his team would have laid a hand on Phoebe, but she'd still been traumatized.

What he needed wasn't groveling though. He needed to know his team had his back, Phoebe's back.

"No one still has doubts about her?" he asked, needing to have that said out loud so they could clear the air and move forward.

"No one," Bear said. The words coming from the man who had the most reason to see anyone associated with Storm

Gallagher brought down meant a lot.

"Then we're good. Dexter Hunt has gone to ground," he informed the others. "Falcon sent in one of the East Coast guys to check out Hunt's place early this morning, found it empty." Prey had two teams based on the East Coast, managed by a team of former SEALs. Both those teams were all women teams and were some of the best operatives he'd ever had the pleasure of working with.

"He knows we're onto him," Arrow said.

"How?" Domino asked. "We watched the footage from the cameras in the hall outside the apartment Phoebe was staying in. No one entered or left other than her, and then us yesterday. To be safe we cleared the apartment, there were no bugs, cameras, or microphones other than the ones Prey already had in there."

"So, he must have someone tailing her," Brick said.

"Phoebe did say that Dexter claimed he had a mole in her office," Mouse said. "Could be whoever it is he left them with orders to keep eyes on her. If he did then it could stand to reason that he saw me take her to Falcon's, then watched the building overnight and saw her go into Prey in the morning. If he did then he could safely assume that she'd told whatever she knew about Dexter to Prey. She doesn't know much, but obviously enough for Dexter to panic."

"Any chance she could have a tracker in her?" Arrow asked.

His stomach soured at the idea of Dexter putting a tracking device inside Phoebe's body without her knowledge or consent. "No, she's clean. Eagle already thought of that and had her checked while she was at Prey."

"So then she's being watched," Bear said. "We need to find her tail. Once we have them we'll get our answers."

"Means they know she's here," Surf added like he didn't already know that.

"No point in moving her. If she's being watched, they'll just follow her wherever she goes. This building is reasonably secure, she should be as safe here as anywhere," he said. The last thing he wanted was knowing a man like Dexter had his address. His daughter lived here and would be coming home this afternoon, now he had the two most important women in his life counting on him to keep them safe. Maybe he should ask his parents to keep Lolly another few days. Phoebe was sick anyway so they couldn't do much, but Lolly was so excited to see her personal superhero again.

"We did a deeper dive into Dexter Hunt," Brick started. "Found something interesting."

"What did you find?" Mouse asked.

"About four years ago, Dexter's spending habits suddenly changed," Arrow explained. "Started buying expensive clothes, upgraded his car, moved to a nice apartment, and started taking regular overseas vacations."

"What gave him the sudden influx of cash?" he asked.

"We're not sure, but right before that there was a problem with his girlfriend. She went to the cops, accused him of beating her and raping her. Seemed like it should have been a slam dunk case. She had the bruises, broken bones, with vaginal and anal taring to back it up," Arrow continued.

"So what happened? How did he get off?" he asked, refusing to even consider the fact that Phoebe had received the same treatment at Dexter's hands.

"One of the best defense lawyers in the country took the case pro bono. They tore the woman to shreds, claimed she was insane and did it to herself," Arrow replied.

"And a judge believed that?" There had to be more to the story than that.

"They produced witnesses who testified in his defense," Domino said.

"They *paid* people to testify in his defense," he corrected.

"Likely," Brick agreed. "Then the lawyer had the whole thing hidden. Deep. Took both Raven and Olivia to dig into everything to get to this. About a month afterward, Dexter helped the man get full custody of his kids."

"They formed a partnership. Dexter was brought into something and had to prove his loyalty by winning the custody case," Mouse said, wondering what this had to do with Storm Gallagher and whoever was pulling his strings. "If Dexter was brought in, then he's not the money man or the power man, he's just a player. What about the defense lawyer, what do we have on him?"

"He died about six months ago. Heart attack." From Bear's tone there was more to it than that.

"Six months ago was right when everything went down with Dove and Isaac, then Mackenzie," Mouse said. "No way can that be a coincidence."

"They're tightening the ranks, cutting off anyone that might be dead weight," Brick said.

"Is Dexter dead weight?" If he was, then the man's disappearance could mean he was already dead or scheduled for death. But there was also the possibility that the man knew he was in trouble and had hidden himself away. Or he could be being protected by whoever he was working with or for in which case they might never get eyes on him again.

They needed to know what Dexter knew and if he'd dragged Phoebe into his mess.

If he had, she would never be safe until they dug out every single person involved in this conspiracy to overthrow the government.

"We don't have enough intel right now to determine that," Bear said, empathy in his friend's voice. No one knew better than Bear how he was feeling right now because Mackenzie was also tied up in this mess. The only way to keep their women safe was to get answers, but unless they could find Dexter, he wasn't sure how they would get those answers.

"Hey." Arrow waited till he was looking at him. "We'll figure this out. We'll find who Dexter Hunt is working with, we'll find who was using Storm, we'll find everything we need to destroy every last one of them. No one messes with our family and gets away with it."

Five determined sets of eyes looked back at him, and he knew with certainty that the words his friend had just spoken were true.

Nobody messed with their family.

No one.

* * * * *

March 8th
1:09 P.M.

Snuggled in a pair of Asher's sweatpants, one of his t-shirts, and a sweater that all smelled deliciously like him, Phoebe yawned as she opened his bedroom door. The only clothes she had here were the ones she'd worn yesterday which Asher must have collected up and folded neatly, stacked on the dresser. When she'd woken up feeling sick during the night, he'd loaned her some of his, and she liked the idea of wearing his clothes.

It felt intimate in a different way than when their bodies had been joined together. That was a physical intimacy with some emotional intimacy. But this ran so much deeper. This was something real and strong developing between them.

He'd been *so* sweet with her, fussing and taking care of her like they were an old married couple instead of being at the very beginning of their relationship. A sexy man with abs to die for, and muscles for days, and dark eyes you could get lost staring into was all well and good, but a man who took care of you when you were sick, that was the real clincher.

That was a man you held onto and didn't let go.

Phoebe was smiling despite the thumping between her temples, her clogged up nose, and the hacking cough as she padded down the hall.

"Hey, honey, you shouldn't be up and out of bed," Asher said as soon as he spotted her. She noticed that he'd chosen the armchair that faced the hall, watching over her even as he worked with his team.

"I need to stretch and move around for a bit."

Asher came to her and kissed her forehead before placing the back of his hand against it. "You're still hot. Are you feeling any better?"

"Not better but not worse, the extra sleep helped."

"Course it did."

"You want me to make some lunch?" The guys were all sitting watching her. It was the first time she'd seen them since yesterday morning when they'd broken into her apartment. While she knew they were good men and wouldn't hurt her, she couldn't say she didn't feel a little antsy around them.

"We ate already, but if you're hungry I'll make you something," Asher replied.

"Maybe later," she replied. Her stomach was still a little off.

"We'll go, let you get some more rest, darlin'," Surf said, offering her a warm smile as he came over and wrapped her in a hug. "Sorry about yesterday," he whispered in her ear.

Phoebe relaxed and hugged him back, a weight lifted off her shoulders. These men were important to Asher, as important as his daughter, parents, and sister. She didn't want them to not like her, and she didn't want to put him in a position where he felt like he had to choose between them and her. "Thanks," she whispered back.

Arrow, the team medic approached her next. He picked up her hand, his fingers touched her wrist, and he checked her pulse. "A little elevated but you'll be fine, our boy is taking good care of you."

Brick and Domino both hugged her as well, then Bear stood before her, silent for a moment before. She saw the guilt in his

178

eyes, the regret, even before he opened his mouth.

"I'm sorry we didn't handle things better," Bear said softly. "Mackenzie is everything to me but you deserved better. Both of you did," he added, shifting his gaze to Asher.

"I forgive you," she gave him the words she knew he needed to hear.

"Mackenzie would love to catch up with you again when you're feeling better. She said she had fun last time."

"I'd like that," she said, and meant it. She'd found a new circle of friends and she was grateful to have been accepted and brought into their little family.

Asher moved behind her, settled her against his chest, his arms strong around her waist, his breath warm against the top of her head as he said goodbye to his friends. When they were alone, he scooped her up and carried her over to the couch, lying her down against the cushions.

"I'll make you some lunch, you need to eat to keep your strength up. My parents are dropping Lolly off soon, but you should be able to get another nap in before they get here."

"I should go back home, I don't want to pass on this cold to Lolly." Plus, it was selfish of her to want to soak up Asher's time and attention when he should be looking after his daughter.

"Uh-uh, stay right there, butterfly. First off, that's not the way this works, we're together, I take care of you, simple as that. Second, Lolly is a kid, kids get sick, colds run rampant at elementary schools. If she catches the cold, she'll get over it. Third, she knows you're sick and was already excited about playing nurse and making you all better when I talked to her on the phone earlier."

"Really?" Lolly was an absolute sweetheart.

"Yep, she told me she was going to Google remedies to help with colds."

She huffed a laugh that turned into a coughing fit, and by the time it eased Asher had a glass of water ready for her to sip on.

"Thanks," she said as she accepted it.

"Rest and I'll make you some lunch."

Phoebe only intended to close her eyes for a moment, but the next thing she knew she could hear whispered voices and quiet giggles. A pleasant warmth encapsulated her as she listened to them, a sense of home settling around her. Even though most of her life had been happy with good parents, good family, and good friends, those few months with Dexter had made her forget how nice it was to just be surrounded by people who cared about you.

When she blinked open heavy eyes and sat up, she saw Lolly and Asher had built a fort with pillows and blankets on the floor in front of the TV. They were currently in the process of stringing up fairy lights across the furniture.

For a few minutes, she watched as they tried to be quiet. They were so adorable, they teased one another, the love between father and daughter obvious. And Asher wanted to share that daughter with her, it was the most amazing gift anyone had ever given her.

"Phoebe," Lolly squealed when she saw her watching them. "You're awake."

The little girl flew across the room but stopped just short of throwing herself onto the couch, then very gently leaned down and hugged Phoebe.

"Hey, peanut," she said, wrapping her arms around the little girl and hugging her tight.

"Daddy and I made you chicken noodle soup. And we have lots of orange juice and tea with honey and lemon. I looked it up, that all helps get rid of your cold," Lolly said proudly.

"You organized all that for me?" Tears misted her vision. How did this little girl and her daddy manage to get sweeter and sweeter?

"My daddy always takes care of me when I'm sick, it's our job to take care of you now," Lolly said like it was the most obvious thing in the world.

"Couldn't have said it better myself," Asher said, slinging an arm around his daughter's shoulders.

"We made the chicken soup from scratch," Lolly announced.

"How long was I asleep?" A look out the window showed it was dark out.

"Around six hours," Asher replied.

"I didn't realize it had been so long, feels like I just closed my eyes."

"Your body knows what it needs."

"We made a pillow fort to eat dinner in and then we can watch movies," Lolly said, her blue eyes dancing with excitement.

"Disney movies," Asher whispered loudly, adding a dramatic shudder.

"Daddy, you like Disney movies, you told me you do," Lolly said.

"Shh, we don't want anyone else to know that," Asher joked.

This was so nice. Even feeling crummy with a cold didn't diminish the enjoyment of her first family moments with Asher and Lolly. This could be her future, cozy family movie nights, laughing and teasing, pillow forts and fun. In the future there might even be more kids cuddling up with them.

"Let's go grab some of that delicious soup you two made," she said, moving to stand.

"No way," Lolly stopped her. "Daddy and I are serving you tonight, that's what he said."

"I don't make the rules." Asher grinned and shrugged. "Well, I do, but this is a good one."

Leaving the daddy-daughter duo to go to the kitchen and organize dinner, Phoebe eased off the couch and into the pillow fort, snagging a blanket and wrapping it around herself. Even though she was enjoying every second of this, there was some primitive part of her gut that was tingling and issuing a warning, but she wasn't quite sure what it was trying to tell her.

Brushing aside the concerns as a byproduct of being sick, she focused on the memories she was making tonight.

CHAPTER EIGHTEEN

March 9th
11:46 A.M.

"You're not overdoing it?" Mouse asked into the phone. He hadn't wanted to leave Phoebe and Lolly alone this morning. Not because he didn't trust her with his daughter, but because she was still sick and should be resting, not caring for an active, bubbly, energetic seven-year-old.

"We're fine. We drew and painted this morning, made our own Playdough and played with that for a while. We're about to make French toast for lunch, then this afternoon we're doing a virtual scavenger hunt," Phoebe replied.

"Babe, I didn't ask you what you'd done today, although I'm glad you're both having fun. I asked if you were overdoing things."

He could hear her coughing for a moment before she replied. "I'm not. Lolly and I are having fun. After the scavenger hunt, we'll put on a movie, okay?" She sounded like she was trying to pacify him, and he couldn't help but smile.

"All right, I'll bring something home for dinner so you don't have to cook anything."

"Sounds perfect. Be safe, okay?"

"Promise. You guys too." There was no evidence to suggest that Phoebe was in any immediate danger, but that didn't mean he wasn't going to worry. Until they knew more about Dexter's involvement in the conspiracy to overthrow the government, they didn't know whether her ex was the only threat hanging over her head or not.

"How's our girl?" Surf asked from the driver's seat when he ended the call.

"Says she's not overdoing things."

"Sure she's not," Arrow said with a snicker.

"What am I going to do with that woman?" he joked, shaking his head and rolling his eyes. Really though, he loved the bond growing between his daughter and the woman he was falling for a little more each day.

"Hold on and not let her go," Brick said.

Mouse couldn't argue with that. There was no way he intended to let Phoebe go, she was his and she was starting to realize it too. Although she'd been uncertain about sleeping in his bed last night with Lolly there, worried the little girl would question it, there was no way he was sending her home alone while she was miserable with a cold. Nor was he sending her to Falcon and Hope's for them to look after. She was his and he took care of his own.

Twenty minutes later, they were pulling up outside the house of Marcia Mients. The woman was a relatively new hire at the firm Phoebe had worked at. According to Phoebe, Marcia had befriended her but had been full of questions, questions that upon consideration had been not only excessive but also intrusive.

Since they knew Dexter had a person at the firm who had been monitoring Phoebe, and Marcia had been the one to bring her the letters with the blank sheets of paper and the one with the engagement ring, she was a logical starting point. Adding to that the fact that the woman had quit just a day after Phoebe had, and that the woman had recently bought herself a brand-new house, and she was definitely worth taking a look into.

On the drive here they'd hashed out a plan. Since they had no proof Marcia had done anything other than work at the same family law firm as Phoebe, certainly not a crime, they couldn't go in guns blazing. So, they were taking a more subtle approach. He was going to go and knock on the door, pretend he thought Marcia was a friend of Phoebe's, pretend he was Phoebe's boyfriend—okay that part was the truth—and that she'd run. If Marcia thought he just had a few questions about where she thought Phoebe might go then the woman might let her guard down. That was when he would strike with more pertinent questions.

His team split up surrounding the house. They'd move in once he had the woman's attention. There was always a chance that if the woman was involved she was dangerous. Mouse could certainly take her on his own, but his team would be there for back up.

As he approached the small house, he knew she was watching him. He couldn't see her, there were no shadowy figures in the windows, no faces behind the curtains, but he could feel eyes on him and knew that it was the woman in the house.

It took a solid couple of minutes for the front door to open after he knocked, but he wasn't giving up, wasn't walking away. Not when this woman might be the key to finding out just how much danger Phoebe was in.

Hammering on the door every few seconds, when Marcia obviously realized he wasn't going anywhere, the door flew open and an irritated woman in her early thirties stood there.

"Who are you?" she asked, obviously annoyed. Yet despite the question there was recognition in her eyes. She knew exactly who he was.

"You're Marcia, right? Marcia Mients?"

"I'm sorry, you didn't say who you were." Marcia planted her hands on her hips and glowered at him. Was it his imagination or was there a light sheen of sweat on her forehead? Was she sick?

"I'm Asher Whitman. Phoebe's boyfriend."

Her eyes widened, but now he was suspicious of her motives. Was she surprised because she didn't know Phoebe had anyone in her corner or because she hadn't expected him to admit it?

"I didn't know Phoebe was dating anyone," Marcia said.

"It's new. You are Marcia, right? You worked with Phoebe. I

remember her mentioning you. I was hoping you might have spoken to her today."

With a sigh the woman finally stepped back and indicated that he should follow her inside. "Yeah, I'm Marcia. Phoebe and I did work together, but she left." There was an odd note to Marcia's tone, almost anger like Phoebe had betrayed her in leaving.

"Yeah, she's trying to rebuild her life after a bad relationship. Her cousin got her that job, she wanted to stand on her own feet again and get a job that she got all on her own," he said, wanting to remain as close to the truth as possible.

"Phoebe implied her ex cheated on her," Marcia said slowly as she led him down a hall and into a dark kitchen. The blinds were all drawn and the only light came from a dull globe hanging from the ceiling above the stove.

Mouse wasn't surprised she'd allowed Marcia to think that, it was what Hope had assumed so Phoebe had obviously decided to use it as a cover. "I'm surprised she told you about her ex."

Marcia shrugged. "She didn't. Not really. When I kept trying to set her up, she said she wasn't ready to date, told me there were no good men around anymore." Mouse could have sworn Marcia muttered something else under her breath, but he didn't catch it and let it slide. The woman was fishing for information just as he was, he could play the game, dance around, knowing he would be the one to get what he wanted in the end.

"I can assure you her ex certainly wasn't a good man."

Again, there was an odd flare in Marcia's eyes as she dropped—almost wearily—into a chair. "Why do you want to know if I've heard from Phoebe?"

"She left this morning, haven't been able to contact her."

"Maybe you're not a good man either. Maybe she left for a reason."

"I would never hurt Phoebe."

With a weariness that belied her young age, Marcia sighed. "All men hurt you in the end."

There was a glassiness to Marcia's eyes, a flush to her cheeks he didn't like and a heaviness to her breathing that had his pulse spiking. "Arrow, get in here. Now," he ordered into his comms. "Marcia, what's wrong?"

"If you're here then you know," she said, leaning down to rest her head on the table.

Dropping to his knees beside her he touched his fingers to her neck and found her pulse weak and erratic. A moment later the back door banged open, and Arrow dropped down beside him.

"What happened?" Arrow demanded.

"Don't know, she's been going down since she let me in. I think she took something. Marcia, did you do this to yourself?"

"Better this way. If they get their hands on me, they'll make my death slow," the woman murmured as Arrow began checking her vitals.

"Who are they?" If the woman had taken something to end her life, he needed to get everything out of her that he could right now.

"Like Dexter they're not good men."

"How do you know Dexter?" he asked, not liking the concern on Arrow's face.

"We've been together for a couple of years off and on," Marcia said. Her eyes had been closed but now she opened them and locked her gaze on his. "I'm sorry."

Dread pooled in his gut. "For what?"

"You seem like you really care about her, she's a nice woman, already too late for her."

"What do you mean?" he growled.

"Didn't have a choice, had to do it." Her gaze wandered to a cell phone on the kitchen counter.

Leaving Arrow to tend to the dying woman, he snatched up the cell phone. It didn't require a passcode, fingerprint or facial ID to get into, almost like Marcia had regretted what she'd done and wanted to try to make it right however she could. Mouse brought up the messages, found the last one Marcia had sent.

His blood turned to ice as he read it.

It was only seven words.

Seven words that could irrevocably change his life.

Take from him the woman who had firmly lodged herself in his heart the moment he learned she had risked her life to save his daughter's.

They know. You'll have to take her.

* * * * *

March 9th
12:12 P.M.

Why had she been worried she wouldn't be able to do this?

As Phoebe worked side by side with Lolly in the kitchen making French toast for lunch, she found she felt completely at ease with the little girl. She hadn't spent a whole lot of time around kids, she liked them and all that, and had always assumed she would have a couple one day, but she'd been worried she wouldn't know what to say to Asher's daughter, that things would be weird and awkward.

But they were the opposite.

Things with Lolly felt almost more natural than they should. A sign perhaps that she and Asher were destined to be together? Phoebe wanted to believe that. She wanted to believe that the bad days were behind her, that her future would be bright and sunny, but at the same time, she still felt that black cloud hovering overhead.

A worry for another day though.

Because today was all about bonding and fun.

"Phoebe?"

"Yeah, peanut?" The peanut nickname had stuck. Although it had slipped out by accident the first time, Asher hadn't asked her to stop, and Lolly didn't seem to mind, so now she used it because she wanted to.

"Could we do makeovers later? After we watch a movie so you can rest," Lolly quickly added. Phoebe knew that Asher had given his daughter the same talk he'd given her about not overdoing things today. He'd also given her his parents' numbers in case she felt worse and needed to call them, they were on standby and could be here in ninety minutes.

"I don't see why not." She snagged a tissue from the box on the table and blew her nose, tossing the tissue and washing her hands.

"Yay!" Lolly clapped her hands and bounced excitedly from foot to foot. "Grandma doesn't think little girls should wear makeup, but Daddy lets me do makeovers with him sometimes. It's not the same though, all my friends do makeovers with their moms."

Her heart cracked for the little girl. Growing up without a mom was rough, and even though she had her dad and grandparents it wasn't the same, not even close. Lolly was so bright and bubbly, but she knew underneath the girl was hurting. Not only did she not have her mom, but she missed out on huge chunks of time with her dad as well.

"Phoebe?" Lolly asked, her voice serious. "Are you and my daddy going to get married?"

"I don't know, sweetie," she answered honestly. She liked Asher a whole lot, and they were both serious about seeing where things went, but she didn't have a crystal ball so she couldn't know how things would turn out.

"I hope you do, then you'll be my new mommy."

Taking the couple of slices of toast out of the frying pan, Phoebe turned off the gas and led the little girl over to the kitchen table. "Lolly, I'd never want to take your mommy's place. She loved you very much, and no matter what happens with me and your daddy she'll always be your mom. But if your daddy and I are together then I will love you just as much as if you were my baby." She'd decided she was going to be honest, so she added, "Even if your daddy and I aren't together, I'll still love you like you were my baby."

Who was she kidding, she already loved the kid. From the moment the little girl gave her the stuffed kitten to help her sleep better so she wouldn't be alone, she'd fallen for the child, and being with Asher or not wouldn't change that.

Lolly flew into her arms. "So even if you and my daddy aren't together, we can do makeovers? And paint? And cook?"

"And go to the park, and read, and play games," she added with a laugh as she hugged the child back. "Now how about we have our lunch, then do our scavenger hunt. After we watch a movie we'll do makeovers, and your dad said he's going to bring home dinner."

"Ooh, I hope pizza," Lolly said as she went to the counter to get the plates.

"Pizza's your favorite, huh?"

"My absolutely bestest best favorite."

"Have you made your own pizza before?" she asked as she collected maple syrup, sugar, and lemon juice.

"No, but sometimes Grandma buys pizza bases from the supermarket and lets me choose my own toppings."

"That's fun, but I have a really good recipe to make our own pizza bases, and we can make our own sauce too." Grabbing orange juice from the fridge, and two glasses she joined Lolly at the table and poured them both some juice.

"I want to do that." Lolly immediately latched onto the pizza idea.

"Maybe you, your daddy, and I could make them together one day," she suggested.

"And brownies for dessert, brownies are my favoritest dessert."

"Sounds like a plan. What are you having on your French

toast?"

"What are you having on yours?"

"Well, my mom always put a little lemon juice and a sprinkle of sugar on mine when I was a little girl, so that's what I'm having."

"I'll have that too," Lolly quickly said.

Phoebe hid a smile at Lolly's obvious attempts to be just like her. While she still felt like given her recent history she wasn't the best role model for the child, at least there were some things she could teach Lolly. Most importantly was that if you needed help don't let anything stop you from getting it. If she hadn't been ashamed, she would have reached out to her cousin the first time Dexter hit her.

Second was don't let anything keep you down.

She was working hard to rebuild her life. It wasn't easy, she still had a lot of doubts and insecurities, but she was doing her best not to let them control her. Her confidence would come back, she was seeing her therapist, she'd got her new job, she was saving for a new place, and she hadn't let her fears keep her from forgiving Asher and moving forward with him.

Nothing was going to stop her from fighting to get her life back on track.

With an amazing man and the sweetest little girl offering her their love and support, how could she possibly fail?

Lolly was chattering away about makeovers when her cell buzzed on the table beside her. On the screen was an image of the hall outside Asher's apartment, he'd hooked her phone up to his security system. Standing outside the door was an elderly man, he looked worried, and was leaning heavily on a cane.

"Peanut, do you know an old man with lots of gray hair?" she asked. Asher had cautioned her to be careful, but assured her that there was no reason to believe she was in immediate danger from anyone other than her ex. Still, there was no way she was opening the door to anyone she didn't know.

"Mr. Gilbert?" Lolly suggested.

"Does this look like Mr. Gilbert?" She held up the phone to show Lolly.

"That's him. He lives in the apartment across from ours. Sometimes Daddy helps him with things, like fixing things, and putting away groceries. Last Christmas we even saved him some dinner and took it to him so he wouldn't be alone," Lolly explained as she jumped up from the table.

So the old man had probably come round because he needed something. She was happy to help, and while her cold was better today, she was still coughing and sneezing so didn't want to make an elderly man sick, but also couldn't just leave him there. Not if he needed help.

Phoebe followed Lolly through the apartment, her phone buzzed with an incoming call this time. The smile was automatic as soon as she saw Asher's name. He was probably checking in with her again, he'd already done that several times since he and his team left this morning. Even though she gave him the same answer every single time, he didn't seem to get tired of making sure she was okay and not overdoing things with Lolly.

"Can I open the door, Phoebe?"

"Sure, peanut," she gave permission, unable to see any possible way the elderly man could be a threat.

Until she answered the phone.

"They're coming for you," Asher's voice yelled down the line.

"Lolly, don't," she screamed a split second too late.

The little girl opened the door. The old man's terrified eyes met hers. Another man stepped up behind him.

Phoebe launched herself at Lolly.

The sound of the gun firing sounded exorbitantly loud.

Mr. Gilbert dropped.

Lolly screamed.

Phoebe clutched the little girl to her as a man with baby smooth skin, soft strawberry blond curls, and the greenest pair of eyes she had ever seen stepped into the apartment. The man had a scar that ran from his temple down along his right cheek, stopping millimeters away from the corner of his mouth.

If it wasn't for the complete lack of emotion in his eyes as his gaze moved from the dead body to her and Lolly, she would have thought he was some sweet young man who worked as an accountant or something else equally as boring and mundane.

But as he reached for the little girl, yanking Lolly from her arms, she knew this man was both evil and deadly.

One wrong move and she'd get herself and Lolly killed.

Asher knew she was in trouble, but his warning had come too late, just as he would. By the time he got here, she and Lolly would be gone, trapped in the clutches of the most soulless man she'd ever come into contact with.

CHAPTER NINETEEN

March 9th
12:33 P.M.

"Phoebe!" Mouse screamed into the phone.

No, no, no, no, no.

This couldn't be happening.

"Phoebe!" he yelled again.

"What's going on?" Bear asked as he joined Mouse on the sidewalk outside Marcia Mients' house.

"We're too late," he said in a strained voice that sounded nothing like him. He'd been in terrible situations before, situations he thought he wouldn't survive. He'd hit rock bottom when he'd lost Emily and been left a single parent to a newborn baby girl.

At least he thought he'd hit rock bottom.

Now he'd found a place so far lower that it had to be one stop above Hell itself.

A gunshot came down the phone line, followed by a thump that he knew for certain was the sound of a body hitting the floor.

Whose body?

"We have to go," he said as he ran for the car, painfully aware of the fact that they were too far away to be of any help to Phoebe and Lolly. "Phoebe? Talk to me? Who's there? What's happening?"

There were no answers to the questions he fired off and his anxiety amped up several notches.

His daughter and the woman he was falling for were alone with a very dangerous man. One with ties to a conspiracy that could change the entire world. He wasn't there to protect them.

How many times had he told his daughter he would never let anyone hurt her?

How many times had he promised Phoebe he wouldn't let her be hurt again?

Fail.

Fail.

Failure.

He hadn't been able to keep his wife alive, and now the two most important people in his world had been taken from him. The best he could hope for was that Phoebe and Lolly had been taken and not killed outright.

"Why go after her now?" Arrow's voice cut through the fog of fear, and Mouse found they were all piled into the truck and driving, he presumed back to his apartment.

"Because Marcia Mients told them to," he snapped.

"She was afraid enough of them to end her own life," Brick said like he hadn't spoken.

As if he needed another reminder that whoever had broken into his apartment could kill both Phoebe and Lolly without breaking a sweat.

"Dexter brought her into this. Looks like the two of them have known each other since a conference around five years ago," Surf said. "Dexter has been seeing her regularly ever since, cheated on our girl the whole time they were together."

If that was all the damage the man had done to Phoebe, then he'd thank his lucky stars.

If abusing Phoebe was all the damage the man had caused, he'd thank his lucky stars.

Because this new trouble was around a million times worse than both of those things put together.

"I heard a gunshot," he said dully. Had he told them that already? His mind was in a mess, not a good thing when his daughter and his woman were in danger.

"I know, man, you told us. Hold on, okay, we're getting to

your place as quickly as we can," Domino said, resting a hand on his shoulder.

"Phoebe knew she was in danger, she wouldn't have just opened the door for anyone," Surf said.

"The door cam." He should have realized to check that already. This morning before he'd left, he'd set it up so it sent alerts to Phoebe's phone as well, but it would still come to his. As a precaution the footage saved itself, when the server was full it bumped off the oldest footage first.

Even though there had been nothing but silence on the other side of the phone ever since he'd heard the gunshot and the sound of a body dropping, Mouse found himself unwilling to end the call, break what could very well be his last connection to his girls.

What if this was it?

There was every chance that when they got to his apartment, they'd find both Phoebe and his daughter already dead.

As far as he could tell there was no good reason to take either of them alive. Killing Phoebe was likely a precaution, his daughter would be killed so there were no witnesses. That his daughter's life would end just so that a killer didn't have to worry about her testifying against him seemed the absolute definition of unfair.

Even if they took Phoebe to find out what she may or may not know, there was no need to take Lolly. She was expendable.

His beautiful, bright, bubbly little girl was nothing but an inconvenience to be eliminated.

Because it could be the only thing standing between his girls and certain death, Mouse disconnected the call, feeling the loss down to his bones. It made no sense, there was no one on the other end. Whatever had happened to Phoebe and Lolly, they weren't talking to him, weren't answering his pleas, but still it felt like he'd just cut off a part of his body.

His hands shook as he brought up the door cam app. It must have sent him an alert he'd ignored in his panic to try to get a warning to Phoebe before it was too late. "It was Herbert Gilbert, the elderly man who lives across the hall," he said, holding the phone up for the others to see.

"Lolly know him?" Arrow asked.

"Yeah."

"So she would have told Phoebe he was trustworthy," Brick said.

"Yeah, she would, the guy usually gives her candy." In trying to teach his daughter to care about the people in her community and help the vulnerable when you were in a position to do so, he had inadvertently put her at risk. "There's no way the man could be involved in this, he's a vet, served for twenty years, but he could have been threatened into getting the door opened."

"Dexter was having Phoebe followed, we knew that, so we knew they knew where she was. It makes sense this guy would look for a weak link. The old man provided him the perfect way into the apartment," Surf said.

"Gunshot would have alerted the whole building," Bear stated from the driver's seat.

"So, he has to get them out quickly," Brick said.

"Or kill them," Mouse said, a horrible ache in his heart causing him to lift his hand and rub at his chest as though he could rid himself of the feeling.

"No, if he went to the trouble of risking exposure then he took Phoebe," Domino said thoughtfully. "Marcia was given orders to alert anyone if we came around, probably because that meant Phoebe knew enough to possibly be a threat. The message said take her not kill her. If they took Phoebe, then they took Lolly."

He wanted to believe that so badly. "We don't know that."

"Yeah, we do," Domino said firmly. "Because they need a way to control Phoebe. To get her to follow commands, make sure she doesn't fight back, and make sure she tells them everything. They took Lolly."

That made sense, but making sense was beyond him right now.

The second the car stopped moving he was out and running into his building. Bypassing the lifts which would take too long, he headed straight for the stairs.

The burn in his chest had nothing to do with the physical exertion, it had everything to do with what he would find when he got to his apartment.

There had only been one gunshot, but that didn't mean they would find only one body.

Mouse knew better than most there were plenty of ways to kill with your bare hands, especially when one of the victims was a seven-year-old child.

Air wheezed in and out of his chest and his steps slowed to a walk as he reached his floor. This was it. His worst nightmare could be about to come true.

Images of the night Emily had died filled his mind.

Her screams of pain.

The blood.

Her weakening voice as she slowly bled out.

A pair of shoes were visible, propping open his front door. Cops were in the hall, approaching with their hands on their weapons, and neighbors milled about.

All of that faded away.

Brushing past the cops he shoved his door the rest of the way open and stepped into his apartment.

He staggered.

Hands closed around his shoulders.

There was only the one body.

Just Herbert Gilbert.

No Lolly.

No Phoebe.

Relief made the world spin around him for a moment. If neither of his girls were here, then for now at least they were still alive.

Alive but gone.

On the floor by the door was Phoebe's phone. Without a care for forensics, Mouse crouched and scooped it up.

She'd changed her lock screen background since he'd last seen the phone. Changed it to a photo of him, Lolly, and herself in the pillow fort last night. Lolly sat between them, perched on both their laps, and he had his arm slung around Phoebe's shoulders. They were all smiling, all happy.

His little family.

Didn't matter that he hadn't known Phoebe long, he'd known from the second that he learned she'd saved his daughter's life that she was his.

Now they were both gone.

Possibly forever.

* * * * *

March 9th
7:40 P.M.

Keep Lolly alive.

Keep herself alive.

It didn't seem like a lot, only two things, and yet they were the two most important tasks Phoebe had ever faced.

Failure here was not an option.

Not at all.

For now, she had to play along, do as she was told, there was no way she would risk Lolly's life by disobeying. Threatening the child was an excellent way at gaining her compliance. Whatever they said she did immediately, the sight of the gun, aimed constantly at the little girl was a reminder of what would happen if she didn't.

Lolly was counting on her, the terrified gray-blue eyes had barely wavered from her in the last several hours. So long as she was able to contain her fear, hold it together, then Lolly was as well. This sweet, loving little girl needed her and she wasn't going to let her down. Last time she'd managed to save Lolly's life and she was determined this time she would have the same outcome.

Even if she had to sacrifice herself to do it.

There was nothing Phoebe wouldn't do to get Lolly home to her father.

Nothing.

"Turn here," the man—who had told her to call him Scar—ordered.

After killing Asher's elderly neighbor, Scar had snatched the little girl from her arms, pressed the barrel of the gun against Lolly's temple, and calmly told Phoebe that she could either come with him quietly or he'd kill the girl, then shoot out both her knees and drag her along with him.

If it was just her, she might have risked it, tried to fight back, but the only thing that would have gained was a dead seven-year-old. So, she had followed the man down the stairs and out to a car. Scar had climbed into the backseat with Lolly and ordered her into the driver's seat.

For the last few hours, she had been following directions. She had no idea where they were going, but with each mile that passed, she felt her hope draining away. Asher would have known immediately that something was wrong but there was nothing he could do to help her.

Nothing he could do now either.

For the time being she was on her own. It was up to her to keep herself and Lolly alive, and she would do it.

Determination flooded her as she made the turn.

There was a strength that had been missing during those months with Dexter. He had squeezed it out of her bit by bit, but she was stronger now. And the fact that Lolly's life was in her hands added a motivator that hadn't been there before.

They drove down a long, tree lined driveway and an old farmhouse came into view. The house was nice, it was painted a crisp white, the trim looked like it was a dark green, although it was a little hard to tell in the dark. Behind it she could see a big red barn, and what looked like an orchard off to the right of the house and a vegetable garden to the left. If she wasn't here as a kidnap victim this would be a beautiful place to live.

"Park in front of the house," Scar ordered.

With no choice but to obey, she did as he asked, turning off the car engine. No sooner had she done that than the door to the farmhouse opened, light spilled out onto the porch, and two large men strolled down the steps.

Behind her Lolly whimpered. Although she was every bit as afraid as the little girl, Phoebe somehow managed to cling to control. "It's going to be okay, Lolly."

"Very good, Ms. Lynch," Scar praised. "That's absolutely true. So long as you are honest with us, answer all of our questions, then the child can go free. There is no need for her to be hurt in any way. Her fate is in *your* hands, Ms. Lynch, don't forget that."

No mention of her being set free.

Phoebe gulped down a whimper of her own. They may or may not allow Lolly to go if she told them what they wanted, but Scar wasn't even pretending that she'd be let go. It was likely that he was lying to her. Lolly had seen his face, he couldn't really let her go, but letting her think he would would make her more compliant.

Even if he did let Lolly go, he'd kill her. That threat was evident. Not that it changed anything, she would always pick saving Lolly over her own life. She already loved the little girl, was half in love with her father too. If it wasn't possible for her to get home and have her happy ever after with Asher, she could at least make sure he didn't lose his daughter. He'd already lost his wife, it would be the unfairest thing in the world if he lost his little girl as well.

The car door was opened and one of the men reached in, unbuckled her seatbelt, and dragged her out. He stunk of cigarette smoke, the smell almost enough to make her gag, but she was afraid to do anything to upset any of these men. So, she opened her mouth and breathed through that to counter the smell as she was pulled up the porch steps.

Lolly and the other man were right behind her. The two of them were taken upstairs and down a corridor to a room with several locks on the outside. Didn't take a genius to figure out that's where she and Lolly were going to be kept.

As predicted, Scar opened the door and the two men set her and Lolly inside. "I know it's late, but dinner will be sent up shortly. While you wait, you're welcome to take a shower or bath. It's been a long day so I'm sure you're both anxious to get some rest. Tomorrow we will begin our questioning."

With that ominous threat hanging over their heads, Scar smiled politely as though he'd just checked them into a high-end hotel.

The sound of the locks being secured seemed to echo in her mind, and for a second Phoebe almost fell apart, gave in to the terror pressing down upon her, trying its best to smother her. If it wasn't for the small fingers that curled around hers, she very well might have succumbed to the need to sob out her fear, beat her fists against the heavy wooden door, and scream out her frustrations about the unfairness of being dragged into this mess by a man who had already hurt her so badly.

But falling apart would scare Lolly, so she clawed at the lid keeping her emotions in place and pasted on a comforting smile. "It's going to be okay, peanut."

Lolly looked up at her with somber eyes much too mature for such a little girl. It was clear she didn't believe the lie that hung between them, but she didn't call Phoebe out, just edged closer. "Can we take a bath?"

"I don't think we should, sweetie," Phoebe replied. What if there were cameras in the bathroom? The last thing she was going to do was allow these sick men to watch a naked child if that was their thing. "Do you need to use the toilet?" They'd stopped only twice on the drive here. Both times Scar had insisted they both use the bathroom, but the last stop had been a couple of hours ago.

"No," Lolly replied softly.

"Dinner will be here soon," she said, stroking the girl's hair.

"I'm not hungry."

"No, baby, I'm not either, but we'll eat anyway."

"How come?"

"Because I'm sure your daddy would tell us that we need to eat to keep our strength up so that when it's time for us to make our escape we can," she said, attempting to inject confidence into her tone. Her number one priority was getting Lolly out and making sure she was safe. She would watch carefully for an opportunity to do just that.

"Phoebe?"

"Yeah, peanut?"

"Do you really think we're going to get out of here?" Lolly asked.

The trust in the child's voice said that whatever answer Phoebe gave she would believe. This time she didn't just attempt to inject confidence into her tone, she made sure that she sounded like she believed one hundred percent what she was about to say. "I know we are, peanut."

Lolly nodded once then wrapped her arms around Phoebe's waist and rested her head against her chest. "I wish Daddy was here."

"Me too, sweetie, me too," Phoebe agreed as she swept a hand up and down the child's back.

If Asher was here, he would have killed Scar before the man could take them out of the apartment. He would have known what to do in the car to make sure they never wound up locked in a farmhouse. And he would have been able to handle Scar and the two other men all on his own without a weapon.

But Asher wasn't here.

And he might not be able to find them in time to help.

This wasn't the first time she'd been alone to face a monster, that was her entire relationship with Dexter. But this time she had someone else counting on her to survive, to get away, and to not give up.

She couldn't let these men win. She couldn't fail.

Whatever it took, she had to get Lolly home safely. Dexter might not have been able to break her completely, but not saving Asher's little girl would end her life as effectively as whatever Scar had planned for her.

CHAPTER TWENTY

March 10th
4:14 A.M.

"In position," Mouse said softly into his comms as he watched the beach house from the dark shadows of the sand dunes.

Finally, they'd got a location on Dexter Hunt, the man must have been making his way back to New York to get to Phoebe again. The beach house was a beautiful three-story structure and probably worth a small fortune. It was also remote which meant they wouldn't have to worry about taking him and transporting him somewhere else. They could perform their interrogation right here.

Not getting information out of the man wasn't an option.

His daughter and Phoebe's lives were hanging in the balance.

There had been no signs of them since they'd been taken well over twelve hours ago. Twelve long, horrible hours where any number of things might have happened to his girls.

Twelve hours was plenty of time to have interrogated Phoebe then killed both her and Lolly and buried their bodies somewhere no one would ever find them.

"Move on my count," Bear's voice came through the comms.

With a ruthlessness he'd perfected over almost twenty years in the military, Mouse shoved away his fears, locked down his emotions, and focused on what they had to do.

One step at a time.

It was the only way he could function, and functioning was the only way he could get his girls back.

"Let's go," Bear said.

On his friend's words, he moved toward the house. There was only the one car parked in the driveway, and the drone's scans indicated there was only one heat signature inside the house. While it was obvious that Dexter Hunt worked out, the man also clearly had no training, and he wasn't expecting there to be any difficulty in getting the man restrained. One untrained lawyer against six former special forces operators, this wasn't a fair fight, but he didn't care about fair, he only cared about answers.

It took him all of five seconds to pick the lock of the back door and enter a large, spacious kitchen. The airy open plan living area was decorated in whites and blues, a beachy feel in everything from the colors to the pictures on the walls, to the soft sound of the waves crashing on the beach.

There were two smaller rooms at the front of the first floor. From the floorplan they'd been given, they knew one was a media room, and one was a study. Mouse bypassed both as he headed to the staircase. The second floor held four ensuite bedrooms, and the third floor had the master suite complete with a balcony with amazing views across the ocean.

The heat signature indicated that Dexter was on the third floor, and he headed silently up the stairs. There was no movement, no sounds, no indication that Dexter was aware his life was about to take a turn he hadn't anticipated.

When he eased open the door to the master suite, he saw the huddle in the middle of the bed. He huffed a disgusted breath. If the man was going to get himself involved in a conspiracy to destroy the government, then he really should take personal security a little more seriously. That was the trouble with wealthy men like Dexter, they thought their money was enough to save them from any and all situations. Too bad for him his money wouldn't save him from this.

Domino was at his six as he crept across the room toward the bed. Just as he reached for the covers, Dexter sprang into action.

A glint of light on metal caught his attention.

"Gun," he yelled.

The warning was enough for both him and Domino to weave to the side, missing the bullet's path.

Launching himself at the man in the bed, Mouse slammed a fist into Dexter's jaw, immensely satisfied by the crack of his knuckles hitting bone.

Dexter's howl of pain was even better, a soothing balm to the riotous emotions churning inside him.

"I would love nothing more than to give you a taste of what you put Phoebe through, so don't test me," he growled as he hauled the man out of bed, wrenched his arms behind his back, and secured them with plastic zip ties.

"What are you doing here?" Dexter whined as they dragged him down to the kitchen.

"Getting answers about what you got Phoebe into," he snapped.

A smug smirk met him when he shoved the man into a chair, securing him with more zip ties. Dexter thought he still had the upper hand, but he was about to learn that they were the ones holding all the cards.

Pulling up another chair, Mouse turned it around and sat to face Phoebe's ex, his arms propped on the back of the chair. "We know what you're mixed-up in."

There was one small flicker of confusion before the man hid it. "You know nothing."

"We know that you were working with or for Storm Gallagher before he died. We know that Storm Gallagher had plans to bankrupt the government using vets to do it. We know that Storm Gallagher was being used by someone with more power and money," Mouse said.

"Phoebe saw you and Storm in your office talking about getting him custody of a child. We know Storm's plan was to impregnate his sister, we assume that's the child he was talking about," Arrow added.

Surprise filled Dexter's deep blue eyes, but it quickly morphed to anger. "I knew she heard something. She started asking questions at the office about me. She lied, said she wasn't, that she didn't know anything." An evil sneer curled his lips up. "I taught her a lesson though, one I don't think she'll be forgetting any time soon."

His fist was moving before he even realized it. Would have slammed it into the man's head, but Bear grabbed his wrist. "He's not worth it, he's trying to goad you."

"You're working with whoever was pulling Storm Gallagher's strings, no point in denying it. They're dangerous men, Mr. Hunt. I don't think you know what you've gotten yourself involved in," Surf said calmly. "If you want protection, we can offer it in exchange for your testimony."

"My testimony? You must think I'm crazy if I'm turning on them. They'll kill me."

"They'll kill Phoebe," he snarled. "They took her thanks to you. They'll kill her like they killed Marcia."

Grief covered Dexter's face. "Marcia?"

"Committed suicide yesterday when we showed up at her house to talk to her. She was your mole at Phoebe's firm, the one you had watching her. She's involved enough in this to be so afraid about what they'd do to her that she took her own life. Now Phoebe is in their hands." Helplessness washed over him. They might have Dexter, and they might be able to get answers out of him, but what if it wasn't enough?

Like he'd already grieved for Marcia and moved on, Dexter's smug grin returned. "I have Phoebe. I have a man watching her. I called him last night from the airport and told him it was time to make a move. Then I flew out here. He's bringing her here later today. Did you really think I would just let her walk away? Phoebe belongs to me."

That couldn't be right.

Marcia had texted someone around lunchtime to tell them to

move in on Phoebe, by last night she'd already been with her abductor for several hours.

"Do you know this man?" he asked, pulling out his phone and bringing up an image of the man with strawberry blond curls who had kidnapped Phoebe and Lolly.

"That's Scar," Dexter replied. "Why do you have a picture of him?"

The door cam filmed so long as there was movement within its range. They'd watched the man with the curls enter the apartment and then leave it a few moments later with Phoebe and Lolly. From the way he kept Lolly close to his side, they assumed he'd held a gun on her and used it to control Phoebe.

"He took Phoebe and my daughter yesterday. Lunchtime," Mouse added.

Dexter's brows drew together. "I didn't call him until around seven."

"He wasn't following your instructions. He was following someone else's. Marcia's." They'd assumed Dexter had been drawn into this by the defense lawyer and he had been the one who had then brought in Marcia. But what if they'd gotten it backward? What if Marcia was the one who had brought him in?

"You're going to tell us everything you know about Scar and about the people you've gotten into bed with," Mouse ordered.

"You've lost your mind if you think I'm telling you anything about Scar. He's the best mercenary in the business."

And that man now held his daughter and the woman he was falling for.

"Let me put it this way, you tell us what you know, or I'll do to you everything that you did to Phoebe," he threatened.

Dexter opened his mouth, no doubt to offer some snide comeback. But the crack of a gunshot split through the kitchen, and half of Dexter's head disappeared.

* * * * *

March 10th
6:58 A.M.

It had been a long night.

While Lolly had dozed off and on, curled against Phoebe's side on the bed, she had laid awake watching over the girl and trying to figure out a way to get them both out of here alive.

So far, she hadn't come up with any sort of viable plan.

It was obvious that this house had been used before to hold hostages. There were bars on the windows, the door had all the locks, and there were several armed guards. Still, she couldn't accept that things were hopeless.

Every time she felt her hope dwindling, all she did was picture the way Asher had dragged Lolly into his arms that day at the park. His fear had been a tangible thing, filling the air around them, his love for his child evident in the way he'd thrown her to the ground when he thought she'd hurt Lolly. There was no way she would make him lose his daughter on her watch.

She *would* find a way to get Lolly out of here. She had to.

"Breakfast," the cigarette man announced as he dropped two plates onto the table, one in front of her the other in front of Lolly. The plates were piled high with toast, eggs, bacon, and hashbrowns. Apparently, they liked to feed the people they kept captive here.

Lolly looked to her before making a move to touch anything on her plate, and the fact that the little girl had such faith in her almost stole her breath. It was such a big responsibility to live up to, but she vowed she wouldn't fail.

"It's okay, peanut," she told the child, picking up a piece of toast and taking a bite. It was unlikely they would bother to kill the two of them with poison, when they got what they wanted, chances were they'd shoot her and Lolly. It was more important that Lolly keep her strength up in case she got an opportunity to get the girl out of the house.

For the next ten minutes they ate in silence. The food felt like a rock sitting heavily in her stomach, but she also needed to keep her strength up, so she ate everything on her plate and drank several glasses of water.

That food very nearly came right back up when the man with the curls stepped into the room.

Even before he spoke, she knew why he was here.

Her time was up.

"I trust you enjoyed your breakfast, Ms. Lynch," he said politely. The man had a really nice voice for a hitman, or mercenary, or whatever it was he called himself.

"It was nice, thank you," she forced out. The man terrified her. He might look like an angel, but she knew he was really a demon in disguise.

Scar moved until he stood behind Lolly's chair, his slender hands resting on her shoulders. She understood the threat without him needing to verbalize it. If he thought she was lying when he asked her whatever questions he had, he wouldn't hesitate to take it out on Lolly.

It was a smart move. While she might have lied if they inflicted the pain on her there was no way she could in good conscience allow them to hurt Lolly. The little girl had nothing to do with this. In fact, if she hadn't allowed Asher to draw her into his life then she would be safe at home right now with her dad and her grandparents.

"Do you know why you are here, Ms. Lynch?" Scar asked.

Phoebe swallowed the lump in her throat. "Because of Dexter."

"What did you see in that man?" Scar asked with a disgusted roll of the eyes.

"I don't know," she answered honestly, that was an easy question.

"Then you will be happy to know the man is no more."

She froze.

Did he mean what she thought he meant?

"Dexter is dead?" she asked.

"The man had become a liability. He served his purpose, brought in many wealthy benefactors who were willing to pay whatever price to procure custody of their offspring. I never fancied the idea of having children myself. Too much work," he said, giving the little girl in front of him a thoughtful glance. "Although some days I do wonder what it would be like to be loved so completely."

Huh?

So, the mercenary was contemplating fatherhood. The man was the strangest person she had ever met.

"You had him killed?" she asked. Whatever information she could get would help Asher and his team find who else was involved in the conspiracy. Assuming of course she lived long enough to see him again.

"He came back to New York because he ordered me to bring you to him."

"But you killed him?" Who would have thought that criminals could be so confusing.

"I wasn't working for him, he just believed I was. He was always brought here to be taken out. You on the other hand, were taken because we realized you knew more than we thought you did."

"I don't know anything," she protested. She'd received more information from Asher than she had from Dexter. To her, Dexter had just been her abusive boyfriend. She'd had no idea that he was somehow mixed up in a terrorist plot.

Scar's hands tightened on Lolly's shoulders causing the little girl to flinch.

"I don't. I swear," she said in a rush. "Please, don't hurt her."

"That's not quite true, is it, dear?" Scar said slowly. "I mean, you sent your posse to my Marcia's house. She messaged to say you had to be dealt with and then she took her own life."

The spark of rage and grief in his green eyes barely registered as she felt the shock hit hard that the woman who had been so sweet to her when she'd first started at the job Falcon arranged for her was involved in all of this.

"Marcia knows you?"

"We have been together many years. Marcia knew your Dexter as well. Intimately. She is the one who first thought he might be of use to us."

Too many shocks coming so close together had her trembling. Marcia was the mole at the office watching her, but she was also both Dexter and Scar's lover.

"You sent your men to her, so you must have had reason to suspect she was involved."

Phoebe hadn't even known where Asher and his team were going, they hadn't told her, so whatever reason they had for looking into Marcia had never been known to her. "I don't know anything. I swear. Just that Dexter was involved with a man named Storm Gallagher, who wanted Dexter to secure custody of a baby for him. I don't even know who Storm is, I just saw him in Dexter's office. I swear, that's the only thing I know."

From the frown on Scar's face, he didn't believe her, but before he could ask another question one of his men entered the room and waved to get his attention.

Wanting to take advantage of this temporary reprieve to prepare Lolly as best as she could for what was coming, Phoebe asked, "Please, may we use the bathroom?"

"Fine," Scar tossed over his shoulder.

The cigarette man took her arm, and Lolly practically jumped out of her chair to run and wrap her arms around Phoebe's waist. They were taken down a hall and shown into a small powder room. "Two minutes," the man said before slamming the door and locking it from the outside.

"Lolly, I know you've been so brave, but I need you to be …"

Phoebe trailed off as her gaze landed on a small window above the toilet.

The window had no bars on it.

There was no way she could fit through it, but Lolly could.

"Phoebe?"

The first genuine smile she'd had since Scar had barged into Asher's apartment lit her lips, and she felt almost giddy with excitement. "Hurry, peanut, get up on the toilet," she said, already grabbing the girl and lifting her up.

"You can't fit through the window," Lolly's voice wobbled.

"But you can and that's all that matters." Her goal had always been to get Lolly to safety. If she managed to get away as well, she would have gone, but this way she could make sure she got Lolly a head start.

"But ..."

"No buts, sweetie. I need you to be brave, I need you to climb out there and run. You find somewhere to hide until you see the men go past you, then you run as fast as you can in the opposite direction. Can you do that, baby?"

Lolly's blue-gray eyes were watery, but she gave a firm nod of her head. "I can do it."

"When you find someone you trust, you tell them your name and ask them to call your daddy."

"How will I know who to trust?"

"Because you're a smart little girl, your daddy's daughter. You'll know."

"One minute," cigarette man called out as he knocked on the door.

"Hurry, sweetheart." Phoebe coughed to cover the sound as she shoved the small window up and helped the little girl climb through it.

Lolly hesitated once her feet hit the ground. "Phoebe?"

"Yes, peanut?" As much as she wanted the child to hurry up and get to safety, she also wanted to offer whatever reassurances she could.

"I love you."

"Oh, peanut, I love you too." Phoebe blew the little girl a kiss and with a last longing look, Lolly turned and ran.

As the child disappeared around the corner of the house Phoebe sagged in relief. Lolly was gone, hopefully safe, but as soon as the bathroom door opened they'd know she was gone. She had to buy as much time as she could for the little girl to find a hiding place.

Sliding the window closed she picked up the toilet tank lid and stood in front of the door, waiting for it to open. All she had to do was hold them off for a few minutes, whatever time she could buy would help. They'd punish her for getting Lolly away, and for fighting them, but she didn't care. Lolly was safe, Asher hadn't lost her.

"Coming in," cigarette man announced and a second later the door opened.

Phoebe didn't hesitate, she swung the chunk of china right at the man's head. It connected with a horrible crunch and he dropped.

Jumping over him she ran out into the hall. The front door was up ahead, but if she ran for it she was leading them right toward Lolly. Instead, she headed back toward the dining room. Too bad the cigarette man must have left his gun behind, but if she could find it and get hold of it maybe she could kill Scar and the others.

Before she had a chance to look for it, there were shouts, then several of the guards appeared, coming at her from multiple angles.

She spun in a slow circle, weighing her options.

They wouldn't kill her, not yet, Scar wasn't finished with her.

Using that knowledge to her advantage, Phoebe threw the toilet lid at the first man who came toward her.

The man swore and jumped back.

But it didn't matter. There were too many of them.

Determined not to go down without a fight, Phoebe kicked, she clawed, she swung her fists, and snapped her teeth at anything that came close enough.

It wasn't until something slammed into her temple that the world shimmered around her.

Still, she didn't stop.

Her fist connected at least twice more with hard muscle.

The second blow to the head was too much.

Pain speared through her.

Her vision dimmed then disappeared altogether.

Phoebe's last conscious thought before the black, pain filled void sucked her in was a prayer that she had bought Lolly enough time to get away.

CHAPTER TWENTY-ONE

March 10th
7:42 A.M.

Lolly ran.

She didn't want to.

She didn't want to leave Phoebe behind in the house with the bars on the windows, the locks on the doors, and the bad men with guns, but she did because Phoebe said it was the only way.

The only way for them not to die.

Die like her mommy had.

Die like Grandma and Grandpa's old dog had the year before. She'd loved that dog, loved having it snuggle beside her on her bed when she slept at their house, loved throwing a frisbee in their little backyard, and leaning against the dog's side as she laid on the grass and read.

But Daisy-Mae had died the same way everybody died.

The same way her daddy could die every time he left her.

The same way she could have died when those men in the park made her go with them.

The same way Phoebe could die if she didn't find any help.

So, Lolly ran.

As far and as fast as her legs could carry her.

She wished she was a grown up. If she was a grown up, then the man with the scar wouldn't have been able to use her to make Phoebe go with him. Lolly might be only seven, but she knew that was her fault. Phoebe had done whatever the scar man said because he had threatened to hurt her if Phoebe hadn't.

Just like Phoebe had stayed behind in the house because Lolly was just a little girl and she wanted her to be safe.

But Lolly wanted all of them to be safe. Even though she tried really hard to be brave, it scared her when her daddy left to go to work. She knew he might not come home to her one day. But she didn't want him to worry about her while he was gone, so she always pretended to be okay. She didn't want her daddy to die because he was worried about her.

She was scared now too.

Really scared.

Only she didn't have Mrs. Fuzzy to hold on to, and she didn't have her daddy, or Grandma, or Grandpa, or Phoebe.

She was all by herself.

That meant she had to be a big girl. Phoebe needed her to find someone safe, someone who could get her help, and who could take her to her daddy. Her daddy could save Phoebe because her daddy was a superhero. He said he wasn't, that he had just learned how to fight bad men, but Lolly still thought he was a superhero, and superheroes could save anybody.

There were lots of big trees around the house. Phoebe had said to hide until she saw the bad men go past her and then go back the other way. Could she hide in the trees?

The branches were high, above her head, but she could reach them if she put her arms up. Could she swing up onto them like she'd done with the monkey bars at the park the day they'd met Phoebe there?

Phoebe had been able to swing up and around the bars so easily. All the kids had thought it was so cool, Lolly had too, and Phoebe had promised to teach her how to do it but they hadn't gone back to the park.

What if she couldn't do it?

What if she wasn't a big enough girl to find help for Phoebe?

What if she was too small? Too scared?

No.

She couldn't be too scared.

If she was too scared, then the bad men would kill Phoebe. She knew that. They were going to be mad with her, and they'd … hurt her. Her daddy got mad at Lolly sometimes, but he never hurt her, he just made her miss out on dessert, or go to bed early. Grandma made her sit on the time out chair when she was naughty, but Grandpa never punished her, sometimes he even slipped her dessert even though her daddy said she couldn't have any.

She wished one of them was here with her right now, maybe then she wouldn't feel so scared.

And so small.

Normally, she didn't mind being small, she was the fourth shortest in her class, but her daddy always said good things come in small packages. He'd told her that her mommy was short, and Lolly had always wanted to be just like her mommy. Her mommy was beautiful, and smart, and Daddy said she was the best lady he'd ever known. He loved her mommy a lot even though she was gone.

But Daddy liked Phoebe too.

Lolly could tell by the way they looked at each other. They stared at each other the way she stared at a new toy when she wanted to convince whoever was with her to buy it for her.

Phoebe was beautiful too, and smart, and brave. She'd saved Lolly from the bad men at the park, and she'd protected her from the bad men in the house and helped her get away.

She had to be brave too.

For Phoebe.

She already loved Phoebe, and she wanted her to be her new mommy. If the bad men killed her then she couldn't be her new mommy, and her daddy would be sad. Then he would have lost two women that he loved.

She didn't want anybody to be sad, and she didn't want anybody to die.

Lifting her arms, she curled her fingers around the lowest

branch. She could just reach it, but it wasn't like the monkey bars. The wood was rough and scratchy, and it hurt her hands a little as she hung onto it, but she didn't let go.

There was no other branch nearby for her to swing her legs up to, so she was going to have to swing them up and onto the same branch she was holding onto.

It was hard, but Daddy said you didn't not try something just because it was hard. He said the only way to get good at something was to practice, to try your very best and keep trying until you got it.

That's what she'd do.

Just like Phoebe had told her, she held onto the branch and swung her legs, using her body's mo-mom-momentos—no, that wasn't quite the right word, but she couldn't remember what Phoebe had called it. She swung bigger each time until her body swung right up and she was able to scramble onto the branch.

She'd done it.

Lolly beamed even though she was still scared. If she could climb just a little bit higher then maybe the bad men wouldn't see her.

Last year she'd fallen out of a tree and broken her arm, she was still a little bit scared of being up high, but being up high was less scary than the bad men finding her, so she climbed.

And climbed.

And climbed.

When the ground looked a long way away, she stopped. Was she high enough? Would they see her if they walked past?

What if they never walked past?

How long should she stay up here?

Now that she didn't have anything to do but sit here, Lolly got more scared. She wanted to go home, she wanted her daddy to be here, or Phoebe. She didn't want to be up in the tree all by herself.

Tears stung her eyes, but she didn't want to cry. Crying was for babies. Well, her daddy told her that everybody cried sometimes and that it was nothing to be 'shamed about. But he also said big girls only cried when they had something to cry about, that big girls didn't cry just because they didn't get what they wanted, or because they didn't win a game.

This was something to cry about though, right?

It didn't make her a baby if she cried just a little bit.

So, she sat there and cried and hoped she wasn't a baby, and tried to be brave, and hoped that Phoebe was okay, and the bad men weren't hurting her too bad.

"The kid has to be around here somewhere. How far could she have gone?"

The loud voice made her tears dry up real quick.

It was one of the bad men.

She could see him below her, he and another man were walking between the trees, and they had guns in their hands.

Were they going to shoot her?

Lolly squeezed up to the trunk of the tree and clung to it. She tried to be really quiet, and really still, pretending they were playing dead fish. She never won when they played that at school, she always got itchy and then tried to scratch the itch without her teacher seeing, but Mrs. Matheson saw everything.

"Maybe she didn't come this way," the other man said.

"Well, she's around here somewhere and the boss is really mad she got away."

The boss had to be the scar man. He was the scariest of all the bad men. If he was angry, he was hurting Phoebe.

Lolly tried not to cry again, tried to be really brave, tried not to get itchy, and wriggle, she had to get help. That was her job.

It seemed like it took a real long time, but the men disappeared. Even after they were gone, she stayed where she was, just in case they were tricking her. Daddy did that sometimes when they played hide and seek.

When it seemed like hours had gone by, she very carefully climbed down the tree, trying not to think about falling and breaking her arm again.

But she didn't fall. She got to the ground and then looked at where the men had gone. Sometimes she got confused about left and right, so she lifted both her hands and held her pointer fingers up and thumbs out, finding which one made the letter L. The men had gone right which meant she had to go left.

Because she didn't want the bad men to hurt Phoebe too badly, she started running as fast as she could go. She had to find help.

Lolly ran for a long time.

Her legs were tired and she had a pain in her side. She wanted to stop and rest but every time she wanted to she thought of Phoebe and kept running. Phoebe had said she would know who was someone she could trust when she saw them, but what if Phoebe was wrong?

Or what if she never saw anybody?

Just when she didn't think she could run any more she saw a road. Roads meant cars. Cars meant people. People meant help.

Slowing down, she stayed just hidden by the trees but followed the road. When she saw a car, she could jump out and wave it down.

But what if it was the bad men looking for her?

Lolly was too scared to wave down the first car she saw.

And the second.

And the third.

She wasn't being brave like she was supposed to, but she was so scared that the people in the car would take her back to Phoebe, and then Phoebe would die. Maybe she would die too. If she died, then her daddy would be all alone.

She didn't want her daddy to be alone and sad.

Another car drove past her, but it was slowing down and then stopped a little way up ahead.

The bad men?

Had they seen her?

Lolly almost ran back into the trees, away from the road, but then she saw a woman get out of the car. The woman opened the back door and a little boy climbed out. The boy was smaller than her, he took the woman's hand, and she walked him into the trees.

"Next time you go to the potty before we leave," she heard the woman say as she crept closer.

"But I didn't have to go then," the little boy whined.

The lady didn't sound too angry, just a little bit mad. There hadn't been any women or little boys at the house, so these people had to be safe.

With a sob of relief, Lolly ran toward them and threw her arms around the woman's waist, clinging to her.

"Please," she cried, "you have to help us or the bad men are going to hurt Phoebe."

CHAPTER TWENTY-TWO

March 10th
4:07 P.M.

Mouse's heart was hammering in his chest.

The last twenty-four hours had felt like an eternity, but the last few had been the worst of all.

Ever since they got the call.

Eagle Oswald had called him to say Prey had received a phone call from local cops in a small town about four hours away from New York. The cops said a woman had been driving and stopped to let her four-year-old son pee in the woods because the child had been desperate, and they'd been approached by a little girl claiming she needed help.

His little girl.

Lolly had been found.

Apparently, she was alive and unharmed, but he would believe that only when he saw her with his own eyes.

Phoebe wasn't with her.

They'd been a couple of hours in the other direction, and it had taken them far too long to finally get to the police station where his daughter was waiting for them.

The second the car stopped he was out of it and running inside the building. "Lolly?" he yelled as soon as he was inside. If he didn't see his daughter soon, he was going to lose it. Although they'd been told Lolly was okay, he knew that only meant she was likely physically unharmed. No way could she have gone through what she had and not be psychologically harmed by the ordeal.

"Sir, if you'll just—"

"Lolly? It's Daddy," he yelled again, ignoring the cop who left the front desk and walked toward him.

"Sir ..."

"Daddy?" Lolly's voice echoed from somewhere in the building and a door off to his right banged open.

Then he saw her.

She was wearing the same blue jeans with the flowers on the knees, and the same pink sweater with the bunny on it that she'd had on when he'd kissed her and Phoebe goodbye yesterday morning.

Was it really only yesterday?

Felt like he'd lived a lifetime in those one and a half days.

Mouse didn't remember moving, the next thing he knew he was dropping to his knees in front of his daughter and dragging her into his arms.

As soon as his arms closed around her, she began to sob noisily, and his heart cracked into a million pieces. He'd underestimated the men they were up against and thought that Dexter was the only real and immediate threat. His daughter had paid the price for those assumptions.

"Shh, bumblebee, I'm here now. Daddy's here," he crooned as he lifted her off the floor and stood with her in his arms. She clung to him like a little monkey, wrapping her arms tightly around his neck, her legs around his waist. "It's all right, baby girl, it's all right."

"No, Daddy, it's not all right." She wept against his neck.

"It is, baby, I won't let anyone hurt you again, you're safe now."

"But Phoebe is still there," Lolly cried.

His daughter was more upset about Phoebe than what she'd just been through? Mouse had never been more proud of his daughter in his life than he was in this moment.

"Let's go in here, man," Bear said softly, his hand on Mouse's shoulder propelling him through and into the same room Lolly had just left. It was clear this was where his daughter had been while she was waiting for them to arrive. Remnants of lunch and snacks covered a conference table, there was a tablet someone must have rustled up for her to play with, and someone had gotten her a teddy bear as well.

Someone pulled out a chair and he sunk down into it, Lolly still wrapped up in his arms. "Did they hurt you, Lolly?" he asked. Just because he'd been told she had no injuries doesn't mean he had believed it yet.

"No." Lolly kept her face pressed into his neck and her small body was trembling in his hold. While she might have been able to escape the attempted abduction in the park with minimal emotional scarring, there was no way she would be that lucky this time.

Especially if they didn't get Phoebe back alive.

No.

He couldn't allow himself to go there.

As far as they knew, Phoebe was still alive and he would get her back. He had to. There was no way he could accept anything else. Lolly was his daughter, his heart walking around outside his body, but Phoebe was the woman who was curling around his heart and sliding her way inside it. He wanted a future with her, a family with her, Lolly, and maybe more kids in the future.

There was no way he would let that future be ripped away from them.

No way would he allow that beautiful, brave woman who had risked everything to get his daughter to safety, lose her life.

Mouse didn't have a doubt in his mind that Phoebe had done whatever it took, including putting herself in grave danger, to save his child.

A mother's love.

While Phoebe may not be Lolly's mother, she had shown the same love he would expect of a mother, willing to put everything on the line for their child. And damn if that didn't make him realize that he already loved Phoebe. It was a new love, fresh and beautiful, just starting to grow, but he couldn't deny that those feelings were there.

Fear for Phoebe, who was far from safe, was the only thing that had him drawing Lolly back enough that he could see her tear-streaked little face. The exhaustion of the last day was etched into his daughter's face, her red puffy eyes, the dark circles beneath them, and the tight line of her lips. His instincts were to protect her from further pain, to hold her, rock her, and continue offering promises that everything would be okay.

But those would be empty promises, and Lolly knew it.

His daughter was strong, strong enough to get herself away from her kidnappers and find help. Coddling her wasn't going to work, she needed to feel like she was doing something to help Phoebe.

"Did you see the faces of the men who took you?" Mouse asked.

Lolly nodded, and his resolve wobbled. If they hadn't hidden their faces, they'd had no intention of letting either Phoebe or Lolly remain alive. If Phoebe hadn't gotten Lolly out of that house, he would have lost both of them. He could still lose Phoebe.

"Is this the man who took you, honey?" Arrow asked, showing Lolly a photo of the curly haired man they'd seen on the door cam.

Lolly nodded again.

"Can you tell us what happened?" Surf asked gently.

"He had a gun, he shot Mr. Gilbert." Lolly's voice trembled but then she firmed it. "He made us go in a car, and he sat in the back with me and his gun and made Phoebe drive."

"You're doing great, baby," he encouraged. "Do you know where you drove to?"

"We stopped at McDonald's, and then at a gas station. He bought us food and let us go to the bathroom," Lolly explained.

"Then we went to a big house, it had a barn, and an orchid, and a vegetable garden. He took us inside and put us in a bedroom. It had locks on the door and bars on the window. Phoebe said I should go to sleep, but I kept waking up."

"That's good, bumblebee, really good, I'm so proud of you. You're such a brave, big girl." With a description of the property she'd been taken to, and the location of where Lolly had been found they would be able to narrow down a search area.

"Do you know how many people were in the house, honey?" Brick asked.

Lolly shook her head. "There were lots of bad men."

"Did the bad men hurt Phoebe?" he asked tightly.

"No, but …" Lolly trailed off and his gut clenched.

"But what, baby girl?" he asked, forcing his voice to remain even. The last thing he needed was Lolly to feed off his fear when she had enough of her own.

"But they'll hurt her because I'm gone," Lolly said, her voice hollow. Every time he thought his heart had already shattered it somehow cracked further. His little girl was smart enough to know what Phoebe had risked in getting her out.

"We will find her," he vowed, not a promise he made lightly. Anything less than getting Phoebe home was unacceptable.

"Do you promise, Daddy?"

"I promise," he said without hesitation. "But I need your help to do that. I need you to tell me everything you remember about where you drove, about the house he took you to, about the men you saw there. If we're going to find Phoebe and bring her home to us, then we're going to do it together. You've been so brave, such a big girl, and Phoebe and I are both proud of you."

Determination sparked in Lolly's eyes. They were Emily's eyes, but that determination reminded him of both Lolly's mother and Phoebe. Phoebe was strong, determined, and tough. If there was anyone who could hold on until he got to her then it was Phoebe.

* * * * *

March 10th
10:25 P.M.

Pain cloaked her like a shroud.

It hung heavily on her shoulders, weighing her down, making her weak and vulnerable.

Phoebe was powerless to fight it off. It marched through her head like a never-ending army heading out to fight a battle. The battle it was waging was between her temples and the pain was so excruciating that all she could do was hang limply from her chains and waver in and out of consciousness.

Time held no meaning, she might have been hanging here for a minute, an hour, or a day, she had no idea.

There were various other aches throughout her body, but the pain was very heavily focused in her head. She had a concussion, that was a definite. Already she had thrown up a couple of times, the stench a constant in her semi-conscious state. There was the metallic smell of blood as well, so she knew at least one of the sources of pain in her aching body was because of a bleeding wound.

Aside from the pain, the nausea, and the dizziness that felt like she was stuck inside a tornado, there was also cold.

A bone deep chill that added another heavy layer of suffering.

Every time her body shook—which was a near constant—pain rattled through her. A never-ending cycle, the more she shook the worse the pain was, but the worse the pain was the more her abused body shook.

Darkness took hold of her again and she was swept away in its black folds.

Voices surrounded her the next time she surfaced.

Angry voices.

They chattered around her like a flock of squawking birds.

The sound pierced right through her skull, and she flinched away from it.

Or at least she tried to. Her arms had been pulled above her head and secured with metal cuffs around her wrists. Whatever she was attached to left her hanging, her feet a good foot off the floor.

Helpless.

Phoebe thought she knew the definition of the word. She'd felt helpless when she was with Dexter, trapped in a nightmare she couldn't escape from, but maybe at the back of her mind she'd always known that when she gathered enough confidence she could leave.

There was no leaving here.

Her only way out was in a body bag.

Scar and his men weren't going to let her go. They never had been. There was the smallest of chances they might have released Lolly once she no longer served a purpose, but Lolly had seen their faces so she doubted they would let the girl live.

But she'd gotten the child out.

Nothing they could do would change that.

She was sure that if they'd found Lolly they would have paraded the little girl in front of her, making sure she knew that she had failed, likely telling her that now the child's death was her fault.

No Lolly meant the little girl was still out there somewhere. Still safe. She prayed that Lolly had been able to find help, that she was inside somewhere now, warm, and fed. Maybe Asher had come, and Lolly was back with her daddy where she belonged.

If she was going to die here, at least she could die at peace knowing she hadn't cost Asher his daughter.

"I said, wake her up," a voice she recognized as belonging to Scar snapped.

"We're trying, she keeps going in and out," another voice said in something close to a whine.

"I told you not to hit her so hard, you've given her a concussion," Scar complained.

"We had to hit her, you saw her, she was going crazy. She knocked Camden out, broke Tubman's nose, bit almost straight through Derringer's hand."

Phoebe grinned despite the pain. She'd really done all that? The raging headache was a small price to pay for knowing she'd inflicted that sort of damage and allowed Lolly enough time to get away from the house.

"Boss, looks like she's awake," a third voice announced.

Even though her eyes were closed she felt someone step closer, standing right before her. The good thing about her concussion was that she felt so miserable and was in so much pain that there wasn't really any room left for fear.

Of course, she knew she was in a bad situation. With Lolly gone, if they wanted answers and she didn't give them then they'd hurt her. When they were done, they would kill her. They might even make her suffer first just for fun because she'd outsmarted them when she'd gotten Lolly away.

But there was only so much her body could handle and right now it was all tapped out dealing with the concussion, she'd take that as a small win and enjoy these few moments fear free.

"You are playing an unwise game, Ms. Lynch," Scar told her.

"I'm dead no matter what," she slurred, her voice sounding weak and insubstantial even to her own ears. There would be no more fighting, not physically with the way she was strung up, not mentally with the way her head pounded, and consciousness came and went. The best she could do was remain brave and stoic until the end. Either way, her death would be inevitable, but she wanted to die knowing she hadn't flinched when looking death in the face.

"It did not have to be this way. If you had answered my questions, if you had not made the child run away, it would have gone easier on both of you."

"You weren't letting her go, you would have killed her."

"I did not intend to kill the child. I never did. I do what is necessary but whatever you think of me, Ms. Lynch, I don't take pleasure in murdering. But death was not in the cards for you or the girl."

Lies.

That was a lie, they'd seen his face, he couldn't let them go.

"She can identify you."

"Which is why she would not have been returned to her father, but that doesn't mean I would have killed her. There are other ways to make sure someone is not a threat."

Trafficking.

He was talking about selling Lolly.

And her too.

That might have been a fate worse than death.

A cold hand touched her shoulder, the one Dexter had dislocated, the one that was currently screaming with pain in a battle with her head to see which would be the worst. His hand trailed a lazy path down to one of her breasts. His touch was not sexual despite the body part it was on. After lingering for a moment, it swept further south. Down across her stomach and stopping just above the apex of her thighs.

"I would have liked to keep you for myself, I have no doubt that breaking you would have been an amusing and entertaining prospect. But alas, I do not have the time for such an undertaking. I have not yet made up my mind whether to sell you or kill you. Do you have a preference?"

The question sounded genuine, and Phoebe wondered just what kind of psycho this man was. He kidnapped and murdered without hesitation, yet he was polite and well spoken. He'd let them spend the night in a clean bedroom, then fed them breakfast, and now he was giving her a choice as to what her future looked like.

Too bad both of those options sucked.

"Hmm, perhaps you need a little motivation to answer my questions like a civilized person."

Since her eyes were closed, she had no idea what was going on around her. A poor tactical decision perhaps but she was just too weak and in too much pain to bother trying to gather information about her surroundings when they wouldn't do any good in helping her get free.

Because of that, the sudden blast of freezing water that assaulted her body caught her completely by surprise.

Phoebe screamed in pain as the powerful spray attacked her body with the ferocity of a million icy hammers.

Her eyes popped open, the dull light of the room piercing through her skull as though it wished to rip it to pieces. Instinctively, her body tried to move to avoid the water from the pressure hose, but hanging from the ceiling there was nowhere for her to go.

All moving did was make the pain in her shoulder worse as she struggled fruitlessly to get out of the water's path.

It didn't stop.

Hitting her body in a steady stream.

She'd be covered in bruises by the time Scar lost interest in torturing her.

The spray sent water splashing into her face. Phoebe coughed and spluttered as she tried not to swallow it. The last thing she needed was to wind up with water in her lungs.

Tears streamed down her face, mingling with the water, the combined pain of her head injury, her shoulder, and the bruising force of the water was too much.

Phoebe choked on the water that battered at her lips, and when unconsciousness came calling, she hurried to accept its invitation of blissful ignorance.

CHAPTER TWENTY-THREE

March 11th
1:18 A.M.

Mouse was itching to get inside that farmhouse, get his girl, and bring her home.

If his team wasn't here and they had to breach carefully then he'd already have gone running wildly inside, screaming Phoebe's name.

The need to see her and touch her was overwhelming. As hard as leaving his little girl had been, he'd done it because Lolly had been every bit as desperate to get Phoebe back as he was. For now, Lolly was safe. His parents were with her, back at the station a couple of miles away from the place where Phoebe was being held.

Miles.

His little girl had run for miles to find help.

He had never been so proud of her as he was these last couple of days. She had been amazingly brave for such a little girl, and it was only because of her that they'd managed to locate the farmhouse where Phoebe was.

Prey had responded swiftly, getting access to property records, then they'd gotten drones up in the air, located the white house with the dark green trim, big red barn, orchard, and vegetable garden that Lolly had described. They'd also been trying to get an identity on the man with the blond curls and scar, but so far, they'd come up empty. It was like the man didn't exist, although they knew he did because they had footage of him, and Lolly had seen him herself. It was clear he had some powerful friends, some of whom were capable of wiping him from every database that existed.

Sooner or later, they would find out who he was but for now it didn't matter.

Only getting Phoebe back mattered.

He prayed alive and in one piece.

When Bear gave the order to move in, Mouse sighed in relief. Time to get his girl back.

Even though he couldn't see them, the rest of his team would be moving in on the house at the same time that he was. According to the info the drones had gotten them there were a dozen men here. Given that when they'd moved in on Dexter Hunt there had been a sniper nearby, they'd searched the woods carefully before taking up positions.

To be extra cautious, Bravo team were here too. They would keep watch on the woods, make sure there wasn't a sniper waiting till they were distracted before moving in, while he and the rest of Alpha team located Phoebe and took out the men in the house.

Taking at least one of the men alive was the goal but given that Marcia had committed suicide rather than be taken into custody he didn't hold out much hope.

The first shot came the second he stepped through the front door.

Mouse quickly located the man on the stairs and took him out. Domino followed him through the door, Bear and Surf would be entering through the back, and Arrow and Brick through the side door. With all exits covered, they knew nobody would be escaping. If someone managed to get out through a door that wasn't on the house's blueprints, then Bravo team would take care of them.

They cleared the foyer and started up the stairs, the others would clear the downstairs. More shots peppered the hall as they reached the second floor.

Mouse took out one, then a second. That made three

confirmed killed out of the twelve they knew were on the premises.

A grunt of pain had him glancing over his shoulder.

"Domino is down," he said into his comms. "Dom?"

"Fine," came the grunted reply. "Got me in the vest."

Still a round to the vest was enough to crack ribs or possibly puncture a lung.

"I'm fine," Domino repeated as though knowing where Mouse's mind had veered. "There are another two up here."

"We've eliminated four down here," Arrow told him. "I'm on my way up."

"Domino says there's another two up here," Mouse said, covering his teammate as he scanned the hall. There were still another two doors closed, and they hadn't cleared the other three rooms either. Including the two men up here that still left another three men as of yet unaccounted for.

"Got another," Brick said.

Two unaccounted for.

When Arrow joined them at the top of the stairs, he left Domino with the medic and continued down the hall. At the end he could see a room with several locks on the outside of the closed door. That had to be where Phoebe and Lolly had been kept. Was Phoebe in there now?

A hint of a sound to his right had him spinning around, a head shot eliminated the target before he could fire his own weapon. Nine dead now, three to go, one of which was up here.

Reaching the locked room, he grabbed the keys hanging on the wall beside the door. According to Domino—who seemed to have a sixth sense about these things—there was one more tango up here. Was someone in the locked room with Phoebe?

"Another one down," Surf said through the comms. "None are our curly haired scarred man."

"Phoebe?"

"No sign of her yet," Bear replied.

Could they have moved Phoebe somewhere else after Lolly got away, afraid the child could somehow lead law enforcement back here?

Mouse unlocked the door, swinging it open carefully. When he scanned the room and saw no heat signatures, he called out, "Phoebe?"

There was no answer.

The crack of a gunshot in the hall meant the other tango up here had been neutralized. There was only one man left now, the other eleven had been taken out. Was this man guarding Phoebe? Had he killed her when he realized the property was under attack?

"Mouse, kitchen, now," Bear ordered.

Hurrying back downstairs, he paused beside Domino and Arrow. "He all right?"

"He's fine," Domino growled, but hissed in pain when he tried to stand.

"Couple of broken ribs," Arrow replied.

Leaving the medic to help Domino down the stairs, he took them three at a time and hurried into the kitchen.

"Found the last man," Brick said, gesturing to a body lying beside what looked like a hidden entrance to another room. One that hadn't been on the floorplan Olivia Oswald had gotten for them.

They hadn't taken anyone alive, but then again, that was what they had expected. Whoever these men were working for was dangerous and powerful enough that they'd rather be taken out now than suffer the consequences of failing their boss.

"Looks like it leads to a basement," Surf said from the entrance to the room.

The others all stepped back, allowing him to take the lead as he headed down a narrow staircase.

As soon as he reached the bottom, he saw her.

She was hanging from her bound hands, cuffed at the wrists, the cuffs had been attached to a hook embedded in the ceiling.

Her head hung limply against her chest.

There was a puddle of water beneath her, partially drained away into a drain in the ground. The room was lit by a lightbulb hanging from the center of the ceiling, while dim, the light was enough for him to see bruises on her, including a large lump on the side of her head.

"Clear," Bear announced.

Barely breathing, Mouse crossed the room to stand beside Phoebe's limp form. Curling his hand under her jaw, he pressed two fingers against her neck. Her skin was cold as ice, but he could feel her pulse fluttering beneath his touch.

Lying on the floor was a discarded hose and from the water dripping off her and the bruises he could see forming on pale skin, he knew exactly what they'd done with the hose.

Tortured her.

Rage burned inside him, but when he reached out and gathered Phoebe into his arms his touch was gentle. "We need to get her down."

"Ambulance is on the way," Bear said softly beside him as he unlocked the cuffs.

"She's hypothermic," he said as he held her close, trying to use his body heat to warm her.

"She'll be okay, man, we'll take care of her," Surf assured him.

Carrying Phoebe's too still form up and out of the basement, Mouse tried to believe that the worst was over. Phoebe was alive. Despite the fact she was hurt, hypothermic, likely concussed, with who knew what other injuries, none of them appeared to be immediately life threatening.

He had her back, but would he get the Phoebe he'd been falling in love with or had she been irrevocably changed by her ordeal.

"Tank brought the car around," Brick called out from the front door.

Mouse took her outside and slid into the backseat with Phoebe tucked on his lap. Arrow got in beside him, Brick into the front where he cranked the heat up high. Taking the emergency blanket Arrow handed him, he covered Phoebe then touched his lips to her forehead.

"Come on, butterfly," he whispered, "come back to me."

"Pulse is weak, but steady," Arrow told him. "Let me see her head."

Careful to keep her covered so he could get her temperature up, Mouse angled her head so Arrow could see it. Arrow checked her eyes and probed the lump on her head, then slipped his hands under the blanket and ran them up and down Phoebe's still body, checking for injuries."

Her naked body.

It hadn't escaped Mouse's notice that they'd stripped her. Had she been sexually assaulted on top of everything else?

"Phoebe, honey, can you hear me? It's Asher, I'm here, I have you, you're safe now. Lolly is fine too. You saved her, sweetheart, you saved my little girl and you kept yourself alive till I could get to you. You did good, babe, but now I need you to wake up for me. Can you do that?"

Like a miracle her lashes fluttered on her too pale cheeks, and then a moment later he was looking down into the most gorgeous pair of baby blues he'd ever seen.

"Hey, sweetheart," he said as tears made her face shimmer.

She was alive, whatever she'd been through they would deal with it, they'd get her help, Lolly too. Hell, maybe he needed counselling as well because he couldn't imagine this knot of fear lodged in his chest ever loosening enough to disappear.

"I love you, butterfly," he whispered as he feathered the lightest of kisses against her lips. Love might not solve anything, but it was the only thing strong enough to get his family through this.

* * * * *

March 11th
8:33 P.M.

She was warm, out of pain, safe now, yet Phoebe couldn't relax.

How could she when she'd brought such a nightmare right to Asher and Lolly's doorstep?

Every time she drew a breath, felt the pounding in her head, the roughness in her chest, she was reminded of how close she had come to dying. Of how close Lolly had come to dying.

Asher's parents had brought Lolly to see her earlier, and the little girl had given her Baby Kitty, telling her the stuffed animal would help, but it wasn't. All it was doing was reminding her of the danger she'd put the sweet little girl in.

How could Asher sit there beside her, cradling her hand in his, knowing that because of her he could have lost his daughter?

He should hate her.

He should have walked away the second he knew she was safe.

He should have done anything other than sit beside her, watching her with what could only amount to love in his eyes.

She couldn't take it anymore.

"Why are you here?" she asked, hating how broken she sounded. Was she broken? If she was it wasn't because of what Scar had done to her, it was because of the man beside her and the little girl she already loved as though she were her own. It was knowing how very badly she'd hurt them that tore her to shreds.

Instead of confusion, instead of pulling away at her question, Asher smiled and leaned in to kiss her forehead. "There she is."

"What?" Phoebe asked, wincing as she furrowed her brows and it aggravated her headache. She wasn't really in pain, the drugs dripping through the IV into the back of her hand had taken care of that, but moving her head too much still made it throb.

"My girl is back." One of his hands cupped her cheek, his fingers impossibly gentle and tender as they caressed her face.

"Your girl?"

"I told you I love you. Lolly loves you. I'd say that makes you ours."

Just like that the dam broke.

Sobs built like a volcano and then burst out in chest-heaving cries. Tears streamed down her cheeks and her entire body shook with the force of her sobs.

Asher moved immediately, lowering the bar on the side of the bed so he could sit beside her and gather her into his arms. He set her on his lap, tucked her face against his neck, and rocked her gently, crooning soothingly in her ear.

Phoebe had no idea what he was saying, but it didn't really matter, the sound of his voice was like a lighthouse guiding her through the storm of her tears and out the other side. By the time her sobs eased and eyes dried, she felt completely and utterly spent. Every last drop of strength she possessed had been squeezed out of her the last forty-eight hours.

Yet she had to know.

Couldn't rest until she had answers.

"You love me?"

"I know it's soon," Asher said as his hand stroked her hair. "But I don't care. I don't want to waste time just to say we didn't exchange I love yous too soon. You saved my daughter's life twice, you've made her smile and laugh in a way I haven't seen before, you've filled a part of me I didn't even realize was lacking. I thought I was fine on my own, thought Lolly was fine without a mom, then along you came, and I realized how much we were both missing out on. We need someone like you in our lives, someone who fights for those she loves, and who would sacrifice anything to protect her people. Someone who loves with her whole heart and sees the good in people. We need you in our lives."

"But ... but ... but ..." she stammered. "But Lolly was almost killed because of me."

"Oh, baby, no." His hand stilled in its rhythmic stroking of her hair to hold her tight. "Lolly was almost killed because a group of men and women have decided that they don't like our government and want to take it over. Because they tried using a mentally ill man to do it and were prepared to throw him under the bus in the process. Because they brought in people who didn't care who they hurt, because nothing is more important to them than their own schemes. None of that is your fault."

"But Dexter ..."

"Hurt you, used you, brought you to the attention of those men. That doesn't mean what happened is your fault."

"But ..."

Asher laughed. "Stop with the buts, butterfly. We were already on their radar before you came along. We went through Marcia's phone. We believe she felt guilty about her part in everything because instead of deleting everything off her phone she left it for us. She was the one who arranged Lolly's kidnapping that day we met you. Because we were the ones who took down Storm, we got ourselves on these people's radar. Going after the Oswalds is too risky, they all have bodyguards, but me and my team we're the ones who killed Storm, so they thought going after us—Lolly specifically—would get Prey to back off. It's just coincidence that Dexter was also mixed up with them and that's what got you on their radar. So, you see, even if you hadn't come to New York that wouldn't have changed anything. They just would have gotten Lolly the first time."

She hadn't known that.

Although she'd given a statement once she was in the hospital, she'd been too out of it to say much, too busy being poked and prodded, sent for tests, too depressed at the pain she'd caused Asher and Lolly to care about asking questions.

"Are you sure?"

"Positive. They might have taken Lolly because she was an easy way to control you, but they'd already gone after her once. Probably thought once she'd served her purpose with you, she could then be used to blackmail Prey into stopping going after them."

"They were going to sell us," she said softly.

Asher froze. His hand, which had resumed is gentle smoothing along her hair, stilled. "Scar told you that?"

"Mmhmm. In the basement. He said he wished he could have kept me himself but that he didn't have time to train me. He said that he'd never intended to kill either me or Lolly, that there were other ways of getting rid of problems."

A shudder rippled through Asher, then she felt his lips on her head, dropping kiss after kiss. "I'm sorry I didn't make sure you and Lolly were better protected. I won't make that mistake again. Prey has agreed to put someone on both of you."

"Oh, Asher, that's not ..." Phoebe trailed off. She was going to say it wasn't necessary, but was she really going to argue about something that would in fact make her feel safer? "Do you think we need it?"

"I'd rather be safe than sorry. No one is ever going to hurt my girls again."

Phoebe smiled as she snuggled against Asher. "I like when you call me your girl. I like knowing you're mine too."

"Always, sweetheart. I'll always be yours."

It occurred to her that even though he'd told her he loved her a few times now she was yet to tell him that she loved him too. "Asher?"

"Yeah, butterfly?"

"I love you. I was scared to say it before because I was worried that you really must hate me after I almost got Lolly killed, but it's true. I do. When I thought I was going to die I realized how much I was going to miss out on. I wouldn't get to make love to you again, would never get to marry you, wouldn't get to be Lolly's stepmom, or add more kids to our family. I wouldn't get to grow old with you."

"We'll have all of those things, honey. We'll have a wonderful life together. We'll travel the world, raise kids, spoil grandkids, watch sunrises and sunsets, and we'll laugh and cry. Through it all you will always know that you are loved and treasured."

"Kiss me, Asher."

"Butterfly, you have a concussion, you swallowed a whole bunch of water, you have more bruises than I can count."

"I don't care. I need to feel you, I need to feel your love, I need to feel something good. Please."

"Oh, honey, you don't ever have to beg. Not with me. Not ever."

His thumb hooked under her chin, and he tipped her face up, then his lips found hers. Their touch was soft, more a whisper than anything else, but it was just what she needed, an affirmation that she was alive and that she had survived. Not only survived but found her place in the world, her home.

When she'd fled California, she'd thought she would never be able to trust a man again. She'd thought she was weak and had been ashamed of what she'd let happen to her. But Asher had earned her trust, reminded her that there were good men in the world. She'd fought for Lolly's life, and for her own, reminding herself that while she'd made a mistake in trusting Dexter, she hadn't done anything wrong.

She was stronger than she'd given herself credit for.

Phoebe had a feeling the man kissing her so tenderly would remind her of that regularly.

CHAPTER TWENTY-FOUR

March 13th
3:29 P.M.

Mouse couldn't wipe the smile off his face, nor did he want to try.

After more than forty-eight hours in the hospital, Phoebe had been discharged. She'd had a whole battery of tests, the doctors had been a little concerned about water in her lungs, but so far, she seemed okay. She'd been hooked up with a surgeon who would operate on her shoulder, fixing the damage Dexter had caused, when she was stronger. Her concussion was serious, doctors thought she'd taken several hits to the head, and when she told them she'd sustained the injuries on purpose by attacking Scar's men so Lolly could get away he'd almost lost it.

This woman was utterly amazing.

She was everything that he'd ever wanted in a partner, and he could hardly believe that she wanted him back.

When they'd first gotten her to the hospital she'd been so subdued, felt so distant like an entire chasm had opened up between them. He'd known she was in shock, struggling to process everything she'd been through, so he'd been there, holding her hand, sitting beside her bed, going with her while she underwent tests. It wasn't until she'd finally emerged from the haze enough to voice her fears that he'd finally known everything was going to be okay.

Now his family needed time to heal.

Phoebe was moving in with him and Lolly. When she was recovered, they'd look for a new place, one that was all of theirs instead of her feeling like she was living in his and Lolly's place. He wanted a house with a yard. It didn't matter if it was a small one, but a place to plant flowers, grow vegetables, kick a ball around with Lolly and the kids he knew he and Phoebe would have one day.

He wanted the whole family fairytale.

"All right, chatterboxes, we're home," he told his girls who were both in the backseat. Lolly had been doing most of the talking, Phoebe was still weak, sensitive to light, a little nauseous, and had a killer headache. He'd be watching her carefully over the next few days and knew the signs to watch out for that would indicate her getting worse.

For now though, he had to believe that the worst was past them. Smooth sailing from here on out, or at least sailing on only slightly choppy water, no more huge swells for them.

"Daddy, can we make pizzas? Phoebe said she had a recipe to make the bases and sauce and everything," Lolly said. Although his baby girl had had nightmares last night and the night before, and he knew she needed help processing what she'd been through, she was doing at least as well as he could have hoped for.

"Maybe not today, bumblebee. Phoebe needs to rest, remember?"

"Oh yeah." Lolly's face got thoughtful, and he was sure she was trying to figure out what they could do instead.

"I can make pizzas," Phoebe protested, but he could hear the heavy exhaustion in her tone.

"No way, babe, you need rest and that's what you're going to get," he said firmly. If he let them, his two crazy girls would be out swinging on the monkey bars, and making pizzas, and who knows what else.

"What about pasta?" Phoebe suggested. "It's pretty easy, we just mix the flour and eggs then let it sit, then all we have to do is cut it up and cook it."

"Oh, yeah, Daddy, can we? Please? Pretty please with

sprinkles, and fudge, and chocolate chips, and cherries on top?" Lolly asked, bouncing in her seat.

How could he say no to that?

"All right, we can make pasta," he agreed. He was going to have to get used to cooking. Usually, Lolly did that with her grandma, but Phoebe seemed to enjoy cooking too and he'd do whatever his girls wanted if it meant spending time with them. "Wait till I come help you out," he told Phoebe.

Surprisingly, Phoebe nodded her assent. If that didn't tell him how awful she was feeling then nothing would.

Mouse waved at Surf and handed over the keys when his friend jogged over. They'd taken two of Prey's vehicles when they went to search for Dexter, then gone after Phoebe. He'd wanted time alone with his girls so they'd taken one car while the guys had taken the other, now Surf would return this one for him.

"You should take a nap," he said as he helped Phoebe from the car.

"I've spent the last two days in bed," she complained.

"Concussions are no joke. You need to get as much rest as you can."

"I want to enjoy you and Lolly right now."

"Butterfly, you have the entire rest of our lives to enjoy us, right now we need to get you well."

"I'll take a nap later," she promised.

"Then you sit yourself down when we get up to the apartment and you take it easy," he said firmly.

"Maybe," she edged.

Mouse laughed. "No maybe, honey. You'll rest. But don't worry I have something planned to keep us busy."

Waving to the guys as they drove off, Mouse scooped Phoebe up into his arms. She could likely make it up to the apartment on her own, well with his arm around her for support, but he wanted her in his arms. He could hold her forever and never get enough of it, the weight of her against his chest, her soft curves, the sweet

251

floral scent of her shampoo, they were all addicting as hell.

"Daddy, can we make the pasta now?" Lolly asked as soon as they stepped foot in the apartment. Prey had organized to have everything cleaned, and you could never tell that a man had been murdered right inside the front door.

While Lolly didn't give the spot a second glance, too excited about the idea of making her own pasta for dinner, Phoebe's gaze locked on the spot where Mr. Gilbert had died.

"It's going to be okay, honey, it will just take time," he whispered in her ear.

She tore her gaze away and turned it to him and offered up a wan smile. "I know."

"I have the perfect thing to distract you," he said as he set her down on the couch.

While comforting Lolly after her nightmares and watching Phoebe clutch Lolly's Baby Kitty in her arms in the hospital, he'd known his girls needed something to comfort them when he inevitably got called out. So, he'd done something about it, hoping that the gift would provide comfort and be a whole lot of fun.

"You two wait here," he told Phoebe and Lolly. "Grandma dropped something off for us."

"A surprise?" Lolly's eyes lit up in excitement.

"Yep. Hope you both like it." Disappearing down to his bathroom where he'd asked his mom to leave said surprise, he scooped up the basket and carried it back to the living room.

The basket ruined the surprise before he could announce it.

"Did I just hear a cat meow?" Phoebe asked.

"A cat?" Lolly leaped off the couch where she'd been sitting beside Phoebe. "You got us a cat?"

"Kitten," he corrected. "Two of them actually. They're sisters, they were the last two left of the litter, and I didn't want to leave one behind. Besides, when I have to go away, I thought if we had two then one could sleep with you, bumblebee, and one could sleep with my butterfly."

"Can I hold one?" Lolly asked.

"Of course. Which one do you want?"

"This one." Lolly immediately reached for the kitten with the golden-brown fur and blue eyes. When he'd looked for kittens needing adoption and he'd seen this little golden one he'd known it was perfect for his family.

While Lolly sat back down on the couch with the mewing kitten in her arms, Mouse passed the white kitten to Phoebe then sat down between his girls.

"This was the sweetest idea ever," Phoebe whispered as she snuggled the kitten.

"I just wanted to know my girls would sleep easy when I wasn't around. Figured these were better than the stuffed variety."

"The sweetest," Phoebe repeated.

"I'm calling mine Cupcake," Lolly announced. "I can't call it Phoebe, and I already called my stuffed cat Mrs. Fuzzy, so I can't call it that either. We baked cupcakes for Phoebe, and the kitten looks just like her, so I think it's the perfect name."

Couldn't argue with that. "What are you calling yours?" he asked Phoebe.

"Cookie," she said thoughtfully. "Cupcake and Cookie, sounds about as cute as you can get."

Couldn't argue with that either.

The smiles on his girls' faces were everything. Absolutely everything.

Mouse wrapped his arm around Phoebe and pulled Lolly into his other side. The two most important people in the world to him. He'd come so close to losing them, but instead the love between them had only strengthened.

CHAPTER TWENTY-FIVE

June 4th
11:08 P.M.

Darkness filled his vision.

Pain.

His body felt heavy, like he'd been covered in concrete.

Mouse tried to clear the fog in his head, but it was a lot more difficult than it should be. What had happened to him?

His memory was fuzzy and the more he tried to focus the further away those memories flitted.

A cry of pain echoed through the darkness.

Who was that?

It sounded familiar, but for the life of him he couldn't place who the voice belonged to.

Even though he had no idea what had happened, a sense of doom hovered over him. It was important to figure things out. His life might depend on it.

Him and maybe his team too?

Another scream filled the emptiness.

It ate at his gut and filled him with a poison he wasn't sure he would be able to extract.

Forcing himself to concentrate, Mouse focused with everything that he had. He remembered kissing Lolly goodbye before he left.

No.

Not just Lolly.

Phoebe too.

His fiancée.

He'd proposed to Phoebe just a couple of weeks ago.

Although maybe he should have married her. Wherever it was he knew things were bad. If he was going to die, he wished he'd been able to make the woman he loved officially his in the eyes of the law. Now she wouldn't be entitled to any benefits, or his life insurance policy, and they hadn't signed the custody papers to make her legally Lolly's mother.

Now it might be too late.

Panic and pain clawed in unison at his lungs, stealing his ability to breathe.

Mouse wanted more than anything to be holding his fiancée and his daughter in his arms, instead he felt a world away from them.

Because he was a world away from them.

The ground beneath him was cold and hard. Concrete. There was no light. His body ached like he'd been beaten, and he sensed rather than heard the rest of his team nearby.

They'd been captured.

The source they'd come to meet with in Somalia had obviously turned on them and now they were captives. Prisoners.

Another scream echoed through wherever they were being held and Mouse turned his head and threw up.

The scream came from Arrow.

Who was being tortured.

And Mouse had no idea how he and his team were going to make it out of here alive.

Jane Blythe is a *USA Today* bestselling author of romantic suspense and military romance full of sexy heroes and strong heroines! When she's not weaving hard to unravel mysteries she loves to read, bake, go to the beach, build snowmen, and watch Disney movies. She has two adorable Dalmatians, is obsessed with Christmas, owns 200+ teddy bears, and loves to travel!

To connect and keep up to date please visit any of the following

Amazon – http://www.amazon.com/author/janeblythe
BookBub – https://www.bookbub.com/authors/jane-blythe
Email – mailto:janeblytheauthor@gmail.com
Facebook – http://www.facebook.com/janeblytheauthor
Goodreads – http://www.goodreads.com/author/show/6574160.Jane_Blythe
Instagram – http://www.instagram.com/jane_blythe_author
Reader Group – http://www.facebook.com/groups/janeskillersweethearts
Twitter – http://www.twitter.com/jblytheauthor
Website – http://www.janeblythe.com.au

Faith is being sure of what we hope for and certain of what we do not see.

Hebrews 11:1